T0318608

"I will not be a wife in name only."

Rian Connor's proposal of marriage should have been the happiest moment of Catherine Davenport's life. He is her savior, her tutor in the ways of flirtation, the man she wants for her lover. But two impediments bar the way: the vicious assault that may have ruined her ability to enjoy any man's touch; and the vindictive woman who will stop at nothing to regain Rian's affection.

"There can be no turning back once you have given yourself to me."

One exquisite night of completely mutual pleasure proves to Catherine that with Rian, the physical side of their union will bring only joy. But even her new husband cannot protect her from the diabolical scheming of his former mistress. Delivered into the hands of the madman who once delighted in tormenting her, Catherine is swept back to the place where it all began. And this time, the price could be her future with the man she is finally free to love . . .

Books by Carla Susan Smith

A Vampire's Promise
A Vampire's Soul
A Vampire's Honor
A Vampire's Hunger

Corsets and Carriages
Mischance
Resolve

Published by Kensington Publishing Corporation

Salvation

Corsets and Carriages

Part Three

Carla Susan Smith

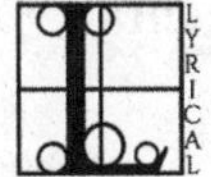

LYRICAL PRESS
Kensington Publishing Corp.
www.kensingtonbooks.com

Lyrical Press books are published by
Kensington Publishing Corp. 119 West 40th Street New York, NY 10018

First Electronic Edition: February 2018
eISBN-13: 978-1-5161-0592-2
eISBN-10: 1-5161-0592-3

First Print Edition: February 2018
ISBN-13: ISBN 978-1-5161-0595-3
ISBN-10: ISBN 1-5161-0595-8

Printed in the United States of America

Chapter 1

"Why will you not see him?" Emily Pelham asked conversationally as her fingers sorted through a rainbow of threads in search of the color she needed.

Looking up from the book she was reading, Catherine Davenport did her best not to appear startled by the question. It was no secret whom Emily was referring to. Catherine wondered if the older woman would be saddened or pleased to know the same question had been on her own mind recently. More than it ought. Untwisting a pale curl from her forefinger, Catherine sighed and closed her book. She had absolutely no idea what she had been reading, but it seemed to her that every sentence began with the same name: Rian Connor.

"I'm not sure I'm ready to see him," she admitted to the woman who had been like a mother to her since she had come to stay at Pelham Manor.

"Why ever not?" Emily asked bluntly. "What are you so uncertain about?"

"I don't know." Catherine shrugged, a movement that spoke volumes.

Rian had returned to neighboring Oakhaven more than three weeks ago, and the very next day he'd called on her for the first time since he'd departed on his mysterious journey north. For a week he continued to arrive at Pelham, day after day, rain or shine, and still she refused to see him. However, it seemed to Emily that at this point Catherine would be hard pressed to say exactly why.

It went without saying that her refusal had sparked a great deal of curiosity in the two households. The Pelham servants, normally staid and unflappable, talked amongst themselves in hushed whispers, trying to decide who would yield first.

And then, without any warning, Rian had stopped coming. Concerned that he might have taken ill, Catherine had made surreptitious inquiries, only to learn he was enjoying excellent health. Now almost two weeks had passed without a visit from him, and she could not explain why his apparent abandonment hurt so much. It made no sense when she had no intention of seeing him. Or did she?

"Catherine." Emily softened her eyes. "This situation cannot go on indefinitely. If Rian has nothing that you desire, nothing you want from him as a man, then be kind and tell him so. Release him from this hopeless pursuit."

The tears, hot and stinging behind her eyelids, came without warning, and her lower lip trembled as she whispered, "But you're wrong. He is everything I desire, all I could possibly want."

Putting aside her needlework, Emily came to sit next to her. She placed an arm around her shoulders. "Then why not tell him?" she asked, kissing Catherine's forehead.

"But how?" Catherine stared at her best friend's mother with a forlorn look. "How am I supposed to tell a man like Rian such a thing?"

"Well, I think it might be helpful if the two of you were in the same room at the same time." Emily gave her a small squeeze. "The words will come, but it won't help if there's no one to hear them."

"Am I being ridiculously silly?" Catherine sniffled.

"No. You are simply being cautious, that is all." The words were reassuring. "There is still so much of your past that is unknown to you because of the amnesia you suffered, and now you are on the threshold of making a decision that could very well affect the rest of your life. None of us can know the future, but you owe it to yourself, as well as Rian, to see if perhaps you want to continue your life's journey in his company."

It was the kindness and concern in Emily's eyes that helped Catherine realize that avoiding the issue any longer was pointless. Now was the time to take a deep breath and face her insecurities. She had spent too much time already playing games of 'what if.' Emily was right. Felicity was right. As Rian's sister-in-law and Catherine's best friend, she had been encouraging his visits in the hope of seeing two of her favorite people in the world united at last.

"Is Felicity due to visit soon?" Catherine asked.

"Yes, actually both she and Liam are dining with us tonight." Emily smiled, always delighted by a visit from her only daughter and new son by marriage.

"Would you mind terribly if I did not join you?"

"No, of course not." Curiosity gnawed at Emily. "But, won't you be hungry?"

"I'm sure the kitchen at Oakhaven will be able to provide for me."

A puzzled frown creased Emily's brow. "I'm sorry, perhaps I wasn't clear. Felicity and Liam are dining here tonight."

Catherine gave her a warm smile. "Precisely. They are dining here, which means Rian will be at Oakhaven. Alone."

Chapter 2

"Are you certain I cannot persuade you to change your mind and come with us?" Felicity asked. "Mama and Papa would be most happy to see you."

"I think I have caused your parents enough consternation with my comings and goings these past few weeks," Rian answered. "I have no wish to ruin what should be a pleasant evening for you all."

"You don't truly think that, surely?"

"Ah, but I do." Seeing the look on his well-meaning sister-in-law's face, he explained. "If I accept your gracious invitation to dine at Pelham Manor, then I predict one of two things will happen." He held up a finger. "Catherine will suddenly develop a headache and keep to her room, or"—he held up a second finger—"she will dine with us, but do her best to ignore me. Conversation would no doubt be difficult, even if I were to bring up the exciting topic of crop rotations."

"Who in their right mind would find the subject of crop rotations exciting?" Felicity asked, looking puzzled.

"Who indeed?" his brother Liam murmured from across the room.

"The point I am making," Rian continued, "is that regardless of which scenario unfolds, a pleasant evening will have been ruined." Hearing Felicity's sigh of frustration, Rian took her hands in his. "I appreciate your concern, but you must stop fretting over this. It will work itself out one way or another."

"But I feel horribly guilty, especially as it was my idea that you ride over to Pelham every day. I truly believed the situation between you and Catherine would have been resolved by now. That she is still refusing to see you, speak with you, defies all reason."

"She does have a considerable stubborn streak, I'll grant you that."

"Perhaps I ought to speak with her about—"

"You'll do no such thing," Liam said. "This is between Rian and Catherine, and no one else."

The arched brow that appeared in response to Felicity's sudden pout was a warning. A warning not to interfere. Felicity gave a mild snort of frustration and looked away. Not wanting the newlyweds to share a carriage cross with each other, Rian squeezed her hands.

"Your intentions were good, and no one knows that better than I, but Liam is correct. This difficulty between Catherine and myself will sort itself out. One way or another."

"I don't see how when you can't even get her to stay in the same room with you."

Rian raised a sardonic brow. "It's a challenge, Felicity, nothing more." His smile turned rakish. "Besides, I think Catherine was beginning to look forward to my daily visit and the chance to refuse me."

"So is that why you stopped riding to Pelham?" Felicity asked. "Because she was expecting you to?"

"Partly, but I also wanted to save the sensibilities of your servants."

"How are they involved?" Liam asked.

"Catherine's excuses for not seeing me were becoming increasingly inventive, and also more preposterous." Rian grinned at his brother. "The last time I rode to Pelham she denied me the pleasure of her company because she was so engrossed in a book, she did not wish to lose her place in the narrative."

"Did you not suggest a solution to her dilemma?"

"Of course. My proposal was to slip a ribbon between the pages of the book, thus securing her place." Rian nodded at his brother. "It is something I have seen your wife do on more than one occasion."

"Reasonable enough," Liam acknowledged, having also witnessed Felicity mark books in this manner.

"Unfortunately, the only ribbon at hand for such a purpose was the one woven in Catherine's hair, or one of those securing her stockings. Using either would reduce her to a state of unacceptable undress, or so I was informed." The corner of Rian's mouth lifted in amusement. "Given a choice, I would have much preferred the loss of a stocking, but then I am man who knows little about the intricacies of women's hair."

"What was she reading?" Liam asked.

"Does it matter?"

"No, I suppose not. I was just curious."

"I cannot believe she would actually mention her stockings." Felicity sounded slightly aghast.

"You should direct your sympathy toward the poor footman who delivered the message. I've never seen a grown man so distressed at repeating someone else's words."

Letting go of Felicity's hands, Rian watched as she moved away from him, shaking her head and making tutting sounds. "I was so hopeful," she told him, her words sounding apologetic. "She seemed settled, more sure of her own mind, especially while her dear friend Lord Barclay was visiting. But now he is gone, she has once again become indecisive and unsure of her feelings."

"Perhaps she now regrets not leaving with him," Rian offered in a low voice.

Now that Catherine had recalled her name and much of her former identity, it had not been difficult for Rian to travel north to the village where she'd once lived. His discovery of her childhood friend, Edward Barclay, had prompted a visit from that gentleman, and Rian sensed that the young man had come with a proposal for Catherine in mind.

"No, I don't think that is so."

The surety with which the words were spoken made Rian turn his head and look at his brother. It was no secret that Catherine had an easier time talking to the younger Conner. But then Liam was able to concentrate on her words when all Rian wanted to do was kiss her. More than once. Having already tasted her lips, he was eager to repeat the experience.

"Has Catherine shared some secret knowledge with you, brother?" Rian asked. "You seem very sure of yourself."

"Catherine has told me nothing, either in confidence or otherwise. I've seen no more of her recently than you have, Rian." The elder Conner's gaze shifted towards his sister-in-law, making Liam add, "And Felicity has shared nothing with me either. Well, nothing that concerns this awkwardness with Catherine," he amended.

"Then how do you know she suffers no regret about not leaving with her childhood playmate?"

"Because her childhood playmate told me so."

"When did you talk with Edward, and why did you not tell me?" Felicity asked in an annoyed voice.

"He stopped by on his return north, and in truth, it did not seem so very important. I assumed he was telling me facts already known to you."

Liam watched in bafflement as his wife threw her hands in the air and began muttering about the idiocy of the male sex. He was certain he heard a few more unflattering observations regarding his gender, but he wasn't so foolish as to ask her to repeat them. He did take comfort in seeing an equally bewildered look on his brother's face. Taking advantage of Felicity's distraction, he poured her a glass of sweet wine, and apologized for his shortcomings.

"So, what was your impression of the young lord?" Rian asked.

"I won't lie," Liam replied, frankly. "I liked him. I liked him a lot."

"So did I," Rian agreed with a satisfied nod. "Now tell me, what did you and young Edward talk about?"

"Mostly we discussed some new innovations in farming." Interrupted by the rude, snorting sound made by his wife, Liam waited until she gave her leave for him to continue. "He was, however, disappointed that you had not yet returned, and asked me to convey his thanks for providing him with Catherine's whereabouts."

"And just what possessed you to do such an addlebrained thing?" Felicity snapped, paying no attention to her husband's sigh at this further interruption. "Sending a potential rival directly to her?"

"Was he a rival? I thought he would be a welcome face from her past. Someone who might help restore some memories."

"You didn't think he might be in love with her?"

"Oh, I know he is, and probably has been for most of his life," Rian observed, "but he is also betrothed."

"He wouldn't be the first man to change his mind," Liam pointed out.

"No, he wouldn't be, but that would be Catherine's decision, not his."

"You knew she wouldn't let him do it," Felicity stated, staring at Rian in mild astonishment. "You knew, even if he offered, she would turn him down."

"Knew? No, I didn't know, but I did hope."

"You took a big risk," Liam said. "What if he hadn't mentioned his engagement and Catherine *had* returned with him? Would you have let her go?"

"Did Lord Barclay strike you as the kind of young man who would not be truthful, especially regarding any involvement with another woman? Besides, he and Catherine have known each other since they were children. I suspect they would each know when the other was hiding something."

"Even so…" Now it was Felicity who seemed to view his reasoning with a certain measure of skepticism.

Rian watched as her hand, the one not holding the glass of wine, fussed with the buttons on her bodice. The rapid movement of her fingers reminded him of a small bird. "Even if Catherine cannot find it within herself to forgive me for what happened on the night of your Oakhaven ball," he continued in a low voice, "I could not let a chance at happiness slip away from her. The decision had to be hers to make."

Turning away, Felicity downed her drink with a most unladylike gulp.

"You're right of course," Liam said. "And he did tell Catherine he was to be married to someone else."

"And?"

"And it is my understanding that their friendship was rekindled, but nothing else. I believe she offered him her warmest congratulations, and some keen insight on how to treat his new bride. So you see, brother mine, if there is something troubling Miss Davenport's mind, I do not think it is her decision not to travel north."

"Are you sure you will not come to dinner with us?" Felicity asked once more. "Catherine may be more amenable, now that it has been some time since she last saw you at Pelham."

Rian looked confused. "But she hasn't seen me," he clarified.

Felicity's laugh was something only another woman would appreciate. "Are you telling me you didn't feel her watching you as you rode away? Trust me, dearest brother, Catherine saw you every time you went to Pelham."

* * * *

Isabel Howard lay quietly, her eyes closed, waiting patiently for the man to be done. His fingers moved gently over her skin, touching her with the utmost care. Finally, it was over and he moved away.

"You may get dressed now, your ladyship," he said, his voice as gentle as his hands, each possessing a soothing quality. Isabel wondered how many other nervous women had been put at ease by just one or two words from him. It was a definite addition to his other professional capabilities. She closed her robe and sat up on the bed, waiting for him to finish washing his hands. She never knew a man so obsessed with keeping his hands clean.

"When?" she asked.

The doctor looked up at the ceiling and calculated briefly in his head. It didn't take much to count to nine but he appeared to enjoy making it a theatrical process. "I would estimate in the winter, possibly November but most definitely by December."

"You are certain?" She knew it was a foolish question before it slipped out of her mouth, but he smiled indulgently at her. No doubt his skill had been questioned before, and she was certain he had seen just as many tears as happy smiles when delivering his news.

“Oh yes, I am quite certain.”

Isabel got off the bed and tied the robe’s sash. Was it her imagination or was her waist already thickening? She went to her dresser and retrieved a small black pouch from a drawer.

“For your discretion,” she said.

The doctor felt the weight of the pouch. A sizeable secret. “Of course. I was never here, your ladyship.”

Chapter 3

The horse Catherine was riding covered the ground with ease, flying hooves gobbling up the terrain as they galloped steadily onward. A light breeze pulled her hair free of its restraining ribbon, making her long tresses stream behind her. Summer had arrived in all its glory and was promising to stay awhile. Wildflowers bloomed everywhere and the trees were thick with their canopies of green, leafy growth. It was a good day and Catherine felt her spirits soar, buoyed by more than just the outdoors. Edward's visit had provided a valuable bridge for her memories, but she had questions he could not answer. Wanting to make certain she did not cross paths with Felicity and Liam making their way to Pelham, Catherine slowed her horse to a canter and then to a sedate walk. Giving the animal its head, she allowed it to wander where it chose, while she gave the same freedom to her thoughts.

Though she had confessed her love for Rian to her childhood friend, and made a promise to share her feelings with Rian, her courage had waned with Edward's departure. How disappointed he would be to see her vacillating, quite incapable of keeping her promise, not to mention the dreadful way she had been treating Rian since his return. But Edward did not know all the details regarding the night of Felicity and Liam's celebratory ball for Oakhaven's tenants.

Catherine would never forget the ecstasy of Rian's kiss, or the humiliation of finding him practically in bed with his former mistress the following morning. It was easy for Edward to brush off Isabel Howard as being of little consequence, but he couldn't tell her that Rian held no regard for his former lover. If Isabel no longer claimed Rian's affection, then Catherine needed to hear it for herself. From Rian's own lips, and that wasn't going to happen if she kept hiding herself away at Pelham Manor.

Emily was right. The situation could not go on indefinitely and it was fast bordering on the absurd. It needed to be resolved one way or another. Rian had made the first move by sending Edward to her, and Catherine was astute enough to know the reason why. But though she loved Edward, and he would always have a special place in her heart, she was not in love with him. Marriage to him had never been her idea, and when she'd sent Edward away, Catherine had made her choice.

She was stronger since the attack that had taken her memory, both physically and emotionally, although Rian had no idea just how much progress she had made. His last image of her had been that awful morning when the pain of his betrayal had made her want to curl up and die. It had been Emily who helped her to consider what she had seen in Rian's bedroom from a completely different perspective. While it was difficult to stomach the thought of him being with Isabel, she was now willing to admit that perhaps there had been mitigating circumstances. Emily had told her quite plainly that Isabel would not hesitate to use trickery and deceit in order to get what she wanted. And she wanted Rian.

The question was, did Catherine want him more?

She closed her eyes and was instantly transported back to that night in the library. Recalling the touch of Rian's fingers caressing her neck before gently dipping into the valley between her breasts sent a shiver down her back. She remembered only too well his hunger, and how desperately her own body wanted to appease that hunger. The situation wasn't complicated at all. Refusing to acknowledge it had been the complication, but now she felt as if a huge weight had been lifted by the sheer simplicity of deciding on a course of action. Rian was alone at Oakhaven. There would be no better time to find out if he was the answer she was searching for.

The sun was making its descent toward the horizon when Catherine topped a small rise and gazed down at the Connor ancestral home. She was near the spot where she and Rian had taken a tumble in the snow, and she had kissed him. Cushioned amongst the lush velvet greenness of the surrounding land, the house sparkled like a jewel, much the same way it had back then. Only this time it was the rays of the setting sun reflecting off the windows that made it glitter instead of bright white ice crystals. And the house was still as beautiful as ever.

Quickly she made her way to the stables, and slipping from the saddle in the courtyard, she handed the reins to one of the younger stable boys. After getting over the shock of seeing her riding unaccompanied, he touched his fingers to the brim of his cap and smiled warmly at her in greeting before leading her borrowed horse to an empty stall. Catherine stood for a moment, her senses drinking in the sights and sounds and smells of the courtyard. It was as if the weeks at Pelham suddenly dissolved, and she had never been away. She entered the house by way of the kitchen door, pausing quietly for a few moments to savor the comforting aromas of the constantly bustling room. It was her maid Tilly who saw her first, announcing her presence with an earsplitting shriek.

"Miss Catherine!"

Immediately every head swiveled in her direction, and Catherine found herself enveloped by a pair of wiry arms as Tilly hugged her with a strength that almost took her breath away.

"You're a sight for sore eyes there's no mistake, lass," Mrs. Hatch said, coming to her rescue by disengaging the maid's near stranglehold. An unexpected lump rose and lodged itself in the back of Catherine's throat. She swallowed, realizing how much she had missed the motherly housekeeper.

"I've missed you too." Catherine kissed her on the cheek. "All of you," she added, looking at the faces gathered around the big kitchen table. She was rewarded by a sea of smiles before Cook good-naturedly scolded everyone back to their chores, while clearing a place at the table and bidding Catherine to sit.

"And what has happened that you feel the need to slink in through the kitchen door?" Mrs. Hatch inquired, folding her arms beneath her ample bosom.

"I wasn't slinking! I just came from the stables and thought I would save my legs by not walking all the way around to the front of the house. Besides"—Catherine glanced up at the housekeeper—"I wanted to see you before anyone else, and thought I might find you here."

"Little minx!" the older woman declared with a chuckle. "Ah well, no matter. 'Tis a blessing to have you back, lass."

"Thank you. Have I missed supper?"

The housekeeper examined Catherine's appearance, allowing just the smallest hint of disapproval at the sight of her hair swinging freely about her hips. "No, and there's just enough time for you to go tidy yourself up a bit," she reprimanded gently. "I'll make sure an extra place is set."

Catherine was almost at the door that would take her out of the kitchen and into the main part of the house when Mrs. Hatch stopped her, her tone cautious. "Miss Catherine, you do know that Master Rian is here alone, do you not?"

She turned back around, feeling the weight of every stare from Cook and Mrs. Hatch to the pot boy and the scullery maid. All of them holding their breath, waiting to see what she would say. Catherine did not disappoint. "Not anymore, he isn't."

A short while later, her face and hands washed, her hair tidied, and the worst of the creases brushed out of her skirt, Catherine entered the dining room. She had been surprised at how quiet the house was with Liam and Felicity gone, but she still managed a sigh of relief to see Rian had not yet come down to dine. A quick glance at the table told her Mrs. Hatch had obviously been distracted as there was still only one place setting visible. She was carrying an extra set to the table when a familiar voice stopped her.

"Hello, Catherine."

Immediately the beat of her heart quickened, and she thought she could hear a faint swooshing as her blood flowed more rapidly, rushing through her veins. She had not realized how keenly she had missed that rich, warm timbre until now, nor the effect it had on her. Not daring to look at Rian, afraid doing so would make her drop the plate she held in her hands, Catherine forced herself to ignore him as she carefully placed it on the table. Then, and only then, did she permit herself to turn her head and gaze toward the open doorway.

She opened her mouth to speak, to return his greeting, but no sound came out. Instead her vocal cords chose now, the most inopportune of all moments, to become paralyzed. In trying to clear her throat, she took in a mouthful of air the wrong way, and embarked on a spectacular coughing fit. Pouring some wine in a glass, Rian handed it to her. She gulped the contents greedily, making him raise his brows in alarm.

"Slowly, slowly," he admonished as he gently patted her on the back. "Too fast will do more harm than good."

Gratefully Catherine handed him back the half empty glass; her throat felt raw but at least the aggravating prickle had now subsided. "Thank you," she croaked, doing her best frog imitation.

Rian handed her the handkerchief from his pocket. Without thinking, Catherine wiped her eyes, and then blew her nose, loudly. She folded the square of linen and put it in the pocket of her dress. Pulling a chair out from the table, Rian motioned for her to be seated. "I must admit I've never seen that particular shade of puce before," he teased, making her blush even more.

"I'm sorry; you took me by surprise, that's all."

It was true. Even though Catherine wanted him there, had expressly journeyed to see him, she had been momentarily stunned by the intensity of her own feelings at seeing him. And his expression said she was not the only one taken by surprise. Now she glanced at the open doorway, wondering how quickly she would be able to sprint through if her plan went horribly wrong. Her glance did not go unnoticed.

"If you are expecting Liam and Felicity to join us, then I must disappoint you." Rian filled his wine glass. He tipped the bottle in her direction, but Catherine shook her head. The remaining half-full glass would be more than enough, if she decided to drink it.

"I know they are dining at Pelham this evening."

"And you have chosen to dine here, with me?"

The idea that Rian might not actually want to see her had never occurred to Catherine, but something in his manner now had her considering the possibility. What if his feelings toward her had already changed? What if she had played the role of reluctant maiden just a little too well? Perhaps he had grown tired of her attitude. Unease suddenly rippled through her, leaving a trail of anxiety in its wake. "If you prefer, I can leave you to your solitude. I don't think anyone would mind if I dined in the kitchen."

"I would prefer it if you stayed. I dislike eating alone."

"Oh, I thought you would be used to it."

He looked at her shrewdly for a minute. "I am, but that doesn't mean I have to like it." Though he kept his voice low, Catherine thought she detected a hint of despondency.

"I'm sorry. I didn't mean for that to come out the way it did," she apologized with a smile that made his stomach flip. "But then everything I say to you always seems to come out wrong, and I don't understand why. I have the words in my head and they make perfect sense there, but then on the way to my mouth they get all jumbled up."

"Perhaps you are trying too hard." He sipped his wine, content to admire the curve of her cheek, the charming scatter of freckles across her nose, the sweep of thick, dark lashes whenever she lowered her eyes. "Would *you* prefer to dine alone?" he asked perversely.

"No, in fact this couldn't be better."

"And why is that?" He sounded more than a little dubious.

Taking a deep breath, Catherine jumped in with both feet. "It seems to me that we have been avoiding each other."

The sound that came from across the table could not be mistaken for anything else but incredulity. She risked a glance and the expression on Rian's face made the heat rise in hers. "Pardon me," she mumbled. "I should say it is I who has been avoiding you, and for too long. It's time we talked, don't you agree?"

Rian could only nod, his mind a whirlwind of things he wanted to say to her, but Catherine was not the only one who was afflicted with words tumbling out in the wrong order. Thankfully they were both saved by the arrival of dinner, although Rian had to wonder if the kitchen staff knew something he did not. The evening meal was usually cold fare, but tonight Cook had added a dish of freshly boiled potatoes to go with the cold leg of lamb.

"Hungry?" Rian asked, picking up the carving knife.

Their meal was a curiously silent affair, unless the polite offer and equally polite refusal of more meat and vegetables counted as conversation. Catherine knew it did not, but she had been hungry and did not want to risk any exchange between them being punctuated by a growling stomach. Finished with her meal, she waited for Rian to speak, but when it became apparent that he was going to follow her lead, she put her elbows on the table, rested her chin on folded hands and said, "Rian, we do need to talk."

Rian drained his glass, pushed back his chair and got to his feet. "Come," he said brusquely. "I think a more comfortable setting is needed."

Chapter 4

Rian sensed Catherine's hesitation as he turned and walked away. In his mind's eye she faltered as she allowed nerves to get the better of her, before she thrust out her chin and followed him. Of course she would follow him. She had come to Oakhaven for a reason. A reason that required being alone with him. And who was he to disappoint her? He headed for the library, pausing at the doorway so she could enter first. The blush on her cheeks did not go unnoticed. No doubt Catherine was recalling what had happened between them the last time they were in this room. He saw her glance up as she passed by, the look in her eye asking if he also remembered. It was something he would never forget, but he was better at masking his emotions than she was.

She refused the offer of a glass of sweet wine, which told him the discussion they were about to have was serious. Of course, it was serious. She had waited until Liam and Felicity had left before confronting him. He just didn't know if, by the time they had finished talking, his heart would be broken. Rian deliberately sat in the same chair he'd used to kiss her that night. A slight smile tugged at the corner of his mouth as Catherine took the seat opposite him.

"How much of your memory has returned?" he asked. He kept his tone neutral, waiting for her to set the mood between them.

"There are pieces that are still lost to me," she answered, "but I believe a great deal is now restored, and I seem to recall more every day."

"Do you know who left you like that, barefoot, practically naked, beaten and—"

"No," she said. "That is still lost to me. I seem to be able to recall most of my life, save for this past year. That remains something of a shambles, although I am confident that eventually even that memory will return." From the way she avoided looking at him, Rian suspected she dreaded the prospect.

"Tell me all that you do remember."

He watched as she composed herself, hands folded together neatly in her lap while she put her thoughts in order. Rian could swear a gentle hum was audible as she rearranged her mind to accommodate his request. But the pucker between her brows also told him she hadn't been expecting him to ask such a question. In fact, he guessed that she hadn't been expecting him to set the tone of their conversation at all. She was the one who'd said they needed to talk, but now she seemed uncertain whether to allow him to dictate the direction of their exchange.

Rian narrowed his eyes slightly as he stared at her. He knew Catherine well enough to take an educated guess at what troubled her. She was worried she would lose her resolve, and not have the confidence to say what she needed to. She was just going to have to trust him.

"Well, for a start," she said, deciding to answer him with a wave of her hand at the books surrounding them, "I can tell you which of these are my favorites as well as those I detest." Her unexpected laugh was a sound full of summer skies and green meadows, and Rian felt himself lifted. He smiled at her and she leaned forward, the change in his expression making her bold. "But I don't think it is my literary taste that interests you. Tell me what is it you really want to know?"

His answer was given without hesitation. "Everything about you."

"Everything?"

"All you can remember…every detail."

And so Catherine spent the next hour introducing herself to him. Although he had already been privy to two accounts of her life, the written report of the investigator he'd hired and Edward Barclay's narrative, listening to Catherine speak of her childhood made it seem as if he was hearing it for the very first time. Her voice filled every part of him, and her words glided gently across his skin as he quickly became lost in the spell of her storytelling. He paid attention to the intonation of her speech, which started out shyly, but then moved with a joyful, tumbling quality as she opened up and shared confidences with him. Now he understood what Liam had meant about hearing Catherine's true voice. Her accent was a reflection of the hills surrounding The Hall where she'd grown up. Her words a softer, sweeter version of the local accent. She filled her own story with all the nuances and inflections that ink marks on parchment failed to convey. Everything she told him was unique to her perspective.

No matter how close their friendship, Edward Barclay could not possibly know her feelings on those matters most personal to her.

Hearing Catherine recall her life, Rian was quietly astounded by her calm acceptance of all that had befallen her. She left nothing out, made no excuses, no attempt to justify the cruel twists and turns that had shaped the path of her life: her mother's death at an early age, her father's inconsolable sorrow and subsequent drinking, the loss of her home to pay creditors after his fatal fall from a horse. The only time Rian felt she was being untrue was in her recollection of her father's death. The sense of falseness was not in the details of the accident itself, but more in her emotions as she spoke. It seemed as if the only way she could articulate the details of the incident was to distance herself. Recount the day as if it had happened to someone else. It told Rian she had not yet come to terms with her father's death, and its aftermath.

"I can even tell you the name of the boy who first kissed me in the hay barn." She finished with a silvery laugh he found captivating.

"Edward." It slipped out by accident and he cursed under his breath seeing her look of surprise.

"Yes, it was Edward. I forgot you had met him."

"Did you enjoy your visit with him?" He tried to make it sound as if she had been visited by an elderly uncle or some equally distant relative. Not someone who held so important a place in her life as Edward Barclay.

"Yes, thank you. It was wonderful to see him again." The genuine pleasure in her voice made him instantly jealous. "And kind of you to send him to me."

"It was nothing."

"No, it meant a great deal to me." She leaned toward him, her hands clasping the arms of the chair as she turned serious. "May I ask you a question?" He tensed, wondering if she could sense the battle raging within him. Every time she opened her mouth, he fully expected her to tell him that it was over between them. Something that had barely begun would be given no chance to flourish. He wasn't sure how he would react once the words fell from those perfect lips. Not trusting his voice enough to reply to her question, he answered with a curt nod of his head. "How is it that you knew to go to Edward?"

"Excuse me?" Momentarily flustered, Rian decided he would be better served if he stopped letting his mind wander. He would need no warning when Catherine decided to destroy his world, and it would serve no purpose if he had one.

"Edward," she repeated."I was asking how you found him."

"Ah well, credit must be given to Stuart Collins, an investigator I hired." Seeing her brows rise, Rian understood he had just widened her circle of acquaintances with the introduction of another. He told her it was Stuart who had first discovered where she was from, and Stuart who had suggested he make the journey north. He did not fail to notice that she narrowed her eyes slightly at the investigator's idea, and he wondered what he would say if she asked him why the suggestion was made in the first place. Or worse, why Rian had acted on it.

"So it was Mr. Collins who told you to seek out Edward?"

Rian shook his head, and swirled the brandy in his glass. "Not directly. Meeting Edward was no more than a fortunate happenstance, but one I admit taking full advantage of."

He proceeded to relate the circumstances by which he had crossed paths with Lord Barclay. His tale did not take as long as hers, and he did not try to conceal his frustration with the local populace who refused to talk about her family until they were sure of his intentions. A wistful smile played on Catherine's lips as she sat listening.

"You know exactly what I mean, don't you?" Rian said, waving a finger at her as he talked about the tight-lipped locals.

"Oh, aye, lad, we knows 'ow to mind our business, and when t'open shop!" She tapped the side of her nose with a forefinger. Rian couldn't help but laugh out loud.

"They're good people," Catherine told him.

"Yes, they are."

"May I ask you another question?"

"You may ask me as many as you like." He got up and replenished his brandy.

"Why did you feel you had to look for my family?"

"Because I needed to know if anyone had been searching for you." Rian paused. "Or still was."

"And if there had been?"

"I don't know," he answered truthfully. "It was a bridge I did not have to cross."

"I have no family left, not anymore," she told him softly.

"I know."

For a few moments neither of them spoke. And then, as if deciding the conversation was in danger of becoming far too gloomy, Catherine perked up. "What else did Edward tell you about me?" she asked, and the sudden playfulness of her tone said she was eager to hear any secrets her childhood friend had revealed.

"Well, for the sake of truthfulness, he never did say he kissed you," Rian confessed. "That was more of a lucky guess on my part."

She clapped her hands together. "I knew he would not tell! I made him promise, and he kept his word. After all these years." She shook her head in mild disbelief, and her voice softened. "Did you like him? Oh, I so want you to like him, Rian."

"Yes, it's hard not to. He's a very personable young man." Jealousy pricked his heart as he wondered why his opinion was so important to her. "Did Edward tell you…anything, Catherine?"

Did he tell you that I love you? Did he tell you how clearly he saw through me? Can you not see that for yourself?

She paused before saying, "He told me a great deal, and the rest I remembered."

"Did he know why you left your home?"

"No. That he didn't know. I was already gone by the time he returned from burying his own father, and the reason is as much of a mystery to him as it is to me."

Rian was relieved. The thought had crossed his mind that, for reasons of his own, Edward might have withheld some knowledge from him when they talked. Something he might prefer to reveal to Catherine in private. But the young man had not done so.

"Unless my memory returns we will never know why I abandoned my home."

Rian said nothing. There was nothing he could say. It would be wrong of him to selfishly declare his gratitude for whatever reason had compelled her to leave. If she had not, she would not be here now, with him. He swallowed down his brandy and let the burning fire punish his throat.

"Edward confessed he was betrothed." Good Lord, had the fiery redhead kept *anything* to himself? "And he offered to break his engagement should I wish it." Catherine's voice dropped to a whisper.

"Did you want to accept his offer?"

Rian wasn't sure how he managed to get the words out as his heart, squeezed so tightly by unimaginable envy, was barely able to beat.

"I am still here, am I not?"

"That's not what I asked," he chided in a husky rasp.

She dropped her eyes and looked down at her hands, which had resumed their demure position in her lap once more. "No, as generous as it was, I did not want to accept his offer."

"Why not? You have known him all your life. Who would make a better husband?" Rian knew that the rest of his life was going to pivot on her answer, and he suddenly felt as if he had stepped into quicksand and was slowly being pulled under.

Catherine snapped her head up and stared at him, hard. Her earlier doubts rushed in again, making her believe she had waited too long before coming to him. Was it possible that he no longer wanted her? Why else would he ask such a thing? A voice in her head told her to leave. Get up from her seat with as much dignity as she could muster and simply walk away. Away from him. But the voice in her head didn't appreciate fate's sense of humor. Rian sat between herself and the door, and she knew him well enough to know he would not allow her to leave without giving him an answer.

"A husband I was in love with." She sounded almost insolent, and actually raised her chin as if daring him to contradict her.

"I beg your pardon?"

Catherine's eyes were dark in the low library light. She couldn't believe Rian was going to make her repeat herself. At some point in the last few seconds she had unconsciously moved her hands from her lap to the arms of the chair, and her fingers now gripped the furniture with enough strength to turn her knuckles white as she spoke.

"I want a husband I'm in love with, and that is not Edward," she said, taking care to enunciate clearly and avoid the possibility of any misunderstanding.

The claw that was compressing Rian's heart flexed and loosened its grip. "But you do care about Edward?"

"Of course, and I always will." The insolence was replaced by conviction. "That will never change."

"And are you always going to allow him to call you Cat?"

Her unexpected peal of laughter diffused the tension between them. "He always has, ever since I was a little girl, and you find it extremely irritating, don't you?"

"What makes you say that?"

"The look on your face when you say the word *Cat* is quite horrifying."

"I find it a difficult appellation for you."

"Edward will always see me as Cat no matter how old I am or what changes my life may bring, just as you will never see me as anything but Catherine."

"True enough," he admitted grudgingly, "but I think Catherine suits you better."

"I would ask you to allow Edward this small indulgence. He has his own burdens to bear."

Rian frowned. To his mind the affable redhead was too young to have much in the way of burdens. Seeing his expression, Catherine softened her tone.

"It's awful to have such a joyous occasion marked by death," she reminded him. "And speaking of awful, did you get to meet his mother?"

The unexpected spitefulness of her tone was a door opening to a darker side of Catherine. A side that Rian found totally at odds with the young woman he had come to know. Whatever Edward's mama had done to hurt Catherine, the wound ran deep.

"No, I did not. Edward said she was visiting his betrothed." He paused, waiting to see her reaction.

"Wanting to be certain she knows her place, I'll wager."

"Surely not. She is, after all, his mother's choice." A slight frown appeared. "Did Edward not tell you that?"

"Yes, he did, but it doesn't mean her life will be any the easier for it. She'll have her work cut out for her."

"You make his mother sound like quite the tartar."

Edward had more or less admitted that his mother had the upper hand in almost every aspect of her son's life, but Rian found this sudden display of open hostility in Catherine fascinating. It occurred to him that perhaps there was another reason Edward called her Cat.

Chapter 5

"Edward's mother will never relinquish her position in that household to another woman, daughter-in-law or not," Catherine said. "Trust me, the young woman had best develop a very thick skin, and be prepared for the fight of her life if she ever wants to be mistress of that house."

Realizing her temper was rising, Rian was at a loss to comprehend why. "For all the affection you bear Edward, it is hard to reconcile such animosity toward his mother."

Catherine sighed and studied her hands for a few moments. She did not look up at Rian as she spoke. "Edward told me he discussed my family with you, so I am sure you already know the details of how my poor papa gambled away his fortune." He said nothing, humbled that she accepted he was already in possession of the facts. "Well, no matter." Catherine continued, "If not Edward then someone else would have revealed the truth."

"Edward and I were childhood playmates, and it is fair to say that a certain fondness developed between us over the years. However, our association was abruptly severed once I reached fifteen. I found out later this was the time our family's circumstances were forever changed. Looking back, it wasn't hard to understand why my papa accepted when we were invited to a special celebration in Edward's honor. I'm sure he hoped that, with the right encouragement, the friendship between us might rekindle, and become something more. Something that would make Edward defy his mother's wishes in his choice of a wife. I think my father always knew I would be strong enough to stand up to her, but she was Edward's mother, and he had to take the first step."

Her smile was tinged with sadness as she picked some imaginary lint off her dress. "I knew what my father was thinking, and if I had refused to attend, the outcome of all our lives would have been very different. But it had been so long since I had been riding, or had a new dress, or been dancing…."She slowly raised her eyes and looked at him. "What a horrible opinion you must have of me now."

Rian wanted to take her in his arms, and tell her that Edward, poor Edward, who still lacked the backbone to stand up to his mother, would never have made her happy. The haunted look in her eyes made him think she already knew this.

"I think you found yourself in a situation over which you had little control," he told her in a low voice. "And you wanted to please your father, someone you cared for very much."

For a few moments the room was very quiet, and then Catherine looked away before continuing, her voice eerily calm.

"Well, I'm sure you know what happened during the hunt that preceded the ball. It was simply awful seeing papa lying on the ground, all twisted and bent. Edward was kind enough to take me away from all those horrible people who didn't care that I heard every cruel, heartless word they said about my father. He took me to the stables, to an empty stall, and he held me while I wept, and wept, and wept. I know I was sobbing for my poor papa, but if I am truly honest, I was weeping as much for myself. I don't know how long we sat there, but it was dark when Edward's mother found us.

"It was awful. She and Edward argued, and it was the first time I could recall him ever raising his voice to her." She sounded almost wistful. "But it made no difference. She ordered him to return to the house and attend to his guests, and then gave instructions to one of the grooms to hitch a horse to a cart so I could be taken back to The Hall with my father's body." Despite the calm with which she spoke, Rian saw the fire in her eyes as the memory of the incident roiled within her. Getting to her feet, Catherine began pacing, her hands clasping and unclasping as she continued with her story.

"Lady Barclay informed me that this would be the last ride they would ever provide for me, and then assured me that lifting my petticoats for her son would prove to be a complete waste of time. As long as there was breath in her body, she would make certain he never married me. It took me a moment before I realized what she meant. She thought, with my father lying dead in a field, that I would try to secure a promise of marriage from Edward using my body." Catherine stopped pacing and turned suddenly, her arms wrapped about herself as tears spilled down her cheeks. "H-h-how could she think that I would do such a thing? Give myself to Edward—or any man for that matter—in that way, or for so mean a reason?"

Experience told Rian she wasn't looking for an answer, though he could have told her such an action was not unheard of. He watched as she sat back in the chair and took the handkerchief he had given her earlier from her pocket.

"I don't suppose I can fault her for thinking such a thing," Catherine said, sounding defeated as she wiped her eyes. "She was only trying to protect her family, but if she thought me capable of such a monstrous act, what did it say about the regard she had for her own son? Edward is the perfect gentleman. He would never do anything so despicable." Pain and humiliation were etched on her face, making Rian wish with all his heart he could pour a magic balm to soothe the hurt. She reached up and tucked a stray curl behind her ear. "I've never told anyone about that until now," she whispered huskily, looking at him from beneath her lashes. "Not even Edward knows."

"It needed to be told, and you may trust I will keep your confidence."

An awkward, heavy silence fell as they both struggled with feelings they desperately wanted to put into words. Fearful of saying the wrong thing, they remained silent. Once uttered, words could not be taken back.

"I suppose it was Edward who told you about the heather," Catherine said, seizing on a less painful topic to discuss.

Rian shook his head, allowing a smile to lift the corner of his mouth. "No, you are wrong. I met an amazing person who claims a long acquaintance with you. Old Ned—"

"Ohhh!"

This time Rian did not hold back. He jumped out of his chair and pulled her to her feet, wrapping his arms around her and cradling her head against his chest, as sobs wracked her body. Talking about Lady Barclay had opened a door Catherine had meant always to keep locked. The hurt was still fresh enough she had not found the charity to forgive Edward's mother her vicious words. And then hearing Rian say Old Ned's name had swung the pendulum to the other side of her emotional arc. Old Ned, the faithful gardener at The Hall who had always been so kind to her. The only one she could count on for help when her father had been so drunk she couldn't manage him alone. Stalwart and unfaltering in his loyalty to the family, he had held both of her hands and cried unashamedly when she told him goodbye.

Two different individuals, each of whom had left their mark on her in different ways and for different reasons—it was no wonder she was crying. And now Rian was holding her in his arms, stroking her hair, offering comfort.

"Catherine…I'm so sorry. I never meant to hurt you."

Feeling the warmth of his body against hers, his strong arms around her, his scent filling her nostrils, only made the pain that much sharper. She pulled her head away and looked up at him with red-rimmed eyes and lashes heavy with moisture.

"Then why did you take Isabel to your bed that night?"

Catherine had not meant to be so blunt. In truth, she hadn't realized she had been thinking about Isabel, but the words tumbled from her lips before she could stop them, and now there was no turning back. He was a man of experience and he could have had Catherine that night. Surely he knew that? She would have gone willingly to his bed. Lord knows she'd offered herself to him, but he had refused her. The rejection had hurt then, and it still did. It was like a thorn in her flesh, one that had to be removed completely or else it would burrow deeper under her skin and fester.

"Why take her and not me?" Catherine demanded in a tremulous whisper. "You said you wanted me…needed me. Was it a lie?"

"No!" Rian shook his head vehemently and tightened his hold on her, but she struggled against him, so he let her go. Running his fingers through his thick hair, his face the picture of perfect misery, he struggled to find the words to ease her anger and hurt.

Felicity had told him to be truthful, but how could he do so when the truth sounded to his own ears like nothing more than a flimsy excuse? Rian knew in his heart and soul that Catherine was everything he had ever wanted in a woman, in a lover, in a wife. He felt the heat rising. His temples throbbed as his pulse pounded, and his heart hammered against his ribcage. She continued to stare at him, her eyes quickly darkening to bottomless pools of deep blue as the gathering storm raged within her, a storm that Rian was more than willing to have consume him.

"Catherine, you must believe me when I tell you I don't remember taking Isabel to my bed. I swear by all that is dear to me, I don't remember lying down with her or making love to her. I swear to you on my brother's life."

She looked at him, aghast. "You admit to making love to her?"

He shook his head, "No—yes—I don't know. She says I did, but it didn't feel like I did."

The air between them suddenly became very thick, and Rian watched Catherine close her eyes and take a deep breath, allowing the truth of his denial to cleanse her. When she looked at him again he saw her eye color had almost regained its normal hue, and her temper was subsiding. She came to him and placed her hand on his arm.

"Tell me what happened that night."

“Are you certain you want to know?”

Unwilling to see the reproof in Catherine’s eyes, Rian dropped his own. The floral design below his feet told him the carpet had been his mother’s choice. All these years, and he had never noticed.

“Yes, I do.” Though softly spoken, the firm determination in Catherine’s voice made him raise his head and look at her. “I was not so drunk I’ve forgotten the words spoken to me by you in this room. Was any of it the truth?”

“Every single word.”

“Then if there is any hope for us, you must tell me what happened after I left you.”

For Rian it was more than a confession. He told her of finding Isabel in his room, of the toast to not standing in the way of fate that she’d proposed, and the brandy they’d shared. He explained his strange reaction to the alcohol and his later belief that he’d been drugged. He even gave her his hazy memories of making love to a woman he’d believed was Catherine herself, and his horror the next morning when he awoke to find Isabel in his bed.

He drained what was left in his glass and waited for Catherine to speak. She stared at him. His body language and the anguish on his face told her all she needed to know. He had not then, nor would he ever again, willingly give himself to Isabel Howard.

“I appreciate how difficult that was for you,” she murmured as she moved toward the door. As painful as the words were for him to say, they had been even harder for her to hear.

“Catherine…” Reaching out, he caught her hand as she passed him. She stopped with her back to him. “Marry me,” he whispered.

Her sharp intake of breath sounded like a whip being cracked, and Rian watched her head snap up and her body stiffen, but she did not look at him. Instead she gently pulled her hand from his.

“If your feelings remain the same, ask me again in the morning.” And for a second time she left him alone in the library, staring after her.

Chapter 6

Rian looked at the almost full bottle of brandy he had carried with him to his bed chamber and seriously considered finishing it off, but the numbing effect would be a temporary salve at best. With a sigh he set the bottle on the dresser and began undressing, cursing his own stupidity as he did so. What on earth had possessed him to ask Catherine to marry him? Not that he didn't want to wed her, but the informality of his manner made the offer seem…disreputable, somehow.

What had he been thinking?

He hadn't and that was the problem. He'd simply blurted out what he was feeling, which was his desire to spend the rest of his life with her. Rian had only ever proposed once before, and that had been a lifetime ago when youthful exuberance could easily be excused for a breach of etiquette. But he had no such excuse now. He was a grown man who really ought to know how to propose marriage to a woman without it sounding so off-the-cuff.

I'm thinking about making an offer for that rather fine stallion Lord Wobbleychops is willing to part with, and if you have no other pressing engagement would you consent to be my wife afterwards?

The problem was he couldn't think clearly when he was around Catherine.

The problem was he loved Catherine.

The problem was he was *in love* with Catherine.

But none of that made any difference now. Her reaction had spoken volumes, shattering any hope he may have held of sharing a life with her. The sudden awkwardness that rose between them, and the fact that she refused to look at him, could not have made her answer more clear. Her request that he ask again in the morning was an obvious ploy. It would give her time to fabricate a refusal that would not cut him to the quick.

One that would spare his pride. Although she was, most likely, hoping he had enough brains not to ask again.

"Damn it all to hell, but you're an absolute ass!" he declared, berating his reflection in the mirror. He was behaving like a lovesick swain when he was older than Catherine by a decade at least, and ought to know better. Well, he had told himself that if she wanted no part of him then, he would hear it from her own lips, and Liam could not fault him for his listening skills this time.

In the morning he would tell Catherine that it was not too late for a future with Lord Edward Barclay. It didn't matter that she was not in love with him. The young man with the fiery red hair was still in love with her, and that could be enough for both of them. She had admitted she still cared for her childhood friend, and always would. Marriages had been built on far less. And if anyone could help the young man find the strength to stand up to his formidable mother, it would be Catherine. The decision made, Rian did his best to ignore the hollow ache in his chest. The grief of loss was already starting to suffuse him. Turning around, he gasped, the breath caught in his throat as Catherine took a step toward him.

The illumination offered up by the lone candle was meager at best, but it was more than enough for Rian to see the apprehension on her face as she gazed up at him. Rian continued to stare, realizing as he did so that Catherine was wearing his robe. It was too big for her small frame, so the hem pooled on the floor and flowed over her bare feet. The sash was wrapped about her waist and now rested over one hip, cleverly fashioned into a bow, and he knew he would never be able to look at his robe in quite the same way again. With her hair gathered in a loose braid that hung over one shoulder, Catherine had never looked more beautiful or alluring.

"Catherine?" He tried to speak but his voice was nothing more than a nervous rasp. Rian felt his heart pounding wildly against his ribs as she delicately gathered the excess length of the garment in one hand, while closing the distance between them. A glimpse of her legs, the pale skin almost luminous in the dim room, was a promise that threatened to steal his reason. A confirmation that she wore nothing inside his robe.

Rian had already removed his vest and managed to pull his linen shirt free of his breeches while mentally berating himself. He now watched as Catherine worked to free the buttons, a task made more difficult by her trembling fingers. If it were up to him he would tear the garment from his body, but he forced himself to resist the temptation by deliberately fisting his hands. However, he could do nothing about the heat that seared through him as she concentrated on her task.

He knew from their recent conversation that she had put her father to bed many times, and was no stranger to loosening a man's shirt. But he doubted her hands had ever trembled so much while attending her father, nor had so much been dependent on it. A small furrow appeared between her brows, telling him she was silently willing her fingers to remain steady. After freeing the last button, Catherine gently opened both halves of the shirt front, pulling the fabric away from his torso and exposing him to her gaze. The play of light and shadow across his well-muscled chest and abdomen made her draw in a breath. She slipped her hands inside the garment, sliding her palms over his skin as she rested her forehead against his sternum. Her breath, now as shallow and uneven as his own, raised goose flesh on his skin, but Rian continued to keep his arms at his sides, hands clenched tightly. He was afraid to touch her, knowing that to do so would be his undoing. There could be no turning back.

His voice was a raw ache as he forced himself to ask, "Catherine, what are you doing here?"

"Seeking the man who asked me to marry him."

The warm moistness of her mouth pressed against his skin, and a dozen wild horses took off in his stomach. He groaned. There was something in her voice, a quiver that he recognized as her own awakening need. Every muscle in his body tensed, making him shudder involuntarily, and he looked down at the same moment Catherine raised her own head and pulled him into the depths of her gaze. Not taking her eyes from his, she moved away, stepping back yet allowing the tips of her fingers to inflame his body by trailing lightly across his ribs and waist before her hand fell. She stopped moving when she was beyond his reach, measuring him with a silent, thoughtful look.

Rian swallowed hard. A tongue of fire licked his skin. It was just a matter of time before he gave in to his need to touch her. The craving she had released deep inside him was ravenous and threatened his grip on all rational thought. Desire beat its own voracious path through him. He needed her. He wanted her, and this time he knew he would not be able to resist the temptation being offered. He did not want to resist, but yet he had to be sure.

"Catherine, you do not have to do this."

"Rian, I cannot…" She hesitated, and his heart plummeted.

He saw her close her eyes, unable to look at him as she suddenly comprehended the jeopardy she had placed herself in. It was beyond foolishness, it was an act of recklessness that put both her name and reputation in peril. The muscles along Rian's jaw tightened as anger flared hot and white. Did she have any idea what a dangerous game she was playing? It was sheer madness to come to him like this. Allowing him a glimpse of what he hungered for, only to deny him.

"I will not be a wife in name only, and I cannot in good conscience allow you to commit yourself to such a union." The words fell from her lips in such a rush, Rian was certain he had misheard. It took him a moment to grasp her meaning and understand this was no refusal, no denial.

"I never asked you—"

Catherine's imperious wave cut him short."If I am to be with you, I have to know…that I can be a proper wife to you. A proper wife," she repeated, "*in every way.*"

Comprehension, like a cool rush of night air, suddenly tempered his lust and dissolved his anger. He knew exactly what she was saying, and why she was here. After the attack she'd suffered, she needed to know she could give herself to a man without succumbing to the nightmares that had bedeviled her.

"No sweetheart, no. You have nothing to prove, Catherine, and I don't need you to do this. Not now, not tonight." He wanted her. God knew his body ached with his need, but not like this. Rian wouldn't have Catherine give herself to him just to prove she could. He wanted—*no, he needed*—her to want him as much as he wanted her.

She opened her eyes and let him see that her desire for him was undeniable, and unwavering. "Yes, I do. I want to…this night." She tugged on the bow at her hip and his robe whispered open. The barest shrug and it slid from her shoulders, down her arms to pool on the floor in a silken cushion.

Rian groaned as his eyes swept over Catherine's naked body. His lust, already awake, broke free from all restraint as he drank her in. Though he had seen her naked before, this time it was different. Now she was offering herself to him, a banquet for him to feast on. And he was a starving man being told to sate his hunger. He gazed at her firm, lush breasts. Each one crowned with a pink nipple that practically cried out for the touch of his lips, the scrape of his teeth, the generous, unending attention of his tongue. He hadn't realized how long her legs were in comparison to her upper body, and he rode the swell of his desire, imagining how it was going to feel to have the silky smoothness of those limbs wrapped around him.

She was giving herself to him.

To him alone.

"Catherine, do you know what it is you are doing? There can be no turning back once you have given yourself. Do you understand what that means?" His warning filled every corner of the chamber.

Catherine could not trust her voice, and nodded slowly in reply. Rian stripped off his shirt, finishing what she had begun. He saw the pulse at the base of her throat quicken and flutter like a small bird's wings. Her body trembled and the end of her loosely fashioned braid danced against her hip as she took a deep, steadying breath. In and out.

"Catherine…" Rian stepped in front of her and placed his fingers beneath her chin, raised her head and looked into her eyes. There was a wariness that made him pause. Despite her declaration, she was unsure of her decision. It still wasn't too late for her to leave with her virtue intact. As hard as it would be to let her go, he knew he should send her away. Permitting her to remain if she had any doubts would mean he could never face her again. Or himself. The tips of his fingers were featherlight as they ran down the sides of her arms. She quivered beneath his touch. "What is it?" he asked in a voice he barely recognized as his own.

"I'm afraid," she whispered.

His hands stopped moving. "You fear me?"

She shook her head.

"Then what?"

"I'm afraid that I have come to you too late. That you have changed your mind and no longer want me."

Inside he groaned. Nothing could be further from the truth. His hands resumed their task though his touch was firmer. Was it his imagination, or did she tremble less?

"There is something I need to know," Rian said, looking down at her. She ran the tip of her tongue across her lower lip, making the heat that flamed his groin jump a few degrees. "How deep is the regard you have for Edward Barclay?"

It was unfair of him to ask her about another man as she stood gloriously naked before him, but he had to quell the last doubt that lingered still. She had said she was not in love with Edward, but neither had she said she was in love with him. And he needed to know that she would suffer no regrets by turning away from a man she had known all her life, for one she had known only a matter of months. He wanted to be enough for her. Rian saw her eyes narrow, her expression turning oddly fierce before it smoothed out.

"I am where I wish to be," she told him, "and with the only man I wish to be with."

Glorious joy washed through him, but still he offered her one last avenue of escape. And this had nothing to do with Edward or himself; this was for her alone.

"This is your last chance," he whispered. "You can leave now, and no one will ever know that you were here. But if you remain, I fully intend to make you my own. In every way."

Reaching up, Catherine put her arms around his neck while boldly pressing against him. He was already hard, but the warmth of her breasts pillowed against his chest made him still harder.

"If I leave, it will not be by my choice." Her mouth desperately sought his.

Wrapping his arms around her, Rian pulled her even tighter against him, the feel of her skin electrifying his senses. With his mouth he greedily plundered hers, his tongue snaking in and out, making promises he had every intention of keeping. He could feel her nipples harden, becoming tight buds pressed against his chest, and he let his mouth move greedily down her neck, his teeth gently nipping and scraping her soft flesh.

With one hand gripping his upper arm and the other buried in his hair, Catherine hung on, buffeted by sensations she never knew existed. She didn't realize her knees were buckling until Rian pulled his mouth away. Scooping her up in his arms, he carried her to the bed. Quickly he shed his remaining clothing, and lay beside her, gently caressing her face. Taking his hand, Catherine turned it over and kissed the palm, her tongue tracing small circles on the surface as she looked up at him from beneath dark lashes. He rolled on top of her, propping himself up on his elbows as he systematically explored her face with his lips. He danced kisses over her forehead, her cheeks, her closed eyes. And this time, when his mouth found hers, he forced himself to be patient and savor the taste of her.

He ran his tongue down the column of her neck, pausing to dip in the hollow at the base of her throat. She shuddered beneath him as he continued to worship her by slicking his mouth across her collar bone, her shoulders, and then down between her breasts. He felt her roll beneath him as his long hair brushed erotically across her skin. Supporting his weight with one hand, Rian stroked her with the other. Gently swiping the underside of each perfect breast, he moved down her belly to the curve of her hip, his hand seeking the sensuous roundness of her buttocks. Little mewling sounds escaped Catherine as her body tingled, and the heat coming from deep inside her flamed ever higher.

Lowering his head, Rian gently suckled one breast, stroking the taut nipple with his tongue before rolling it gently between his teeth. Floundering in a sea of indescribable pleasure, Catherine tried to raise herself off the bed, but Rian was having none of it, and he gently pushed her back on the pillows.

"You want to know if you can be a 'proper' wife to me?" he whispered, moving his mouth and gently worrying her earlobe. With his weight momentarily immobilizing her, he watched as Catherine moved her throat, swallowing with some difficulty, before she nodded, eyes shining and lips parted. "Then I think," Rian continued, "it only fair to show you what type of husband you can expect to receive in the bargain."

Moving so he no longer pinned her body with his, Rian carefully watched her face, looking for the first flicker of fear or apprehension that would halt his continued exploration of her body. His long tapering fingers traced a path between her breasts, pausing before fanning across her stomach and teasing their way through the nest of thick curls. Stroking her inner thigh, Rian patiently waited for Catherine to part her legs, and gently slipped inside her. His finger was immediately coated with her slickness, and he began moving it in and out, increasing the tempo as she writhed next to him. Soft mewling sounds turned into moans, and little rushes of breath became uneven panting. He rubbed the pad of his thumb over her clitoris, feeling the small bud tighten, and was almost pushed back when Catherine unexpectedly surged beneath him. One hand gripped his arm, and the heightened flush of her face told him a storm was gathering inside her.

"Oh, dear God, please!" Her eyes glazed as she ground herself against his hand, an instinctive response to the need pulsing through her. Her breath, uneven before, now became a symphony of harsh, ragged gasps. Her nails dug into his flesh, but Rian merely smiled as he continued to bring her closer to her climax.

Catherine arched her back and raised her hips, her heels fighting for traction amongst the rumpled bedding. Letting go of Rian's arm, she clutched the sheets, twisting them hard enough to make her knuckles turn white. She was lust and desire in its purest form, and with her body she begged him to release her from such exquisite torment.

With one smooth movement Rian rolled on top of her, his thigh pushing her legs open. She opened eagerly, the intoxicating scent of her sex claiming him with its heady fragrance. His unexpected weight made Catherine groan, so he raised himself up on his forearms before leaning down to kiss her. She caught his lower lip between her teeth, sucking hard enough to turn Rian's grin wolfish. He pushed with his hips, watching her pupils dilate at the feel of his cock throbbing against her, awaiting—no *needing*—her invitation. She gave it with an upward thrust of her hips.

"Lift your legs and put them around me, as high as you can," he instructed, feeling the muscles in her thighs tighten as they locked him in place. It was as if she had been made specifically to fit his body, and Rian paused for a moment, caught up in the exhilarating rush of their coupling. Never before had it felt so right. Beneath him, Catherine looked up, her eyes impossibly huge. "Patience, sweetheart, patience," he murmured.

Amazed that he could summon enough discipline to maintain his self-control, Rian was immediately encased by wet heat as he penetrated her. His patience was further tested as he forced himself to wait, giving Catherine time to adjust to the feel of him within her. To accommodate herself to the steady pulsing throb of him. Her gasp was its own exquisite torture, but Rian knew, no matter how willingly permitted, his presence within her was a violation. He felt the muscles in her thighs twitch and jump at the unnatural strain of holding his body between them, and in her eyes he saw the first stirring of panic. His expression became an apology as, with one smooth stroke; he surged forward, rupturing the barrier of silken flesh that was her gift to him.

Rian covered her mouth with his, feeling a sting as sharp teeth sank into his lip in response to the sudden pain spiking through her. He continued to kiss her, his tongue stroking hers, allowing her to ride the crest of exquisite agony until it was swept aside by another sensation entirely. Catherine's body bloomed, opening up to him, and suddenly the ache that came from deep within her no longer felt strange or unknown.

They had both waited too long for this moment, too long to have each other, and Rian, encouraged by her movement beneath him, quickened his pace. Though increasing in intensity, he made certain his movements were still controlled. This was all about Catherine awakening the demands of her own body, and learning there was nothing to fear. The feel of her nails raking across his back, and the firm pressure of her thighs locked against his hips almost broke his restraint, encouraging him to seek his own release. He was grateful she did not yet recognize how close he was to losing himself inside her.

Perspiration matted Catherine's hair at her brow and temples, dotting her upper lip and making the hollow at the base of her throat glisten. Rian watched as a trickle shimmied a path between her breasts. Her eyes glittered and her face flushed. Kiss-bruised and swollen lips parted enough for him to feel the warmth of her breath against his skin. He made a low growling sound in the back of his throat as she rolled his nipple between her thumb and forefinger, increasing the pressure to pinch the hard nub. He felt his self-control slipping, and when he was certain he could not hold back another moment, Catherine shrieked and became rigid beneath him. He felt her tense as muscles clenched and sinews stretched and every nerve, every fiber of her being, exploded at the same time. Riding the swell of her climax Rian found his own release, gasping and shuddering as he joined her in the fiery heat that threatened to consume them both.

Not wishing to cause further discomfort, Rian pulled out and rolled off her. His mouth twitched when he heard Catherine's sigh of relief at having her body returned to her, and he watched as she moved her limbs with a lazy, languid motion. Her expression told him she was blissfully content, from her toes to the ends of her hair. Still caught in the ebb and flow of her fading orgasm, she did not notice when he slipped from her side. Indeed, it wasn't until the soreness between her legs was eased by cool water that she opened her eyes to look at him. Rian gently wiped away the remnants of her virgin's blood with a soft cloth, holding the cool square of linen against her tender skin and lessening her discomfort. He leaned over and lazily kissed her breast, scraping the nipple lightly with his teeth, and making her jump as an erotic echo of her orgasm peaked again.

"Don't..." she admonished weakly. "Let me catch my breath."

He chuckled softly as he returned the basin of water to the washstand and returned to the bed, taking her in his arms. "Take as long as you need, my love."

Turning her head, Catherine looked at him with an expression that was curiously serious. "It wasn't like that...what happened to me...I don't remember ever feeling like that before."

"I know." Rian kissed her tenderly on the mouth. "A woman's virginity is a gift that can only be given once, and you graced me with the honor of taking it."

"I'm glad. I wanted it to be you."

He smiled at her, feeling ridiculously happy. "Hush now, you need to sleep." Drawing the blanket around them, Catherine rolled onto her side and Rian pulled her toward him until her back was pressed against his chest, her buttocks nestling in his groin. She smiled as she felt him stiffen at the contact.

"Rian?"

"Mmm..."

"Will you—can we—" She sounded hesitant, unsure of how to phrase her request, and certain of the lack of decorum in asking.

"Yes, but not just yet," Rian murmured, understanding her completely.

"Oh, you don't want to?"

He sighed and moved a stray curl that was tickling his face. "I think you know that's not the reason," he chuckled. "You need to rest. When you waken—"

"You promise?"

"I promise."

It was an assurance he had no difficulty keeping.

* * * *

Dawn was chasing the night from the sky when Rian swept the hair from Catherine's face and held her close. His lips found her ear and he whispered quietly in the darkness. She replied without hesitation, her voice warm and loving. "Yes," she told him.

Chapter 7

The sound of voices raised in anger could easily be heard even before Rian pushed the door open and entered the kitchen. Almost every servant at Oakhaven was seated around the large table in the center of the room. Only the stable hands were missing, but he knew that their exclusion was due to the nature of their charges. They rarely ate breakfast with the rest of the staff, but the reason for such an extraordinary gathering would be shared with them all at the midday meal.

And speaking of breakfast, Rian couldn't help but notice it appeared to have been largely forgotten. The swell of voices rose and fell in obvious displeasure. Ordinarily he would have been touched by the loyalty of the staff, except it wasn't a Connor that they were pledging their allegiance to. It was the first time in his life he had ever been the recipient of such censure, and he decided he didn't much care for it.

The angry chatter might have continued unchecked if not for a scullery maid who noticed him leaning against the wall, arms folded across his chest, listening to the growing brouhaha. She squealed and dropped the mug of tea she held in her hands. The sound of the heavy earthenware mug shattering on the stone floor brought all conversation to an abrupt stop as every head turned toward him.

"Be careful not to cut yourself," Rian told the girl as he helped to pick up the broken pieces of her mug.

Looking at the faces of his staff, he noticed more than a few were now flushed bright red, but hardly anyone averted their eyes. Even if he had not overheard their conversation, he would have been a fool not to realize the entire household was aware that Catherine had not spent the night in her own bed. And they were not pleased by it. The general consensus seemed to be that he had taken advantage of her. He was, after all, older and more experienced in the ways of the world. Rian felt a muscle in his jaw tighten and it took effort to remain calm and say nothing. Scanning his audience, he noticed Mrs. Hatch was curiously absent, but while the housekeeper could claim the entire house as her domain, the kitchen belonged to another. Cook came toward him, wiping her hands on her apron.

"Did you need something, Sir?" she asked.

Rian took a good look at the large, florid woman as she continued to dry her hands. He found himself inexplicably drawn to the motion, fascinated by the hide-and-seek game her fingers played with the cloth tied around her waist. He found it hard to believe the same woman who could tenderize a slab of meat by pounding it with her fists, could also produce the lightest of pastries. He swallowed and looked her in the eye, the arch of her brow the only indication of his fall from favor. It did not escape his notice that she had called him *sir* and not Master Rian. He gave her his best smile. It was not returned.

"Actually, I was looking for Mrs. Hatch," he said.

"She is in the back parlor. She has a visitor."

"Who is calling on Mrs. Hatch at such an early hour?" He was intrigued both by the visitor's timing, and his housekeeper's need to receive such a person in the back parlor.

"It's Reverend Hastings," Tilly blurted out, earning more than one scolding look.

"Really? Well, well, well, how very fortuitous."

Ignoring the glares being thrown her way, Tilly got to her feet. "Would you like me to take her a message, Master Rian?" she asked.

"Yes—no wait. I think it's best if I speak to her myself, Tilly, but I do need you to do something for me." She waited for him to speak, clearly uncomfortable at the idea of such an unrepentant sinner being in the same room as a pious man of the cloth. Deciding he might as well confirm their gossipy chatter, Rian grinned wickedly. "I think Miss Catherine would very much like a hot bath this morning, and would you also see that a breakfast tray is taken up to her."

"Yes, Master Rian, I'll see to it immediately," Tilly rushed, bobbing him a quick curtsey.

He turned to go, and then turned back. "Where did you say Mrs. Hatch and the Reverend were?"

"In the back parlor."

"Ah yes, and Tilly?" He waited until every person seated at the table was looking at him.

"Yes...?"

"Take Miss Catherine's tray to my bedroom."

The door had almost closed behind him when he heard another mug hit the floor and shatter.

* * * *

It had been a momentous day.

Catherine had been touched when Rian had told her how furious the entire household staff was because he had taken her to his bed. Particularly the stable hands. It appeared that someone had decided waiting until midday would be too long, so they had taken it upon themselves to bring the grooms up to speed.

"I'm convinced they all wanted to give me a good thrashing!" Rian recalled.

"But I seduced you," Catherine protested, concerned and upset by the misunderstanding.

"Well, I wasn't about to tell them that," Rian said smugly, "and even if I had, I doubt it would have made the slightest difference. They're all very fond of you, Catherine, and at least one or two love you almost as much as I do." He dropped a light kiss playfully on the tip of her nose.

Reverend Hastings had arrived that morning to discuss the forthcoming marriage between one of the stable boys and one of the housemaids. Rian took it as an omen, a most auspicious one at that, and had insisted the rector meet with him and Catherine as well. Seeing for himself that Catherine was not being coerced in any way, Reverend Hastings was more than happy to sell Rian a common license, thus allowing them to dispense with the reading of the banns. It also meant they could be married that afternoon. The ceremony took place in the family chapel with almost every member of the formerly disgruntled staff standing as witness. Catherine looked radiant in a pale green gown with a matching bonnet, and Rian was forgiven. Though it took a couple of casks of ale to placate the stable boys.

Now she sat at the dressing table drying her long hair with a towel, and the scent of roses perfumed the air. She looked at herself in the mirror as she continued with her task. The face that stared back at her was the same one she had seen yesterday, but it was also different somehow. There was an awareness that she had not noticed before, the loss of innocence replaced with a woman's knowledge.

After dropping the towel to the floor, she picked up her brush and began passing the bristles through the tangled skeins of her hair. When it was smooth and free of knots, she quickly braided it, letting the heavy plait fall over one shoulder. She thought about tying a bow in the end, but dismissed the idea. Bows were for children or young, innocent women, and she had crossed that threshold last night. Rian had warned her she could not go back. There would be no more bows, at least not in her hair, and besides, she smiled at her reflection, she was wearing enough bows already.

"Come to bed, Catherine."

She turned and looked at her husband, who was propped up on one elbow, patting the empty expanse next to him in invitation. Mrs. Hatch had shooed him out of the room earlier as she helped Catherine prepare for her wedding night.

"I think it's a little late for that," Catherine apologized as the housekeeper poured perfumed oil into her bath water.

"Hush, lass," the older woman had admonished gently. "You were married today and tonight is your wedding night. It matters not what happened before."

Assuming a maternal role, Mrs. Hatch washed Catherine's hair and sponged down her limbs. When she was dry, she dressed her in a lacy item that could barely pass for a nightgown.

"Where on earth did you find this?" Catherine asked in an amazed voice, holding the garment next to her and delighting in the feel of the delicate material.

"It was in your trunk."

"My trunk? But I've never seen this before in my life!"

"Aye, well I think Master Rian has, as it was with the other clothes he bought for you."

"How on earth—why would he?" Catherine shook her head, too bewildered to wonder what had been going through Rian's mind when he'd purchased such an item for her. "It is beautiful though, isn't it?" she sighed, letting the sheer gauze run through her fingers.

"Yes," Mrs. Hatch agreed with a faint blush staining her cheeks. "It's perfect. Now let's get it on you so I can permit your groom to return."

Catherine caught hold of the housekeeper's hand and pressed her cheek against the back. "I want you to know, Mrs. Hatch, we meant no disrespect. It wasn't Rian's fault. I was the one who refused to wait."

The housekeeper hugged Catherine tightly and the look in her eyes said she appreciated the first part of the apology, and only believed half of the second part.

"Come to bed," Rian repeated, his voice a low enticing growl as Catherine crossed the room toward him.

The nightgown covered her from neck to ankles, but as she moved it revealed more of her body than it covered. Just as it was supposed to. Very much a novice in the art of seduction, she stood by the side of the bed, shyly waiting for Rian to tell her what to do. He moved quickly, swinging his long legs over the side and sitting on the edge. Placing his hands on her hips, he drew her gently toward him until she stood between his thighs. His fingers curled around the ends of the bows decorating each shoulder, and he tugged, delighted to see Catherine's mouth form an 'O' of surprise as the garment fell in a whisper about her feet.

"Turn around," Rian instructed.

At first she wasn't sure what was happening, and fear knotted itself in her stomach until she impatiently pushed it away. This was Rian, and he would never hurt her. And then she felt his mouth, soft and gentle, pressing against her back, kissing the faint lines that still marked her skin, and the one violent, angry slash that was never going to fade. Beginning at the small of her back, he worked his way up her body. His mouth caressed each horrific reminder, washing away the poison embedded in each puckered ridge of skin. With his mouth he worshipped her, telling Catherine she was loved wholly and completely no matter what. Her body would always carry the mark of that night, but it was a burden her soul could release.

Catherine closed her eyes as a light fluttery feeling danced in the pit of her stomach. At Rian's urging she took a few steps forward, feeling her husband slide off the bed and sink to his knees behind her. His clever lips continued with their task, making her shiver with pleasure when he found the sensitive place at the back of her knees. Taking hold of her hand, Rian turned her once more, but now it was to move her back onto the bed. Lying against the pillows, Catherine gazed at the man who now came up off the floor, and watched, mesmerized, as the candlelight played with the planes and shadows of his body. Lowering his head, Rian ran the tip of his tongue from ankle to knee before continuing upwards, trailing a silken path across her inner thigh.

She gasped at the sensation and her muscles trembled as her husband repeated his actions on her other leg. Without looking, Rian cupped her breast, casually rolling the pad of his thumb across her nipple and feeling it stiffen instantly. Catherine's moan came from some place near the back of her throat, and she licked her lips. Inside her body a storm was gathering, and Rian breathed deeply, inhaling her musky scent.

Palming her buttocks, he raised her hips, his hair brushing along the sensitive skin of her thighs as his tongue stroked her flesh. She gasped and gave an involuntary shudder as his tongue swept a broad path up her center. Gently Rian probed and licked her sweet flesh, and the more she writhed as her passion built, the deeper he went. He suckled her with his mouth, feeling her heat increase, and knowing she was ready to be taken to heights she never knew existed. Pausing just long enough to raise his head, Rian found himself caught in Catherine's gaze. She seemed to be having difficulty focusing.

With a smile he buried his head back between her legs and fastened his mouth over her sweet spot, sucking gently at first and then with an increasing pressure that had her hand fisting in his hair as he teased her to the edge of her climax, before pushing her over the edge with a final flick of his tongue. Shoulders down and hips raised, Catherine arched her back as she entered her own frenzied vortex. Every nerve in her body exploded as her climax swept through her, followed by a searing heat washing over strained muscles. Rian, grateful she'd let go of his hair, gathered her to him, rocking back and forth while he stroked her skin as she whimpered in his arms. He felt the frantic drumming of her pulse in her throat as the silken thread that had first bound them when she had been in the throes of her fever became stronger and pulled them even closer. When Catherine's breath no longer came in harsh, ragged gasps, and her pulse had slowed to a steady throb, she opened her eyes and stared up at her husband, her lover.

"Will you promise to do that to me again?"

"Of course," he replied, stroking a damp curl from her neck. "As often as you will permit me."

"And what can I do in return?"

With a deep chuckle, Rian rolled onto his back, and showed her how to straddle him. Allowing Catherine to take control, he watched her eyes open wide as she sheathed him inside her body, felt the prick of nails from hands braced against the smooth expanse of his chest. She shuddered slightly when he moved inside her, but the curve of her mouth told him it was in delicious anticipation.

Tipping her head forward, Catherine pooled the heavy rope of her hair on his torso, and Rian held his breath, watching as the woman he had almost seduced in the library slowly emerged. This time there was no need for blackberry brandy to aid in the transformation. Instead he looked on with pride as Catherine shed the last remnants of the girl she had been, and wholeheartedly embraced the woman she would be from this moment on. Eyes closed, lips parted, her body glistening with perspiration, she began moving rhythmically on top of him.

"Slowly, sweetheart, slowly," he told her, guiding her with his hands, "let me find my heaven with you."

A quick study, Catherine adjusted her pace, intuition directing her movements, increasing her tempo, until she followed her husband to the point where neither of them were able to hold back. Giving one final upward thrust, Rian emptied himself inside his wife, holding her tightly in his embrace as she fell forward, completely spent.

Lying quietly in the dark with their limbs entwined, Catherine haltingly told Rian about the nightmares she'd had while staying at Pelham. Nightmares that featured a dark, indistinguishable figure, pain, terror.

"If they come again, hold onto me and I will be strong enough for both of us," he promised. Relieved that he took her word as fact, Catherine relaxed against him. In a matter of moments the even feel of her breath blowing over his skin told Rian she was asleep. He lifted her left hand and gently kissed her fingers, pressing the cool smoothness of the gold wedding band he had placed there earlier to his lips. "I love you," he whispered, his heart soaring as his wife snuggled closer to him.

Chapter 8

Propped up on one elbow, Catherine watched Rian as he slept. He lay on his back, one arm flung carelessly over the pillow, the other resting lightly by his side. The realization that she had never seen anyone more beautiful struck her. Sleep had been late in claiming them, and the sun was now high enough for daylight to reach the bed, bathing the occupants in its glow. And affording Catherine the opportunity to really look at her husband as he lay quietly next to her.

His face was ruggedly masculine. The severity of his dark brows was softened by the long sooty lashes that rested on his cheek. Catherine lightly ran the back of one finger down the curve of his face, following the strong jaw line and chin, now coarse with stubble. With the tip of her finger she lightly smoothed a path down his straight nose, pausing in the dimple above his top lip before following the outline of his generous mouth.

Thick brown hair curled lazily over his shoulders and Catherine smoothed it away from his skin, her palm lingering on the muscles of his upper arm before sliding across the breadth of his chest. Rian did not stir, so she let her hand rest lightly on his sternum, enjoying the steady rise and fall of each breath. Then, empowered by her own boldness, she continued with her exploration. Hungrily her eyes devoured him, this man who was now her husband and lover, as she softly scraped the tips of her fingers over his belly, boldly following the line of dark hair that disappeared beneath the sheet covering his hips.

“Don’t begin something you may not be willing to finish.”

She gasped, and turned her head to find Rian fully awake and staring at her. She didn’t need to be told her face had turned bright red; she could feel the burn plain enough. “I thought you were sleeping,” she said guiltily.

Rian's smile was filled with amusement. "Hard to do when your hand is so arousing."

"And what makes you think I am reluctant to see this through to completion?" she challenged, slipping her hand beneath the sheet and running her nails over his hip, a particularly sensitive place she had discovered quite by chance last night. She felt him jolt under her hand. "After all, I have an excellent tutor."

The amused look on Rian's face quickly changed to something else as his body, already stimulated by her touch, came fully awake. Rolling Catherine onto her back in one swift movement, Rian looked down at his wife and murmured huskily, "Then let us see if you are ready for today's lesson." Her throaty laugh filled his head as she proceeded to show him how willing a student she was.

Later, after their appetite for each other was sated, Catherine stretched and flung a leg carelessly over his with a contented sigh.

"Happy?" Rian asked as he kissed the top of her head.

"Mmmm, yes, very, although…"

"Although what?"

"Felicity and Liam are going to be very cross with us." Intoxicated by the scent of her skin, Rian nuzzled her neck, offering an unintelligible murmur in reply, and earning a playful slap on the arm. "Rian, I'm serious!" Catherine protested.

He stopped what he was doing and looked at her. She was serious, although he knew a few moments more and the serious side of her would willingly wait until the wanton side had finished with him. He had known many women in his life but never had he reached the heights of ecstasy that Catherine took him to simply by allowing him to take her there first.

"When Felicity and Liam see how happy we are, they will forgive us both," he assured her. "You are happy, aren't you?"

"Of course, I am. How could you doubt it?" Her eyes were wide with disbelief.

"A man needs to be reassured from time to time, that's all," he grumbled happily.

"I shall keep that in mind."

When he tapped her lightly on the thigh, she rolled her leg off him and watched as he got out of the bed and crossed over to the bureau. "I have a gift for you."

He returned holding a large flat box in his hands, but Catherine was too busy looking at the rest of his body to pay much attention. Sitting up, she pulled the sheet about her and gave him a thoughtful look before asking, "Who is Sophie?"

Rian stared at her, unexpectedly at a loss for words. "How do you know about Sophie?" He felt certain the only two people who knew of Sophie's existence, his brother and Mrs. Hatch, would not have told Catherine about her. At least not without letting him know of it.

"I am not the only one who talks in my sleep," Catherine told him. "You didn't say anything else, just her name."

The look in his eye told her she had touched a nerve, one that was still raw, and she turned her head away. Strong fingers caught her chin, and Rian made her look back at him.

"Catherine, I will keep no secrets from you," he said seriously.

"Then who is she?"

He hesitated a few moments, as if trying to decide how to tell her, and hoping she would understand. Although the circumstances were completely different, it felt like he was courting danger, explaining his relationship with another woman so soon after his confession about Isabel. "She *was* someone I cared for once. Very much." Catherine could hear the sorrow in his voice. "She was my wife."

"Was?"

"Yes…she died."

Suddenly recognizing there were a great many things she did not know about the man she had taken for her husband, Catherine was immediately curious. How long had he and Sophie been married? Had she borne him any children? How had she died? But she stayed her inquisitiveness, and instead threw her arms around his neck, holding him tightly. "Oh, Rian, I'm so sorry. Forgive me for asking."

He took his time before gently pulling away from her, not wanting to let her go. The strength that flowed from Catherine was like a never-ending pool of cool, sweet water where he would always be able to quench his thirst.

"There, there," he comforted, seeing her eyes glisten. "It was a long time ago, and I promise I will tell you about her, but please, not today. Today belongs to you." He watched as she settled back down, blotting her damp lashes with the heel of her hand. The smile he gave her dispelled the somber moment. "Now, I have a wedding gift for you," he said, placing the flat box on the bed in front of her.

"But…I have nothing to give you."

He kissed her, slowly, deeply. "My darling, what you have given me has far more value than the trinket I now give to you."

Blushing, Catherine stared at the item on the bed. The box had an aged look to it, and spoke of being handled by many through the years. "May I open it?"

The glint of excitement in her eyes made Rian laugh. Like most women, his wife was going to enjoy receiving gifts. Almost as much as he was going to enjoy giving them to her. "Of course, how else will you know what's inside?"

Carefully she disengaged the simple latch and lifted the lid, gasping and opening her eyes in surprise at the treasure nestled on the velvet within. "Rian, I can't—it's beautiful—it's too much—where did you get— *Oh Rian!*" This last was added with a deep sigh.

"It's an old Connor family tradition. Something each first born son gives to his wife. Would you like to try it on?"

She nodded, not trusting herself to speak as Rian lifted the necklace from the box and placed it around her throat, securing the clasp firmly. The setting was plain but elegant, not that the stone required anything to enhance its beauty. As big as an apricot, and almost the same color, the canary yellow diamond sparkled, seeming to draw every drop of sunlight that spilled into the room, and reflecting the light back as a deep gold that dazzled the eye. Rian smiled, delighted to see the play of rainbow light that danced on Catherine's skin as the gem rested between her breasts.

"Perfect," he whispered. "It's just perfect."

"Oh Rian, it's too much!I can't possibly—"

"Hush, you have to take it. It comes with me." He kissed her lightly on the shoulder, watching her face as she tried to make sense of what he had told her.

"What do you mean, it comes with you?"

"Connor family tradition dictates that the first born son give this necklace to his bride."

Ever practical, Catherine arched a brow. "And what if there is no son?"

"Then it falls to the first born daughter, who gets to wear it after she has taken a husband." He reached out and cupped the diamond, feeling the weight of the jewel as it rested in his palm. "Either way, the diamond has to stay with the Connor family," he finished solemnly.

Sensing he was holding something back, Catherine asked, "Why? What will happen if it does not?"

Rian shrugged. "Something about pestilence and ruin and general ill fortune." The twinkle in his eyes told her he was teasing.

"All the more reason to keep it hidden safely away, I would think." Catherine reached up behind her head to undo the clasp but Rian stopped her.

"No, please don't," he said gently. "I like the way it looks on you, and it has been hidden away for far too long." He put his hand against her cheek as she slowly lowered her arms. "Wear it every day or only on special occasions if you wish. It will be returned to the box when you hold our first child in your arms."

"Why? Is that a tradition also?"

"Yes." He chuckled, already hearing the regret in her voice at having to give up the necklace. "But if it's any consolation, you can wear this for the rest of your life." He slipped onto her finger a ring whose single gemstone, though far smaller, was a perfect match in both clarity and color to the one around her neck.

"They are the same!" Catherine was delighted.

"It is rumored both gems were cut from the same stone." Rian gave his wife an indulgent look. "And I think there's enough similarity to give credence to that theory, don't you?"

Holding up her hand, Catherine admired the ring, which sparkled with as much brilliance as the pendant. "Where did they come from?"

"No one knows for certain," Rian admitted with a lazy shrug.

His wife gave him a look of mild alarm, "Rian, what if they were stolen by one of your ancestors?"

His chuckle was a deep rumble. "Knowing some of my ancestors, I'd say that's a strong possibility. I should warn you, rumor has it that the gems are bespelled."

"Bespelled?" Catherine was intrigued. "You mean like magic?"

He nodded. "Legend says that if either the necklace or ring is worn by anyone other than the intended recipient, then the diamond will curse the false wearer."

"How?"

"Absolutely no idea," Rian told her with a devilish grin. "It's never happened as far as I know, but I rather like the idea of sores and boils erupting in unsavory places."

"That sounds a little severe, considering the recipient would always be a woman,"

"Very well then, how about warts and unsightly chin hair?"

"Better," she laughed. "Still, I suspect your curse is actually the result of one of your forebears wanting to keep the jewels together in one place." She jumped off the bed and went to stand before the mirror, pirouetting first one way and then the other, admiring the way the diamond moved with her.

"As I said, a perfect fit," Rian murmured.

Chapter 9

Felicity was filled with a serenity that only women who are blessed with carrying new life possess. It is a feeling universal to all, yet still unique to each prospective mother. She had been disappointed on arriving at Pelham Manor to find that Catherine was not there, but accepted her mother's insight regarding her friend's absence. It was generally agreed the only way for Catherine and Rian to resolve the stalemate between them was to spend time together. Even Felicity's father agreed, and besides, it wasn't as if they would be completely alone. Oakhaven had almost as many servants as Pelham.

However, whatever the outcome with Rian, Felicity had expected Catherine to return the next day. Concern became her companion as the hours passed with no sign of either her friend or her brother-in-law. It was not relieved until an Oakhaven groom, returning the borrowed horse, informed them that Catherine had made no mention of returning to Pelham Manor.

"Is that a good sign, do you suppose?" Felicity asked her mother, unable to keep the worry from her face.

"I think it is a very good sign," Emily answered reassuringly. "Let them be, daughter. If they are meant for one another, then allow them the time they need to discover it for themselves."

A discreet note to Mrs. Hatch requesting further reassurance had brought a reply that was brief, almost to the point of rudeness. The housekeeper informed her mistress that Catherine appeared in good health, and everyone enjoyed having her back at Oakhaven. Whether that included Rian, Mrs. Hatch did not say.

"Were this written in any other hand but Mrs. Hatch's, I would be concerned," Felicity said, waving the paper at her husband.

"Why is that, my love?" Liam chose not to point out to his wife that she was already concerned.

"Mrs. Hatch has corresponded with me many times before, and this is most definitely not her normal tone of communication." She blew out an irritated breath. "There's something she's not saying."

Taking the note from Felicity's outstretched hand, Liam quickly scanned the contents. "She says Catherine is well and everyone enjoys having her back." Confusion knotted his brow as he glanced up from the parchment. "What else is she to say?"

"What's she's obviously not telling me," Felicity replied testily.

Liam sighed. He did not pretend to understand how women thought, and now that the most important woman in his life was with child, he had the distinct impression that he was going to comprehend that process even less. Wisely he decided to offer no further comment on the letter.

Needless to say, Emily and Charles had been delighted with the news of their first grandchild, and it had taken very little persuasion to make their daughter and son-in-law extend their visit. Felicity enjoyed being made a fuss of, and Liam took the opportunity to share with his father-in-law some ideas for the inevitable merger between the two estates.

But they had been gone now for almost two weeks, and it was time to return home. Liam had duties at Oakhaven requiring his attention, while Felicity was eager to make ready the nursery. And scold Catherine for her continued silence.

* * * *

A quick search of both the stables and library, two of Catherine's favorite places, did not reveal her presence, but the hour was still early enough that Felicity reasoned her friend might still be getting dressed, or even abed. After tapping lightly on the door, she entered Catherine's bedroom and stopped, her hand still on the knob as she stared in dismay at the room's shocking state of disarray. Clothes spilled out of half-open dresser drawers with stockings and petticoats tossed carelessly on the floor. Dismay turned to unease. Catherine was by nature a tidy person, and this disastrous mess was not the result of her hand.

Making her way to the dressing table, she noticed the rosewood box that held Catherine's ribbons and combs was missing, as was her hairbrush. Pursing her lips, Felicity looked carefully about the rest of the room, trying to determine what else was out of place. Something nagged at her, but it wasn't until she was on her second sweep that realized what it was.

How could she not have noticed? While the rest of the room looked as if a small hurricane had passed through it, the bed remained immaculate. Neatly made and obviously not slept in. The furniture refused to divulge the whereabouts of the room's occupant or reveal what had taken place within these walls.

Rian!

The thought of her roguish brother-in-law galvanized Felicity into action. Picking up her skirts, she hurried down the hall to his room. Intuition told her that somehow the disaster in Catherine's room was his fault. She had no idea how he was involved, but he had best answer her questions to her satisfaction or else, firstborn or not, he would feel the lash of her tongue!

The man in question had just finished fastening his breeches when Felicity threw open the door to his room and stormed in. He looked at her first with surprise, and then consternation at her obvious agitation. "Felicity?" The high spots of color on her cheeks were an obvious sign of her current distress, and he wondered what could have upset his mild-mannered sister-in-law. "Where's Liam?" he asked, reaching for his shirt.

"Who? Oh, he's about somewhere…" Felicity answered with a distracted wave of her hand.

"I see." Rian slipped his arms into the sleeves of the shirt and began fastening the buttons. He noticed, with some amusement, that Felicity had just registered his state of near undress. The flush on her cheeks deepened, but it seemed that anger superseded any embarrassment she might be feeling as she took a step toward him.

Seeing her hands curled into fists, Rian wondered what Liam had done to cause this rare mood in his wife. He had never seen her so distraught, and it really was most unfair that his brother's doltish insensitivity would make his wife direct her anger at him. Deciding a private conversation with his sibling was necessary, Rian resolved to make it happen soon.

"What have you done with Catherine?" Felicity demanded in an accusatory tone. "Is she well?"

"Catherine is in the best of health," Rian replied, hoping his own composure would counteract Felicity's agitation. He finished buttoning his shirt and straightened the cuffs before looking at her. "Why do you suppose that I have done anything with her?"

The color in Felicity's cheeks was beginning to fade, but Rian noticed she did not look him in the eye. Instead her gaze was fixed on a point just beyond his left shoulder. "I was just in her room…" she began.

"And?" Raising a quizzical brow, Rian folded his arms across his chest. He knew in all likelihood he would catch hell for this later. If not from the woman in front of him, then most definitely his brother, but he couldn't help himself. It was a rare thing to fluster Felicity, and he was going to enjoy the moment.

"I can't find her!" Felicity wailed. "She isn't in her room." The fists unclenched so Felicity could wring her hands instead. "You don't understand. The mess, there are clothes thrown everywhere."

Rian rubbed the back of his neck. "Ah, well that's really my fault, you see—"

"And her bed!"

"What about her bed?" Rian asked suspiciously.

"It hasn't been slept in, that's what!" The tremulous waver in Felicity's voice was a clear indication her anxiety was beginning to climb.

"Oh, is that all."

"Is that all!" Felicity's voice was well within shrieking range. "Is that—" she stopped and shifted her focus, suddenly no longer afraid to look him in the eye. "But you already knew that, didn't you?"

"Knew what?" Holding his hands out in a gesture of surrender, Rian feigned innocence. How long would Felicity insist on pursuing this line of questioning before the truth dawned on her?

"Catherine. You already knew she hadn't slept in her bed, didn't you?"

"Um, yes, actually I was aware of that." He dropped his hands to his sides, powerless to prevent the grin that tugged relentlessly at the corners of his mouth. Apparently Felicity was going to make him spell it out for her, and he was more than willing to oblige, but before he could say a word, she closed the distance between them, and poked him hard in the chest with her forefinger.

"Well, where is she?" Felicity demanded. "What is it you're not telling me? Why didn't Catherine sleep in her own bed?" Each question was punctuated with a hard jab at Rian's sternum.

"Because I'm sleeping in his."

The small, familiar voice came from behind her, and Felicity, finger poised in mid-jab, turned her head slowly to see Catherine sitting in the middle of Rian's bed. The sheet she held tightly about her, coupled with her disheveled appearance, left no doubt what she was doing there. From the moment she'd stepped into the room, the Mistress of Oakhaven had given her attention to only one person. It never crossed her mind that Rian might not be alone. She now stared at Catherine, who was guiltily trying to smooth her unruly hair with her fingers. Felicity's mouth fell open, and for a moment she was thunderstruck, but then she quickly regained her composure and turned back to face her brother-in-law.

"As you can see for yourself, Catherine is quite well," he said quietly.

"Yes…as I can see. Please accept my apologies, Rian."

She turned and gave Catherine a bewildered look before exiting the room with as much dignity and self-control as she could muster. It didn't stop the sound of Rian's rich chuckle from reaching her through the closed door.

* * * *

Liam was alarmed to discover his wife seated in the drawing room with a very large glass of port wine in her hand. "Felicity, darling, is that good for the baby?" he asked, kneeling before her.

She took a small sip. "Oh, I don't think it will hurt. Mama said it would be quite all right." Her manner was distracted and she sound vague.

Taking the glass from her hand, Liam placed it on the table out of reach. "I don't think she intended that you drink it for breakfast."

"Hmmm, what?"

The look she wore told him her mind was elsewhere. Liam took her hand in his. Something was obviously troubling his wife. "Darling, is everything all right? Did you find Catherine?"

"Oh yes." She looked at him and blinked, owlishly, "And it's the most extraordinary thing, Liam."

"What is, sweetheart?"

"She was with Rian."

Noticing the flush on his wife's cheeks, along with the drops of perspiration beading her upper lip, Liam frowned. He would have thought the news that Rian and Catherine were together would be an occasion for joy. Wasn't this what they had been hoping for? The past two weeks here at Oakhaven must have done the trick, giving the obstinate couple a reason to seek each other's company, and to discover they shared enough similarities on which to build a relationship. So why wasn't his darling wife as pleased with this news as she ought to be?

"Catherine and Rian were together," he repeated. "Isn't that a good thing, sweetheart?"

As if realizing he had failed to read between the lines, Felicity tugged on her husband's hand, making certain she had his full attention. "Catherine was in Rian's room," she told him. "In his bed!" she hissed.

The younger Conner didn't know whether to be shocked or overjoyed. Far be it from him to tell his older brother how to conduct himself. He might be more than a little perturbed by his wife's statement, but he knew

Rian well enough to know if Catherine was in his bed, she was there of her own free will.

"Liam!" Felicity hissed under her breath as she tightened her grip on his hand. "What are we going to do?"

Unsure of what they could do, Liam was saved from giving a response by the entrance of the very people they were discussing. He got to his feet as Catherine came toward him, automatically bending down to kiss her cheek.

"It is nice to have you both home again," Catherine told him, before returning his affection. Felicity, however, still seemed to be in a dazed state as Catherine bent down and kissed her.

There followed a heavy, awkward silence. Catherine and Rian positively reeked of guilt while Felicity appeared embarrassed and Liam simply confused. For a full minute they all stared at each other. Felicity occupied with twisting a handkerchief between her fingers, while Catherine attempted to smooth down her hastily put together coiffure. The Connor men just looked at each other, indulging in some private form of communication.

"We're having a baby!" Liam suddenly blurted out.

"A baby!"

"How wonderful!"

"Congratulations, old man, when?"

And then, as three pairs of eyes turned toward her, Felicity burst into tears.

"I c-c-c-can't seem to stop c-c-c-crying!" she wailed miserably, hiding her face in her hands.

It wasn't Liam, but Rian who went to her. Pulling her gently to her feet, he held her in his arms, cradling her head against his shoulder, stroking her hair as she wept.

"There, there, it will pass, I promise," he said, keeping his arms around her until the worst of her crying was over.

Gently he sat her back down on the couch next to Catherine. Both women stared at each other for a moment before Felicity suddenly pulled Catherine into her arms, which initiated another bout of noisy weeping. Their husbands retreated to a discreet distance across the room.

"How long do you suppose this will last?" Liam asked, slightly alarmed. He was positive his wife had wept more this past week than the rest of her entire life.

"For me it is already over, but as for you, little brother, this will get worse before it gets better. You have my word on that," Rian assured him.

A sudden wave of melancholy came over Liam as he recalled the reason behind his brother's certainty, but he remained silent. This was not the time or place to discuss so painful a moment from the past. Taking the same chair Felicity had occupied earlier, Rian now moved it toward the couch and sat down. Felicity and Catherine had their arms about each other's waists and they looked up at him, a matching set of wet cheeks and slightly red noses.

"Felicity, please accept my apologies for my manner toward you this morning. Had I known, I would not have teased you." He leaned forward so he could take her free hand in both of his. "And please believe me when I say Catherine wanted to tell you and Liam right away. I was the one being selfish. I wanted to keep her to myself for just a little bit longer."

Over Rian's shoulder, Felicity gave her husband a confused look. The clarity she was seeking was not to be found as Liam appeared just as baffled as she. For a moment she wondered if this was one of her duties as mistress of the house, being informed when assignations of an intimate nature took place under her roof. If that were so, it was a duty she would relinquish immediately. "What is it you wanted to tell us?" she asked, nervously.

"That we're married," Catherine said softly, shyly holding out her hand so they could see for themselves the plain gold band on her finger. The large diamond had been put aside for the time being.

"Married? Did you know about this?" Felicity asked as she turned pale and shot her husband an accusing look.

"No one knew Felicity," Rian said. "Everything happened very quickly."

"When?" she demanded.

"The morning after Catherine came back to me," Rian answered softly. And he went on to tell them how Reverend Hastings happened to be visiting, and agreed to marry them that afternoon.

"Were you at least married in the chapel?" Liam inquired, happy to see Catherine's nod.

"It was beautiful," she told him.

"But we should have been there," Felicity wailed.

"I know and I am so sorry," Catherine said, putting her arm around her friend's shoulders. "But we couldn't wait. *I* couldn't wait," she added softly, seeing a gleam of understanding shine in the new mother's eyes.

"Who stood up for you?"

"The entire household I think," Rian said with a rueful grin as he remembered the sound of shuffling feet followed by some belligerent whispers as toes were trampled and ribs elbowed.

"Well, that's alright then."

At that moment Mrs. Hatch came into the room, followed by a maid carrying the inevitable tea tray. "Oh, Master Liam, Miss Felicity, how nice you have returned," she said, gesturing to the maid to place the tray on the table. The sound of Felicity blowing her nose brought a worried look to the housekeeper's face. She could see her mistress was on the verge of tears again.

Liam waited until the maid had left before addressing his housekeeper in his best Master-of-the-House voice. "Mrs. Hatch, is there anything you wish to tell us, an event that we should be made aware of perhaps?"

She looked carefully at the faces in the room, gave Felicity a sympathetic smile, and then sighed with relief. She didn't like keeping secrets. "No, Master Liam, I imagine, from Miss Felicity's demeanor, you have already been made aware of what has happened." A glance encompassed Rian and Catherine. "But if I may be so bold, I'd like to say it's well past time, though I daresay many a heart will be broken once it is known he is wed."

"I doubt that," Rian muttered with a snort.

"His only saving grace," the housekeeper continued with a smile, "is his choice of bride. I could have wished for no other."

Felicity dabbed her eyes with a handkerchief before saying, "Mrs. Hatch, I must applaud your skill at keeping such a confidence."

"If you please, I didn't want to keep it from you, but Master Rian tricked me into promising before I had a chance to think."

Rian managed not to wilt beneath the housekeeper's disapproving look.

"Well, he does have that way about him, doesn't he?" Felicity noted.

Looking at the teacup in his hand, Liam addressed Oakhaven's housekeeper. "Mrs. Hatch, you might want to get a bottle or two of wine so all the staff can share in our good news."

"Pardon me, Master Liam, but there's really no need. Master Rian was already very generous in allowing us to toast his and Miss Catherine's good health."

"Of that I have no doubt," Liam said giving his brother a wide grin, "but there's another reason to celebrate. I want everyone to rejoice in the new life that will be born into this house."

Chapter 10

John Fletcher flinched at the sound of the figurine hitting the wall. The delicate statuette shattered into so many pieces, he knew reassembly would be impossible. He sighed. That particular piece of porcelain had been a favorite of his, although he'd be hard pressed to say why. Perhaps it was the way the artist had so exquisitely managed to capture the flush of innocence on the face of the shepherdess. But now she lay in a dozen pieces on the floor, so he turned his attention to the woman pacing angrily about the room, wondering how many more fine objects would be destroyed before her temper ran its course.

"He married that whey-faced bitch?" Isabel shrieked. Her face was turning a most unattractive blend of crimson and purple, but, having seen this before, John remained silent. There was nothing to do until her fury had exhausted itself, and Isabel was once more able to think clearly.

Rian's brief return to the city from his trip north had not included a stay at the family townhouse. Instead, he had gone directly to the home of Matthew Turner and, after concluding his business, had accepted the hospitality offered and stayed with him. It was, therefore, reasonable to assume that Rian had no knowledge of the letters Isabel had sent him before they were forwarded with the rest of the correspondence to Oakhaven. Better to believe that than to think he had read them and chosen to deliberately ignore all her prettily worded invitations.

Despite their parting, Isabel refused to believe that she could not win back Rian's affections. Returning him to her arms, as well as her bed, was just a matter of time. John, however, was not so certain. Though he admired her confidence, he felt it was misplaced this time. Isabel had overplayed her hand. An opinion he was prudent enough to keep to himself.

Unlike the servants who staffed the townhouse, those at Oakhaven proved to be almost rabid in their loyalty to those they served. The promise of a gold coin was not sufficient temptation to make anyone share secrets with him, so the closest he could get was a tradesman from the village whose interaction with the estate consisted of delivering occasional supplies. It was not the best source of information, but it was all John had to work with. Though not privy to any intimate details regarding the family, the man passed on what he knew, and in his longtime role gathering information for Isabella, John had learned that even the most mundane information could prove useful.

The news that Rian Connor had taken a wife had been anything but mundane. John had withheld the information about Rian's marital status for almost a week before common sense told him that suppressing it any longer was foolish. If no one else beat her to it, that gossiping harpy Lady Maitling was sure to mention it.

Isabel's mercurial temper was something to behold, unless you were on the receiving end of it. John waited patiently, watching from beneath half closed lids as she struggled to regain some sense of decorum. She sat with a dejected *whump,* accepting the glass of sweet wine he poured for her and emptying it in one go. For a time nothing was said. He knew Isabel was thinking, her mind furiously tumbling from one thought to the next, deviously plotting her next step. Her plan to win Rian back had been shattered just as irrevocably as the shepherdess figurine. Now with that particular door closed, Isabel's mind set about dealing with her problem from an entirely different angle. Suddenly she looked across the room at John, a wicked smile lifting the corners of her carefully painted mouth. He thought she had never looked more sinister.

"How difficult will it be for you to arrange another meeting with Phillip Davenport?" she asked, getting to her feet and refilling her glass.

John gave a slight shrug. "Not difficult at all." He hesitated for moment before continuing. "However I distinctly recall your desire to never have to deal with him in person again."

"I did say that, didn't I?" She gave him a calculating look. "As a means to an end, he could prove to be a most useful individual, and I'm certain I could hide my revulsion for as long as it was necessary." John accepted the glass of wine she held out to him, wondering what type of scheme would involve Phillip Davenport.

"This news has changed everything," he commented.

"Rian Connor has gone too far," Isabel said, the flare of her nostrils proof her fury still simmered just below the surface. "I will not be humiliated like this. It's time he learned he cannot simply cast me aside without there being consequences." She took a sip of her wine. "Someone is going to have to answer."

What exactly Isabel meant by 'consequences' was something it did no good to dwell on, but John suspected it would not bode well for her former lover. Completely calm now, she walked over to a small side table where a silver tray held an assortment of invitations. Picking them up, she shuffled them as thoroughly as a deck of playing cards, her brow furrowed in concentration. Not finding what she wanted, she dropped them back onto the tray, turned and looked at John. "I don't think the newest Mrs. Connor should be left to flounder in the depths of the countryside, do you? A man of substance such as Rian Connor would surely welcome an opportunity to introduce his wife to society." The smile on her lips turned icy.

"And how do you propose bringing about such an introduction?" John asked, keeping his own expression stoic.

Isabel's eyes glittered malevolently. "What would be better for a coming out than a ball?"

"And who did you have in mind to host such an event?"

The sound of her laughter rang in his ears for a long time.

* * * *

Perspiration ran down Lettie Davenport's back. A rivulet that bisected her shoulder blades as she forced herself to ignore the searing pain that came from dragging her useless leg behind her while she made her way around her bedroom. *One more circuit*, she told herself between gritted teeth, *just one more and then I will rest.* Protesting such abuse, her body sent a spasm of fire to claw along her lower back, hip and down her leg.

Step and drag...step and drag...

Every day the small woman pushed herself a little farther, and every day she got a little stronger. For too long she had kept to her bed. It had been too easy to play the role of the invalid wife. Her only consolation was that the deformity caused by her husband's rage, had also stopped him from demanding his right to her body. For some perverse reason Phillip would not force his attentions on her now that she was physically unable to deny him. Though she had never done so before, the fact that she'd possessed the capability had all been part of his sick fantasy. The possibility, no matter how remote, that one day Lettie might turn on him, was enough. But now, slaking his lust on a body that was broken and damaged was, to his mind, the same as beating a dead dog.

For Lettie it was the silver lining in the thunderhead that threatened her sanity. By choosing to defy Phillip's authority and help Catherine escape, she had sacrificed the use of her leg. It seemed a small price to pay compared to what Catherine had been forced to endure, and what further abuse would surely have been forced upon her had she not escaped.

Regrettably, the actions of that night had brought about other changes. Her servants were being dismissed with no warning, replaced by faces unfamiliar to her. The latest example had occurred this morning when a girl, barely more than a child, had come in place of her personal maid.

"Where's Mary?" Lettie asked, doing her best to conceal her concern at this latest change.

"Gone, Missus," the girl replied, carefully setting down the basin and jug of water she carried.

"What's your name?" Lettie asked, frowning slightly as the girl shifted nervously from foot to foot.

"Grace, Missus." The rough quality of her voice betrayed her street origins. A child of the gutter and back alleys, grateful merely to survive from one day to the next. She would have no expectation of bettering her situation. It was safer for Phillip that way.

Lettie observed the girl's clothing with a small wrinkle of distaste. She had no idea what color the faded dress hanging from her thin frame might once have been. The ridiculous frilled cap covering her head had possibly once been white, but no longer. The girl raised a dirty finger and slipped it beneath the cap, and scratched vigorously at her head. Lettie felt a shiver go down her back. No doubt the child was crawling with lice.

Seeing Grace's look as she struggled to hide her fear and confusion, Lettie realized it was useless to ask anything more about the missing Mary. This child had no answers. In all likelihood she had no idea who Mary was, especially as it was plain to see she had never been in service before. This could very well be the first time she had ever been inside a house such as this one. It was a wonder she had managed not to drop the pitcher of water she'd carried. Compassion stirred in Lettie's breast. Perhaps if she herself stopped acting like a frightened rabbit, it might lessen the girl's anxiety.

"Is Martha still here?" Lettie asked.

"I d-don't know who that is, Missus," Grace stammered.

Quickly Lettie gave a brief description of the woman she was referring to, relieved when the dirty grey cap bobbed a couple of times. The scared look in Grace's eyes was replaced by a hesitant, but intelligent gleam.

"Tell her that I said you are to have a bath and your hair washed. Your clothes are to be taken away and burned and you are not to attend me again until you are clean and presentable. Do you understand?"

Grace nodded, more slowly this time, as she repeated what she had been told. Satisfied, Lettie leaned back on the pillows and closed her eyes. It was a few moments before she realized the expected sound of the bedroom door being open and closed had yet to come. Opening her eyes, she saw that Grace was still standing by the side of her bed.

"What's the matter?" Lettie said, noticing the girl was now trembling. "Did you not understand my instructions?"

"Oh yes, Missus, but I've had a bath once before—"the girl sniffed"—and I didn't like it much."

"I'm not surprised," Lettie murmured under her breath, trying to imagine the conditions under which the child might have endured such an event. "Well, it won't hurt for you to have another one," she said cheerfully. Her smile did not alleviate Grace's fears, and her limbs still shook. At a loss to understand what it was that frightened the child so, she asked, "Are you afraid of getting wet?" Grace shook her head in an emphatic denial. Well, that was a good thing, Lettie thought. "Then what are you afraid of?"

The girl opened her eyes wide. "Mam says I'm not to take my clothes off for no one."

"And your mama is quite right, but it will be easier for you to get clean if you remove your clothing first," Lettie explained.

"But you said to have them burned!" The girl gave her an accusing look. "And I ain't got no others." Her small hands curled into fists and she deliberately placed one on each bony hip. It was such a perfect imitation of an adult stance that Lettie could only smile at the copycat motion. Obviously Grace had seen it many times.

"Grace, where is your mother?"

Huge tears now washed down the small pointed face, cleaning a path that only served to accentuate the remaining grime. "Gone," she mumbled, immediately covering the clean tracks on her face by wiping at them with her sleeve.

"Gone?" What on earth did that mean? As gently as she could, Lettie asked, "Do you mean she has died?"

Grace looked at her with eyes that were too knowing for such a young girl. "No, Missus. Mam's just...gone."

"Where did she go?" Lettie paled at the idea that any mother could simply disappear and leave her child behind. She had to be mistaken, but Grace only shrugged her thin shoulders in reply. Unsure if she wanted to hear the answer, Lettie nevertheless pressed on. "Why did she not take you with her?"

"'Cause she didn't have 'nuff to eat, not with the baby an' all. So she sold me."

"S-sold you?" Lettie's voice was filled with horrified disbelief.

Grace nodded serenely, not at all disturbed by what she had said. Either the child had misunderstood the circumstances that led to her mother's departure, or the exchange of human life for coin was such a commonplace event in her world that its occurrence was not strange. Lettie sincerely hoped that the first reason was the correct one, but a nagging voice in the back of her mind told her that the second was closer to the truth. Phillip had bought the child from her mother. The idea made her feel faint and she lay back on the pillows, fighting to catch her breath as the room swayed ominously around her.

"Missus?"

"Pray give me a moment, child." She heard the sound of water being poured into the porcelain basin, and then small hands were wiping a wet cloth across the back of Lettie's hands. She roused herself, recalling what had initiated this conversation. "Your mother was correct when she told you not to remove your dress," Lettie said, doing her best not to shudder. "Nevertheless you need to be bathed, and your clothes have got to be burned." A look of outrage pinched the child's narrow features, prompting Lettie to hold up a hand. "Tell Martha I said to find you some more clothes to wear after you have been bathed."

The hasty departure of young maids from their service over the years meant there was a variety of garments left behind that could be put to good use. Grace turned to leave.

"And Grace, tell her I said to make sure she uses hot water," Lettie instructed as the door closed.

Every day brought with it more changes, and this unusual child was simply the latest being thrust upon her. Lettie wondered about Mary. What reason had she been given to explain why her services were no longer needed? Had Phillip said anything at all, or had he just dismissed her with no explanation? Worry caused a frown to wrinkle her forehead. Had her husband paid Mary what she was owed in wages? Though she wanted very much to believe the answer was yes, in her heart she thought it unlikely. A tear slowly trickled down her cheek.

Lettie wasn't stupid. It was her position to manage the household staff and she knew exactly what Phillip was doing. He was making sure there was no one left who would remember Catherine had ever been there. No one to recall the punishment Lettie had suffered at his hand for her own defiance. How long would it be before she was the only one left who remembered Catherine? And what then? Would Phillip dispose of her also? She had no doubt he was more than capable of performing such a deed. His fury at discovering her part in Catherine's flight had been the most frighteningly savage experience of Lettie's life. She had thought he meant to kill her then, instead of leaving her broken and bleeding on the bedroom floor, and promising the same for any who came to her aid.

It wasn't until he had mercilessly dragged her by the arm back to her own room that he permitted Mary to attend her. By then the damage to her body had been complete. It might have still been possible for a skilled physician to repair her broken and twisted leg, but Phillip refused to send for one. A doctor meant questions would be asked, questions Phillip didn't want to answer. Eventually the swelling went down and the bones knitted themselves as best they could and Lettie survived. Broken, but still alive.

When she had recovered enough to comprehend she wasn't going to die, she had wept bitter, angry tears and railed at God. What more did he want from her? Hadn't she suffered enough already? But deep in her heart she knew that even if God heard her, he would not answer. If he had not protected her on her wedding night, or at any time since, why should he take pity on her now?

That was all right, Lettie told herself. On the Day of Judgment he would not be able to turn away when Leticia Moreland Davenport stood before him demanding an answer. In the meantime she was determined that her husband should not arrange the meeting before she was ready, and that meant strengthening her body.

In the beginning she had only managed a few faltering steps before falling to the floor, trembling so violently from the exertion it appeared she was having a seizure. Now she could complete five circuits about her room before she began trembling and nausea threatened.

Step and drag...step and drag...

Of course Phillip could not find out she was rehabilitating herself. As long as he thought her infirm and helpless, he would have no reason to lock the door to her room. Something he had been diligent about at the beginning of her confinement, but now had become careless about.

Step and drag...step and drag...

With an exhausted sigh she managed to reach the bed and pull herself back up onto the pillows. Dipping a cloth into the dish of water Grace had left on her bedside table,she wiped the sweat from her face and forced herself to take deep cleansing breaths until her thudding heart resumed a calmer beat.

The clock on her mantel told her it would soon be time for her afternoon coffee, and Lettie didn't want Grace to notice anything amiss. A child of the streets, she saw more than she let on, but Lettie wasn't certain how far she could be trusted. As soon as her hands stopped shaking and she had tidied herself up, she picked up her needlework and resumed her embroidery.

The transformation was amazing. With her skin scrubbed and her hair washed, Grace hardly looked like the same little girl who had stood before Lettie a few short hours ago. As she had predicted, Martha had managed to find some decent clothes to replace the lice-riddled ones that Grace had been wearing. Neat and clean in a dark blue dress with a yellow apron and matching cap, she carefully carried in Lettie's tray.

"Why, look at you!" Lettie exclaimed, clapping her hands. "You look simply delightful. Don't you feel better?" Grace turned bright red at the compliment and, now that she was clean, Lettie estimated her age to be no older than ten, twelve if she was being generous.

Averting her eyes, the girl plucked nervously at her apron. "I'm not supposed to talk to you, Missus. No one is," she mumbled, her voice so low Lettie had to strain to hear her words.

"Who said you can't talk to me?" she asked, whispering to the girl.

Grace looked up and then glanced over her shoulder as if she fully expected to see someone standing behind her. "The master," she answered fearfully.

What a cruel and unfeeling bastard her husband was. God alone knew what lies he had told the new help about the reasons for his wife's confinement. "Well, you don't have to talk to me, but can I whisper to you, Grace?" A sudden gleam of intelligence sparked in the girl's eyes. "It will be our secret, I promise," Lettie added.

Crossing her heart with her finger, she then spit into the palm of her hand as a way of sealing her oath, knowing she had impressed Grace by doing so. No doubt the child believed ladies of quality were incapable of spitting. Unless of course Grace didn't think Lettie was a lady of quality. Now her small brow wrinkled as she wrestled with the prospect of disobeying the master of the house, to become an ally to its mistress. The choice was not an easy one, but finally she made it. Favoring Lettie with a shy smile, Grace bobbed her head one time and then busied herself pouring coffee. After handing Lettie the cup, Grace gave another small curtsey and left.

She returned again later with Lettie's evening meal, and then a short while after that to remove the tray. Lettie was thankful that Phillip had not replaced the cook, at least not yet, because it meant Grace would be able to fill her stomach and eat decently. There was some comfort in that at least. Now, lying quietly in her bed, Lettie's thoughts were interrupted by the sound of voices. After her last visit, Grace had not closed the door to the room properly and it now stood ajar, wide enough for the sound of two distinct masculine voices to reach her.

A glance at the clock on the fireplace mantel said it was past the hour for a social call, but even if it were not, they never received visitors. Step-dragging her way to the open door, Lettie opened it a little farther and pursed her lips as she concentrated on the conversation drifting up from the foyer below. Neither voice was one she recognized. One was commanding, the tone that of a man who was used to being obeyed, while the other's tone was the more subservient manner of a servant. Lettie could only surmise the latter belonged to one of the new staff Phillip had recently engaged, and it seemed he was being given a set of instructions.

"When do you expect Mr. Davenport to return?" the first man asked.

"Momentarily, sir," the servant answered. "Would you care to wait?"

There was a clucking sound, a clear indication of the visitor's frustration at not finding Phillip at home. Ordinarily he would have been here, but Lettie knew the demands of a new mistress were currently occupying his time.

"No, I will not wait," the visitor said.

For the next few moments all Lettie could hear was the sound of the man's heels striking the tiled floor. The visitor was leaving, and she waited for the familiar sound of the front door being opened. Then the man spoke again.

"Make sure this letter is placed directly into Mr. Davenport's hands, do you understand?" He sounded annoyed at having to depend on an underling to complete his task. There could be no doubt it was of some importance.

"Of course, sir," the other man murmured respectfully, "and what name shall I give my master?"

"Fletcher, John Fletcher. He will know it, but make sure he knows that although I am the one waiting for his reply, the request comes from Lady Isabel Howard. It would be in his best interest to make sure he answers without delay."

There was no response from the manservant. Now she heard the door being opened, and Mr. Fletcher, whoever he might be, left. She did not shuffle her way back to her bed until the sound of fading footsteps assured her there would be no more surprises.

The unexpected physical tension that came with eavesdropping had created a dull ache which now spread through Lettie's lower back. She barely noticed the pain however, as her mind was fixed on the conversation she had just heard. The name John Fletcher was unknown to her, but she could not say the same about the name Howard. Once before, a messenger had been sent by Lady Isabel Howard, and, for a while, Phillip had been filled with a secret excitement. Unfortunately it did not last, but Lettie had long ago ceased to be surprised by her husband's mercurial nature.

Lying back and staring up at the faded canopy above her bed, she chewed on her lip. What possible connection could there be between Isabel Howard and Phillip? And why would a messenger demand a reply be forwarded to him, and not her ladyship? The entire episode reeked of secrets and lies, and made Lettie shake her head. She didn't know what was happening but she could not shake the terrible feeling that somehow Catherine was involved. Her husband's obsession with his beautiful young cousin was all consuming. Perhaps Lady Howard had given Catherine shelter? Lettie pulled her wrap tighter as a sudden chill swept through her, bringing with it a dreadful sense of foreboding. No, however Lady Howard was involved, Lettie had the ominous feeling no good would come of it.

Chapter 11

"Are you feeling any better?"

Catherine and Felicity walked arm in arm through what had, at one time, been a formal garden gracing the rolling grounds at the rear of Oakhaven. Any pretense of maintaining the original horticultural vision had been abandoned long ago, leaving the area a riotous tangle of overgrown greenery. Only the boxwood hedges remained recognizable, but even they had reverted back to a less formal growth pattern.

"Mmmm, yes, thank you," Felicity replied.

At breakfast the smell of bacon and the sight of runny egg yolks had sent the expectant mother scurrying to the kitchen, the nearest place to find a sink in which to throw up.

"There, there lass," Cook had said, handing her a wet cloth to wipe her face along with a glass of wine to rinse out her mouth. After she had spit the last taste of the acrid bile from her mouth, Felicity was grateful to take a seat at the large wooden table that dominated the room. The glass of wine was replaced with a warm concoction to help settle her stomach.

"It will all be forgotten when you hold the babe in your arms," the big ruddy faced woman said. She gave Felicity an understanding smile before returning to her task of kneading bread.

Murmuring her thanks, Felicity couldn't remember if she had ever heard Cook say so many words at one time, but she found a measure of contentment as she watched her rhythmically work the dough. She had just finished her drink when Catherine found her. The shawl she carried was draped around Felicity's shoulders.

"You're still looking a little peaky. Do you feel up for a walk?"

"Actually I feel much better," Felicity said, nodding her thanks at Cook. "I think some air would do me good."

The two women went out the back door, passing by the kitchen herb garden. Catherine stopped to pluck a few stems from a leafy green growth, handing it her friend with a smile.

"It's mint," she said as the distinctive fragrance filled the air. "It always helps me when I'm feeling out of sorts."

"Am I supposed to eat it?" Felicity asked dubiously.

"Not unless you want to. I always find the smell is what pleases me the most."

Felicity held the green sprigs to her nose and breathed in the crisp scent. With the morning sun warming their faces, and no particular destination in mind, the two women strolled around the grounds before reaching what was now the sadly neglected center of the once formal garden.

"Are you planning to restore this?" Catherine asked, waving her hand at the unkempt beds where a variety of native wild flowers jostled the few remaining formal inhabitants for growing room.

"I'm not sure restoration is the correct term, but I definitely would like to tidy it up a little," Felicity told her. "I remember, as a little girl, seeing Liam's mother take cuttings from here. She was particularly fond of roses as I recall." She sighed sadly. "I don't think anyone really knew how to take care of it without her guidance."

"I must admit almost every aspect of Oakhaven could benefit from a woman's touch," Catherine said. Looping arms, they made their way to a wooden seat where they could sit and imagine the garden in all its floral magnificence once again. "I'm surprised this hasn't rotted away," Catherine commented, clearing a few leaves from the bench with a sweep of her hand.

"That's because it's fairly new. Recognizing my fondness for whiling away the time daydreaming, my husband made certain I could do so in comfort." Felicity smiled at the notion. "There are at least a half dozen more benches scattered about the grounds."

Catherine doubted scattering had anything to do with it. Knowing Liam's attention to detail, she was confident each bench had been placed with precision in the landscape. It was simply another demonstration of his affection for his wife.

"You know Oakhaven is really Rian's birthright," Felicity said, looking at Catherine.

"I thought his father had disowned him, and the estate passed to Liam."

"Yes, that's true, but I think Liam would gladly return it. Especially now that circumstances have changed."

"Circumstances? What circumstances?" Catherine was alarmed. "What are you trying to say?"

"Nothing," Felicity reassured her. "It's just that when Rian returned, well, he wasn't…" She trailed off, not sure how to say what she wanted without offending the woman who was like her own flesh and blood.

"He wasn't what? Married?"

Felicity nodded once and then turned her head as her cheeks burned a bright red.

"Oh, Felicity! I love Oakhaven, truly I do," Catherine said, taking hold of her hands, "but this is not my home any more than it is Rian's. We are guests here, welcome guests I hope, but nonetheless this is not where we belong. Oakhaven will always hold wonderful, warm memories for us, but it is not *our* home. It will always belong to you and Liam."

"Thank you." The words came out in a rush as Felicity tried her best to disguise her relief. "I just love it so and I thought—"

"Oh, you goose!" Catherine said. "That baby of yours must be giving you these silly, fanciful ideas. Now dry your eyes or else I will have to think up some ridiculous reason to explain your red nose to both our husbands." Removing a handkerchief from her sleeve, Felicity did as she was told. "Now," Catherine continued, "why don't you tell me just how you are going to tidy up this wilderness."

* * * *

Standing by the large French doors that opened out onto the terrace, Rian watched the two women as they strolled through the grounds. Their brightly colored dresses made him think of the exotic birds he had seen in the Caribbean. He sighed. Catherine was happy here, and she loved Felicity and Liam dearly. It was going to be hard to take her away from them, but his brother did not require his help to guide the fortunes of either this estate, or Pelham Manor, and Rian needed to be master of his own house. He smiled to himself as another truth dawned on him. Whether she would admit it or not, his wife also yearned to be mistress of her own home.

He'd received a missive from Matthew Turner telling him he was in possession of all the necessary documentation to transfer ownership of The Hall from Lord Edward Barclay to Rian Connor. All that was required was his signature on the legal paperwork. Matthew had raised a questioning eyebrow when Rian had asked him to draw up a will and word it so that, regardless of any heirs, should he precede his wife in death, Catherine could remain in her family home with sufficient funds to maintain the house for the remainder of her life. Of course she would also have a personal income, but Rian did not want her to use any of that money toward the upkeep of bricks and mortar.

Matthew went on to say that, true to his word, Edward had managed to rehire many of the former staff. They were only too happy to resume their duties. He read that they had been busy cleaning and preparing the house for Catherine's return, but only the most essential rooms had been furnished. The rest of the house would remain empty as Rian had instructed, and would stay that way until Catherine could furnish it as she chose.

He had permitted himself a chuckle when he read that Old Ned would not be returning to his former position. He was enjoying retirement, living with his daughter and playing with his grandchildren. When Miss Catherine was home he would be most pleased to visit her, if she so desired, and offer his advice on restoring The Hall's gardens. Rian had a feeling that Old Ned would be a frequent visitor whose opinion was going to be much sought after.

After rereading the letter from Matthew, Rian stared thoughtfully into the distance. He intended to make sure that former servants such as Old Ned received an appropriate stipend in appreciation for their years of service. Their loyalty to Catherine when things were at their bleakest deserved to be recognized. He would discuss it with her, and get a list of names.

"Have you told her yet?"

Rian turned away from the French doors as Liam came into the room, carrying an armful of large, dusty ledgers.

"No, not yet." He knew what his brother was referring to, but wanting to change the subject, he pointed to the books Liam now put on the table. "What on earth have you got there?"

"Some ideas I want to discuss with Charles, but I want to be sure I have my facts and figures correct before I do. Now, stop trying to avoid the question. When do you intend to tell her?"

Turning back to the window, Rian looked once more for the two women, but they had resumed their walk and disappeared from view. "I suppose I had better do it sooner rather than later."

Indicating the letter Rian was holding, Liam said, "Ah. I see you have received word from Matthew."

"Yes, everything is ready. All that is needed is my signature."

"Then why so glum, brother?"

"Catherine will hate to leave here. She and Felicity have become so close," Rian told him.

"I know, and we are just as fond of her, but you know that no house can have two mistresses. Although, if I was a gambling man, I would wager our wives would be the first to make a success of it."

"What about two masters?" Rian asked with a grin.

"That situation occurs more often than we let ourselves admit," Liam observed. "Rian, you are my brother, and no matter what, Oakhaven is, and always will be, as much yours as it is mine."

"Thank you, but you really must stop thinking like that. I want this to be your children's inheritance, not mine." He spoke sincerely and with no regret. "I'll tell her tonight," he said decisively.

"Might I suggest you do it at dinner? That way you won't have to repeat yourself and everyone will know."

"Everyone?"

"Emily and Charles are coming to visit for a few days."

Something in the way Liam spoke made Rian frown. "Do I sense some misgivings concerning the arrival of your in-laws?"

"No!" Liam exclaimed. "Just the opposite. I couldn't ask for a better mother-in-law than Emily."

"Amen to that," Rian agreed under his breath.

"And Charles is a font of untapped ideas regarding the joining of our two properties. You wouldn't believe how wonderfully clearsighted he is when it comes to the future of agriculture, as well as our responsibilities as landowners." He hesitated. "It's just that…"

"What?"

"Sometimes I feel disloyal to Father, particularly when I feel like Charles is the parent I should have had. *We* should have had." He looked at his brother. "I'm not making sense, am I?"

"Yes, you are, more than you know, and there's no disloyalty in caring for your wife's parents. Ours have been gone a long time. Even before he died physically, Father left us both years ago, Liam. Perhaps if Mama had not died, things might have been different. For all of us." Silence filled the space between the two men as each was snared by his own vision of a different future. It suddenly struck Rian that he and Catherine had both had to deal with fathers who'd changed radically with the loss of their wives. "Besides," he continued with a grin, "you know the church really does frown on siblings being intimate with each other. If I were you, I'd thank my lucky stars Charles is Felicity's father and not ours as well." Liam's laughter banished the dark mood. "Now tell me, what are you looking for in all these old books?"

Liam opened the first book and began turning pages. “Ways to improve our current cash flow for the estate,” he said.

“Financial problems, Liam? You know I have more than—”

“Rian, please!” Liam said. “I am not having any problems, financial or otherwise.” His expression became one of exasperated affection. “But if I were, I promise I would go to you first. No, all I am doing is searching for ways to increase our overall profit margin. Something to act as a buffer during the lean times.”

“You think hard times are coming?” Rian sat down opposite him.

“When all is said and done, we’re nothing but farmers. Our fortune is tied to the land, no matter who turns the dirt and plants the seed, and when you deal with Mother Nature on a daily basis, common sense dictates that there will be hard times.”

Rian nodded his head in agreement. “So, how can I help?”

“Here,” Liam said, pushing a dusty manual toward him. “Let me explain what I am looking for.”

For the next few hours Rian’s respect for his brother grew tenfold as Liam discussed his business plan for agricultural expansion that included the neighboring acres of Pelham Manor. By the time Liam had finished talking, Rian was mentally studying the feasibility of taking some of his brother’s ideas and putting them to work at The Hall. He was looking forward to having a home of his own.

Chapter 12

Dinner was a lighthearted affair filled with as much gaiety as six people who enjoyed each other's company could produce. As usual Cook had outdone herself, making Felicity wonder if there was some unspoken challenge between the kitchen staffs of the two households to see which could create the more inventive dish.

Tonight Catherine had decided to wear the diamond pendant, and Rian felt an odd sense of pride hearing her explain to Emily that she could only wear it until their first child was born. Her voice was a mixture of sadness at knowing she would lose the gem and happiness at the reason why.

"I remember seeing your mother wearing this same necklace as a young bride," Emily told Rian as Catherine allowed her to hold the brilliant diamond in her hand for a closer look. "I never knew a woman so delighted to give up such a wonderful necklace. You must have Catherine's portrait painted while she is still permitted to wear it."

Rian thought it a splendid notion, and wondered why the idea hadn't occurred to him before. Dinner over, the men excused themselves and left their wives alone.

"They've gone to play billiards," Felicity told Catherine as they retired to the drawing room. "Papa does not appreciate the game as a solitary diversion so Liam always plays whenever they are together."

"And my clever son-in-law always lets him win at least one game," Emily added with a knowing twinkle in her eyes.

After making sure they all had a glass of sweet wine, Felicity fixed her mother with a steely stare. "Well, are you going to tell me or must I wheedle it out of you?"

Catherine looked puzzled, staring first at Felicity and then at Emily.

"Wheedle what, darling?" Not having had to resort to subterfuge for some time, Lady Pelham was out of practice and not in the least convincing.

"Whatever it is that you have been dying to tell us since you arrived this evening. Obviously it is news that Papa does not yet know."

Emily took a sip of her wine and then, knowing she had their undivided attention, she calmly revealed her news. "As you know, I have been in town recently, and while I was there I received a call from a most unexpected visitor." She paused as two pairs of eyes fixed on her firmly, and then, unable to contain herself a moment longer, she blurted out. "Would you believe Isabel Howard came to see me?"

The room suddenly went very quiet, the silence disturbed only by the low murmur of servants occupied with evening chores. Catherine thought they sounded unnaturally loud. It was Felicity who finally asked, "What on earth did she want?"

"It's the most extraordinary thing. She wants to give a ball, for Rian and Catherine!"

The salty phrase that fell from her daughter's lips caused a shocked expression to appear on Emily's face while Catherine fought hard to suppress a grin. Who would have thought a pregnant woman's cursing would be superior to her own? It made Catherine wonder if her friend would be willing to share some phrases that she could add to her own limited repertoire. Just in case she should ever need them.

"You don't honestly believe Isabel wants to do this out of the goodness of her heart, do you, Mama?"

"Of course not, but I must admit she was very humble," Emily said, turning her head so her attention was fixed on Catherine. "I also found myself able to understand her reasons for making such a gesture."

Felicity snorted. "Mama, really, the woman is a consummate liar!"

"I didn't say I agreed with her, Felicity, just that I understood her position."

"Why would Lady Howard come to see you, Emily, if she wants to throw a ball in our honor?" Catherine queried. Though her voice was soft, there was no mistaking the bite of steel beneath her words.

"To save face. Isabel is many things, but stupid isn't one of them. She knows all too well that she would never be received if she approached either you or Rian directly, so she decided to issue her invitation through an intermediary."

"And what did you tell her?"

"Only that I could promise nothing, but, if an appropriate moment arose, I would discuss it with you."

"A ball seems rather a grand gesture to get back into my husband's good graces, don't you think?" Catherine toyed with her wine glass. "Let us not fool ourselves by thinking there is any other purpose behind such an event."

"I agree with you absolutely, my dear, but I'm not sure you fully understand the somewhat murky waters the aristocracy inhabit. Trust me; there is a reason why Charles and I limit our visits to town.

. "Some of these people are ridiculously foolish about what is considered 'acceptable and appropriate' behavior. Forgive me, my dear"—she gave Catherine a sympathetic look—"but Isabel and Rian made no secret of the fact they were lovers. The surprise came when Isabel, who has always maintained she would never marry again, let it be known that an offer for her hand would not be unwelcome. Provided it came from Rian."

"Ridiculously stupid of her in my opinion," Felicity muttered.

"I agree," Emily continued, "especially as it's my understanding that Rian had never expressed an interest in asking for her hand. I'm sure you can see how humiliating it would be for any woman to have her expectations dashed so thoroughly. The only way Isabel can possibly save face is to show that Rian's marriage does not concern her in the least, and what better way than by being the first to present his new bride to society? Hardly the behavior one would expect from a woman who thought herself jilted."

"Except she was never going to be a bride," Felicity said sarcastically.

"You make it sound as if all of this is somehow my fault." Catherine's voice was bitter, and both women turned and looked at her. "If Isabel was foolish enough to speak of events that had yet to happen, then she has no one but herself to blame for any embarrassment she may feel. Why should it be of concern to me what her friends think, and how is a ball going to change their attitude?"

"Oh dear, forgive me. I wish I had never said anything!" Emily exclaimed. She had been prepared to meet resistance, even an outright refusal, but she hadn't expected hostility. "You are under absolutely no obligation to help Isabel. Please forget I ever mentioned it in the first place. I don't know what I was thinking. Of course you should refuse to go. Actually, you needn't even do that much. Just ignore her."

Emily began fussing with the folds of her dress, her hand moving across the fabric like a small, agitated mouse, making Catherine regret the sharpness of her tone. Her anger with Isabel was not something she ought to be taking out on either of the two women who would rather die than ever deliberately hurt her. Leaning forward, she placed her hand over Emily's nervous one, giving her a wobbly smile of apology.

"I suppose I can see the twisted reasoning behind the suggestion," she admitted reluctantly, "but how is it she knows Rian and I are now married?"

Emily's peal of laughter filled the room. "Oh, my dear child, I have received more than a dozen inquiries asking me to validate the rumors regarding your marriage. It would seem that good news travels quickly, and as most of my dear acquaintances are aware of the fact, it stands to reason that word would have reached Isabel's ears also."

"Do you trust her?" Catherine asked Emily.

"Not for a single minute!" She patted the back of Catherine's hand, letting her know that her momentary bad humor was both understandable and forgiven. "But, if it's any consolation, Isabel does have a reputation for giving very lavish parties and I feel certain she would make an effort to outdo herself for such an occasion." She sighed wistfully before adding, "It would be a shame to miss it."

"Mama, I can't believe that you're suggesting Catherine and Rian should actually consider attending."

"Why ever not?" Emily refilled her wine glass. "We know from the start that Isabel's motives are questionable, but if we go together it will allow everyone to see we are a solid, united family. Criticize one and you risk the wrath of all."

"I rather like that," Catherine said, smiling over the rim of her glass as she made up her mind. "I think we should make plans to attend. When is it to be?"

"At the end of next month." Emily smiled.

"Well, that doesn't give us very much time to get new gowns made," Felicity grumbled.

"Pish-posh! I have a seamstress that can work magic!" Emily's face suddenly took on a more serious look. "All jesting aside, Catherine, darling, are you certain you want to attend? My earlier remark about murky waters was not made lightly. You have had little exposure to the kind of people who gather at these functions."

"Oh, I think I might surprise you," Catherine said brightly. "If the gossips want to see who supplanted Isabel in Rian's affections, as well as his bed, then who am I to deny them? Besides, it might be nice to enjoy ourselves at Isabel's expense."

"Even though it would be nice for us to go as a family, are you sure Rian will be in agreement?" Felicity sounded doubtful.

"Leave my husband to me." Catherine smiled slyly, raising her glass in a toast. "I can be very persuasive when I need to be."

The men returned a short while later to find Felicity and Catherine happily playing a duet on the pianoforte. Felicity noticed her father looked particularly pleased with himself.

"You let him win," her mother mouthed silently behind her husband's back as he was settling comfortably by her side, a generous helping of his son-in-law's excellent brandy in his hand.

Once Felicity and Catherine had finished and resumed their seats with their husbands, Rian decided this was as good a time as any to speak. "I would like to say something," he began when everyone was settled, "and here, in the company of family, I cannot think of a more fitting moment." Four faces stared at him. Liam's was the only one not registering any sign of curiosity. "I have been gone from this house for many years, and have seen more of the world than I ever imagined I would. For the most part I have been as happy as any man has a right to be. I've known joy and sorrow, but I never doubted that one day I would return to my home…and family."

He smiled at Liam. "It is a blessing to find the unwavering, constant love and loyalty of a brother, the gentle warmth of a treasured sister-in-law, the acceptance of her parents and"—he paused and turned to Catherine—"the love of my life."

She blushed prettily and Rian was happy to see that she was still innocent enough to be embarrassed by so public a compliment from him. "But as you know, our father did one thing right before he died. He gave Oakhaven to Liam, and it could not have been placed in better hands. I think with the right guidance—"he looked at Charles Pelham, who acknowledged the tribute"—you might be able to turn a profit one of these days."

Good natured laughter rippled around the room at this last part and Rian waited patiently for the merriment to subside. "But as we all know, every man needs to be master of his own home and as much as Oakhaven is the home of my childhood, that is all it will ever be. I need to set down roots somewhere else, a place that I hope my wife will be pleased to share with me."

"Any place with you will be home for me," Catherine said quietly as she looked at her husband, her love for him shining like a beacon.

"Well, in that case, I believe you will be doubly happy." He went to the table and returned, holding a rolled piece of parchment tied with a red ribbon and an unbroken seal.

"What is it?" she whispered to him.

"Open it and see for yourself," Rian told her as he leaned down and kissed her cheek. "I love you," he added in a whisper meant for her ears only.

Carefully Catherine broke the seal and unrolled the document, her eyes scanning quickly over the contents. She looked up at her husband and then back at the parchment in her hand. Quickly she scanned the other faces in the room. They were all watching her intently, curiosity gnawing at them except for Liam. Of course Liam would know.

"What is it, Catherine?" Felicity asked impatiently.

"It's the property deed…to my home," Catherine told her, her eyes shining brightly as she tried to hold back tears of joy.

"Why that's wonderful." Emily was polite but her tone clearly said she wasn't sure why Rian would make such a show of letting his wife know they had a house of their own. People bought houses all the time.

"No, you don't understand," Catherine told her. "It isn't just any house, it's *my* house, my home. It's The Hall!"

"Oh my!" Emily exclaimed, immediately grasping the significance.

Any other reaction was lost as Catherine jumped up and hurled herself into Rian's arms, crying and laughing at the same time, raining salty kisses on his face. Her joy was infectious and he laughed with her.

"We truly have The Hall? It is ours? When can we leave?" The questions tumbled out of Catherine's mouth before she could stop herself.

"Yes, yes and as soon as you like," Rian answered, grinning from ear to ear. It was, he decided, the perfect gift for his wife.

* * * *

Catherine snuggled closer to Rian in the big bed they shared. He was lying on his back with an arm around her, enjoying the provocative drape of her leg over his. Both of them were filled with the drowsy euphoria that followed the aftermath of their lovemaking, and, on hearing Rian's contented sigh, Catherine thought it a good time to broach the subject of Isabel's party.

"No, no, no!" Rian sat up so suddenly he almost bounced Catherine out of the bed. "I don't trust her. She's up to something."

"Of course she is, but hear me out." Paying no attention to the pained look on his face, she shared Emily's thoughts on what lay behind Isabel's invitation.

"I still don't like it," Rian grumbled.

"Rian, please, I love you and we are wed. Nothing can change that. Can we not afford to be generous?"

"I don't think my generosity is capable of extending that far," he grumbled, making a rude, snorting sound and looking sulky as he examined the bedspread.

Catherine put her hand under his chin and turned his head until he was facing her. She brushed an errant lock of hair from his forehead. "Darling, what does it really matter? We will be leaving soon to start our lives anew, far away from Isabel. She has chosen the life she wants, and we will never have a reason to see her again. It is a small gesture, Rian, and besides…"

He was instantly suspicious. "Besides what?"

"I confess to having another purpose for wanting to go." She caught her lower lip in her teeth and looked up at him from beneath her lashes. It was an outrageously shameless maneuver on her part, and they both knew it.

"What purpose?" Rian asked, trying his hardest to sound stern.

"I want to show off my beautiful diamond, before I spit in her eye!"

Rian's arms wrapped around her, pulling her back onto the pillows with him, and he shook as the laughter he could no longer suppress burst out of him. He couldn't help it. Would this wonderful, amazing woman he had married never stop surprising him?

"You do know I'm not really going to spit in her eye, don't you?" Catherine amended.

"Ah well now, that's a shame because I think there would be quite a few people who would pay good money to see that happen."

Whatever comment Catherine made in response was lost as she buried her face in his neck. The warmth of her breath sent delightful messages to the rest of his body, and Rian waited to see if she was bold enough to act on those messages. But she remained quiet, long enough for him to suspect the nonchalant attitude she displayed toward Isabel's party was a façade. "Are you troubled at the thought of seeing Isabel again?" he asked, brushing his lips across her forehead.

"Not anymore."

Though her tone was sure, Rian could feel the beat of her heart quicken and knew she was not being completely truthful. He just wasn't sure if the bravado was for his benefit or hers. "I will not leave your side," he told her.

"Promise?" she whispered.

"I promise." And to show her appreciation, Catherine demonstrated just how bold she could be.

Later, when her breathing had turned to the sound of restful sleep, Rian remained awake. A troubled frown creased his brow. He did not trust Isabel. He had learned that every detail in his former lover's life was planned for her own benefit and no one else's. Isabel didn't care what society said about her; she never had. The disdain she held for those who thought to condemn her had been one of the things he liked about her. This talk about needing to save face with her peers was a poorly constructed fabrication. There was more to this ball than met the eye, but he had to admit it had been clever of Isabel to issue her invitation through Emily.

Catherine murmured in her sleep, and Rian shifted as she rolled out of his arms and onto her stomach. In the darkness he kissed her scarred shoulder, and took a moment to inhale the scent of her skin. Isabel, he knew, would not hesitate to spit in Catherine's eye if chance and circumstance allowed. He would have to make sure it never did.

Chapter 13

Phillip Davenport, standing in the same room where he had been summoned once before, quickly recognized the meat and bones of this meeting with Lady Howard had a very different flavor from that first encounter. Her ladyship, not bothering to trifle with polite niceties, cut straight to the heart of the matter.

"Mr. Davenport, what are you prepared to do to guarantee the return of your cousin?" Isabel asked him.

Still playing the role of a concerned relative, Phillip portrayed an anxious expression while his voice took on a simpering tone. "Is it possible? Have you found—"

"Do you want her back or not?" The question was abrupt and the tone enough to make Phillip stop and stare at her. Something wasn't right. Hands on her hips, Isabel tapped her foot as she looked at him. "For God's sake, man, it really isn't a difficult question," she snapped irritably.

"Your ladyship is too kind—" he started, still unsure what he was really being asked.

Isabel threw her hands up in disgust. "Do not try my patience! This act of concern you insist on portraying is nothing but a tiresome pretense." She took a deep breath, reminding herself that it was she who had sent for him. Calming herself, Isabel graced him with one of her many practiced smiles. "It is of no interest to me what manner of debauchery you intend to visit upon the girl. My interest is in knowing if you truly want your dear Catherine back."

"Of course I do, but I must protest your ladyship's suggestion that my interest is anything other than—"

"Mr. Davenport, do you suppose I would not know exactly with whom I am dealing? Your reputation precedes you, sir, and besides"—her smile became predatory—"I have seen for myself the evidence of your handiwork." Stunned by her accusation, Phillip was quick to realize his lack of protest only confirmed what had surely been, up to that moment, nothing more than unproven suspicion. Now he could no longer deny any involvement in Catherine's disappearance. As she faced him, one hunter to another, Isabel's voice became silky when she repeated her earlier question. "What are you prepared to do in order to get her back?"

Continuing with his charade was futile. "Whatever it takes," Phillip Davenport told her.

No more simpering or playing games. If Isabel wanted to deal with the real Phillip Davenport, then so be it. He doubted she would like this version any more than she had the earlier one. But he cared little about placating her ladyship's sensibilities. Instead he listened as Isabel told him how she was going to help him get his precious Catherine back, and what she expected from him in return.

Observing Isabel through half-lidded eyes, Phillip carefully reviewed the plan she put before him. Looking for any flaw that might hinder the chance of success. Unable to find one, he grudgingly admitted she had been most thorough in anticipating every possible scenario. He watched her pace before the large picture window, her movements more thoughtful than impatient. She gave the appearance of a woman who cared little for either his approval or opinion of her scheme. They both knew he would agree to her plan. He'd be a fool not to. Brilliant in its simplicity, it would give him exactly what he wanted.

Phillip allowed himself a ghost of a smile. At their last meeting Isabel had preached caution, the necessity of waiting until the right moment presented itself before striking. No matter how long that might take. But now, it was as if she had decided she no longer had the patience to play the waiting game. He wondered what had caused the change of heart. He glanced across the room and found himself caught in John Fletcher's unwavering stare. The ability to read people had always served him well, particularly at the gaming tables, but this man was different. It unnerved Phillip to not know what Isabel's man was thinking. Particularly when Fletcher's gaze was so fixed on himself.

"Are you satisfied?" Isabel's impatient tone cut through his thoughts.

"Your ladyship seems to have considered every possible eventuality," Phillip told her. "I can find no defect or weakness in your plan, except perhaps…" He stared at John and raised a questioning eyebrow.

"Except for what?" Isabel kept her tone conversational.

"I do not know your man. Does he understand the use of discretion, and can he be trusted?" Though it was Isabel's question he was answering, Phillip kept his stare on John.

"Ordinarily I would break your neck for such an utterance," John told him, his words clipped and precise, "but to do so would compromise her ladyship's well thought out design. Just make sure you are at the rendezvous point at the agreed upon hour."

"I will be there," Phillip said, almost rubbing his hands together with glee at the thought of being so close to achieving his desire.

Isabel took up the conversation once more. "Despite my careful planning, I do need to make you aware of a potential obstacle that has arisen. A wild card if you will." She searched Phillip's face, looking for any sign he was reconsidering, but there was nothing to make her doubt the decision to include him in her plans.

"What kind of obstacle?" he asked.

"It seems that in the time she managed to escape from you, your cousin has been quite busy. She has found herself a husband."

Phillip remained very still. The only outward sign he gave of his rage was the vein that stood out near his temple and the small muscle in his jaw that jumped as he clenched his teeth. He was absolutely livid! A husband not only meant that Catherine was no longer pure, for no man could look at her and not want her for himself, but it was a complication he did not need. Forcing himself to relax and unclench his jaw, Phillip stared at Isabel's back. It took some effort, but he managed to keep his voice free of any emotion as he asked, "Whom has she married?"

"Rian Connor."

Now it all made sense. Phillip had been wondering what Catherine could have done to earn Isabel's contempt, and why she would go to such lengths to help him secure her person. Realizing that it was the result of something as mundane as feminine vanity almost had him laughing out loud, but he knew that would be most unwise. Isabel was not the only one aware of whom she was dealing with. Phillip also knew about her. About her dalliance with Rian Connor. The same man who had foolishly taken another as his bride, and who would now have to deal with the consequences of Isabel's wrath.

Putting his hand to his face, he covered his mouth as if he was deep in serious contemplation, when in fact he was hiding a smile. Women really were such foolish creatures he thought, even those with hearts as black as the one beating in the chest of the woman he was dealing with now. "Will he prove troublesome?" Phillip asked.

"Not at all. I am confident he will not interfere with our plans," Isabel answered. She went to turn away from him, and then changed her mind, facing him again with a soft swoosh of silk. "Tell me, Mr. Davenport, what do you intend to do with your cousin once you have her back?"

Phillip's expression changed suddenly, turning hard and cruel. Why should she care? Across the room John Fletcher silently rose from his seat. The change of expression had not gone unnoticed by Isabel's man, who now glared at Phillip menacingly. Not wishing to provoke the man to violence, Phillip stretched his thin lips into a smile that was more reptilian than human. "Do with her?" he asked, feigning confusion.

John Fletcher's hands became clenched fists.

Arching a brow and keeping her voice as sweet and syrupy as the finest honey, Isabel clarified her question. "Yes, how do you intend to *dispose* of your dear Catherine once your appetites have been satisfied?"

The sweetness disappeared so quickly, Phillip wasn't sure if it had been there to begin with, and now he found himself staring at pure wickedness. The veneer of Isabel's civility had slipped away, revealing the essence of the woman within. She was a vessel filled with malicious cruelty and vindictiveness. It was something he could understand. He smiled; perhaps he and Lady Howard had more in common than he'd realized.

"Oh, there are places where my sweet cousin will never see the light of day. Places where those not so fussy will be more than willing to part with a few coppers for the use of her." He did not need to add that those who ran such places regarded the gentry with suspicion, and Rian Connor's wealth would not gain him entry.

"And it is your intent to put her in one of these places?"

"Once I am finished with her of course."

The lascivious undertone in Phillip Davenport's voice sent a shiver of disgust down John's spine. Isabel however, seemed unaffected.

"Good," she said, turning back to the window. "I do so despise loose ends."

Chapter 14

The few weeks leading up to Isabel's ball were hectic. Rian, anxious to see how much progress had been made to The Hall, suggested to Catherine they leave a few days after the trip to London. Excited by the prospect of returning to her home, their fast approaching departure nevertheless made her remaining time at Oakhaven bittersweet. Not wanting to dwell on all the things she would miss about Liam and Felicity's home, she forced herself to keep busy and made certain her time was fully occupied.

Fittings for her ball gown and meetings with the dressmaker were interspersed with plans for refurbishment and redecoration. It seemed as if Rian had requested proposals from every skilled artisan within a hundred-mile radius of The Hall. And all of them had submitted samples and estimates for her approval. Catherine found herself practically drowning in a sea of detail. And it wasn't just the main pieces of functional furniture that she was being asked to select, but all the accompanying decorative pieces and their embellishments.

Rian gave her free rein, venturing his opinion only when Catherine asked for it. She had the oddest impression that he was far more content to play the role of financier than decorator. Which was a good thing as money was an issue for her. She refused to authorize any changes, commission any work, until she had discussed the cost with her husband, detailing the amount down to the last farthing.

"You will tell me if I'm being too frivolous, won't you?" she asked, worried that the draperies she wanted for their bedroom would be too costly.

"I promise I won't let you beggar me," Rian assured her, approving her choice.

Now she watched his reflection in the looking glass as she brushed her hair. He seemed to be engrossed with a number of sketches scattered before him on the bed. Like his wife, he too was busy with refurbishment, but while Catherine was occupied with The Hall's interior, Rian was focused on the exterior. Pausing her brush, she looked at him in the glass. "Rian?"

"Mmm." He picked up one sketch, turned it first one way and then the other before discarding it in favor of another.

"Do you think it might be possible to get the fountain repaired before we return?" Catherine asked shyly. "It was always so pretty to look at." Separating her thick hair into three equal sections, she began her nightly chore of braiding it while she waited for an answer.

"According to Edward's last letter," Rian said casually as he gathered all the sketches and unceremoniously dropped them on the floor by the side of the bed, "all the repairs had been made, and the fountain is functional once more."

"Edward?" Catherine swiveled around on her seat and stared at her husband. "You didn't tell me you were corresponding with Edward."

"Didn't I?" Rian closed his eyes and put his arms behind his head as he leaned back against the pillows. "Must have slipped my mind." Through half lidded eyes he watched carefully for her reaction as she turned back around, her fingers flying deftly through the skeins of white blonde hair. "The affection between you is mutual, I think," Rian said quietly, closing his eyes. "Edward always asks after you in his correspondence."

"You know perfectly well that Edward is promised."

Rian snorted. "You cannot blame me for my jealousy."

Catherine said nothing, giving her full attention to securing the end of her braid with a length of ribbon. Finished, she came and knelt on the bed, the candlelight making her skin glow through the sheer fabric of her nightgown as she waited for Rian to open his eyes and look at her. He obliged and as always, the sight of her took the breath from his body. He reached for her, but Catherine held up a hand, stopping him.

"Edward Barclay is a good man and has been a very dear friend to me my entire life." Though she spoke softly, Rian heard the weight of her words, and treated them with the respect they deserved. "I would like to continue that friendship, but if it is a source of concern, and you prefer I not see him again, then so be it. However, I think it only fair to warn you he will always hold a special place in my heart, and I will never think of him with anything other than affection." She looked up at him from beneath long, dark lashes and he felt his heart stumble before picking up its tempo. "Make no mistake, Rian Connor; I have no regrets about who I married."

"None?" he asked huskily, watching as she lowered her hand. Reaching forward, his fingers slowly began loosening the ties that held her nightgown closed.

"Not yet," Catherine answered lightly, shrugging but making no attempt to stop his roaming hands, "but the night is still young." Her movement allowed the gown to fall open and slip off one shoulder. "What is done is done, and I thank God every day that you came into my life." Seeing his lips part, she leaned forward and covered his mouth with hers. Kissing him was the most effective way she had found to prevent him from saying something foolish.

Pulling back the bed coverings, Catherine straddled his hips, gasping with sensual delight as she took him inside her body. The feel of his hands as he stroked all her secret places made her shudder with glorious anticipation, but this night she showed him how attentive a pupil she had been. When he whispered in her ear the ways she could please him, it was with a mix of pride and wonderment that she left him shaking and gasping as he spilled himself inside her.

* * * *

It was Liam's suggestion that they leave for the townhouse a week before the ball. Realizing that in all probability, it would be a long time before they would enjoy each other's company again, he wanted to make these last few days together memorable ones. He arranged outings to Westminster Abbey, St. Paul's Cathedral and the House of Lords, as well as visits to Vauxhall Gardens, the venue where the composer Handel had rehearsed his Fireworks Music. Also included was a visit to Ranelagh Pleasure Gardens with its fabulous rococo rotunda and Chinese Pavilion.

"Please assure me your itinerary does not include a side trip to see the Covent Garden Ladies," Rian said, taking his brother to one side.

"Good Lord, man, do you think me mad?" Liam was clearly mortified by the thought of either Felicity or Catherine being anywhere near the city's prostitutes. "I think Mrs. Salmon's wax exhibit in Fleet Street will be our most questionable entertainment." Rian chuckled in agreement. Not a moment was to be wasted. For the first time in a long while he had his family complete and whole, and he was both thankful and determined to enjoy every moment.

The journey to London was uneventful, but Catherine could not prevent the lump that filled her throat as Oakhaven slipped from view. It was all too reminiscent of another time when she'd said goodbye to people she cared for.

With Felicity's permission she had offered Tilly the chance to accompany them, but the young maid's reluctance to leave Oakhaven did not surprise her. They had spent the better part of their last morning together weeping and hugging as Tilly carefully packed Catherine's traveling trunk with her personal items. She was thankful that saying farewell to Mrs. Hatch could be delayed as the housekeeper was traveling to town with them. Leaving the motherly figure behind was going to be especially hard.

The first night in the city was spent in the same bedroom where she had been brought by Rian a lifetime ago, or so it now seemed. By rights the master suite should have been occupied by Liam and Felicity, but they were more than happy to give up this particular suite of rooms to the 'other' newlyweds. Unfortunately it proved to be an unsettling and unpleasant experience. Catherine awoke in the middle of the night, disoriented and wild-eyed, her body shaking and her breath coming in shallow gasps.

The nightmare had returned.

She had forgotten what it felt like to be caught in the grip of such terror because she had not experienced it since she began sharing Rian's bed. He suggested that they change rooms, but Catherine would hear none of it. She doubted that a different bed would keep the dream at bay, and she refused to allow it such power over her. Holding her tightly in his arms and whispering in her ear, Rian lay back down and the comforting rumble of his voice soon eased his wife back to sleep. This time to a more calming and untroubled rest.

Listening to the even sound of her breathing, Rian cursed himself for allowing her to sleep in this room. He wondered about all the other times she had awoken from this same dream, afraid and alone, with no one to hold or comfort her. But Catherine had wanted the familiarity of returning to the room she had originally used. Rian did not know whether it was the room itself, or the change of location, that had brought on the nightmare. Emily had confided to him that Catherine had also suffered while at Pelham Manor, but she'd never experienced the nightmare at Oakhaven. And he was at a loss to know why.

He came to the conclusion that there could be two reasons for the return of the nightmare. One, that Oakhaven gave Catherine a sense of peace and safety she did not feel elsewhere, even when she was lying in his arms, or two, the reason for the nightmares was close to being revealed. It was the last blank spot in her memory, and Rian vowed his wife would never know her nightmare disturbed him as much as it did her.

No mention of it was made by either of them the next morning, and suffering no apparent ill effects, Catherine was anxious to meet with Matthew Turner, who had not only been instrumental in helping Rian purchase The Hall, but who was also advising her husband on new opportunities for the investment of his wealth. A short while after introductions were made, Catherine decided she liked the dour looking Mr. Turner very much. With a great deal of patience and no condescension, he took the time to answer her many questions regarding the deed for The Hall, as well some of the proposals he thought might interest her husband.

"I told you she had a quick mind, and an eagerness to learn," Rian said proudly.

"Indeed," Matthew agreed. "'Tis a pity more of the fair sex do not take such an interest in their futures, especially when it comes to their financial security."

"How can we, Mr. Turner, when the very idea is frowned upon by most of your own sex?" Catherine asked. "Too many women have no independent means, and are, therefore, at the mercy of their husbands."

"Then you are most fortunate, Mrs. Connor, to have a husband who recognizes the value of allowing his wife knowledge of his financial affairs."

"Indeed I am, Mr. Turner," Catherine murmured as she smiled at Rian. "Indeed I am."

Their business concluded, Rian insisted Matthew join them for lunch at a nearby tavern. Catherine was delighted to find the staid and somber man of business had another side to his character. He regaled both of them with hilarious, but still discreet, tales of financial mishap.

"I'm not sure everything Mr. Turner told us was completely true," Catherine said with a wry smile, holding Rian's hand during the carriage ride back to the townhouse.

"Perhaps not, but he was entertaining, wasn't he?" Rian chuckled enjoying the feel of her fingers entwined with his own. "And I feel certain that if he did bend the truth a little, it was only to protect another's good name."

The rest of the afternoon was a whirlwind of activity, giving both Catherine and Felicity barely time to change their clothes, and catch their breath before heading from one delightful distraction to another. That night Catherine fell into an exhausted sleep and the nightmare, if it came, did not disturb her rest. Rian wondered if busyness might be the remedy to keep the black dream at bay, and he was determined to make sure his wife had no time to dwell on it, either in bed or out of it.

Only their eagerly anticipated visit to the theater could be considered a failure, marred by an unforeseen consequence. Liam had managed to arrange for them to see the well-known actor, David Garrick, appearing in an unexpected repeat performance of *The Alchemist*. The comedy was extremely popular, and Mr. Garrick's reputation well-deserved, but Felicity spent the entire performance in tears.

"The baby!" she sobbed quietly into her handkerchief by way of explanation, refusing to let them leave on her account.

Liam found it very disconcerting to be laughing at the antics on stage while his wife was weeping pitifully beside him.

"I hope this doesn't mean the child will lack a sense of humor," Rian whispered in Catherine's ear, earning a poke in the ribs for his remark.

Visits to the Royal Parks with their beautiful manicured lawns and well-kept gardens were a much more pleasant affair. Felicity confided to Catherine her plan to shamelessly steal some of the designs they saw, so she could incorporate them into her own ideas for Oakhaven.

The day before Isabel's ball brought a visit from Emily and Charles, along with the dressmaker and their gowns. All three women spent a good deal of time 'oohing' and 'aaahing' as they selected ribbons, feathers and other decorative accessories, much to the bewildered amusement of their spouses.

"A lot of silly fuss if you ask me," Charles Pelham declared as he sat with Rian and Liam enjoying a glass of fine Madeira after a leisurely lunch.

"Ah, but the ladies do love it all so," Rian told him with a wink.

"Yes, indeed they do," he concurred with a warm smile. "And letting them indulge themselves is just one of the many secrets to a long and happy marriage."

"What are some of the others?" Liam asked his father-in-law, his tone hopeful.

Charles guffawed. "If I told you then you wouldn't have the fun of discovering them for yourself, my boy!"

By mid-afternoon on the following day, there was a definite change in the atmosphere of the house. A tense excitement permeated every room, every corner of every room, and even though Liam tried in vain to get Felicity to rest, he could not help but be captivated by her enthusiasm. Deciding the best course of action was to turn the entire proceedings over to the females in his life, both above and below stairs, Liam sought refuge in his study, only to find his brother had already beaten him there.

"You would think they'd never attended a ball before!" Liam exclaimed as he thankfully accepted the glass of wine Rian poured for him.

"Well in truth, Liam, they probably haven't. At least I'm certain Catherine hasn't."

"There were more people at our wedding than will probably be at Isabel's party," his brother grumbled.

"Ah, but at your wedding Felicity spent most of the time in a state of connubial anxiety at being the center of attention. I guarantee she will have more fun this time as an observer, and Catherine wasn't at your wedding. You really can't compare the two events," Rian told his brother kindly.

"But you're not being backed into a corner and asked ridiculous questions about ribbons and bows. As if I could tell whether a satin bow was more becoming than a velvet one!" Liam muttered in exasperation.

"Come now, Liam, she's your wife. No question Felicity asks should be considered ridiculous."

"It's not *my* wife who's doing the asking," he retorted.

"I'm sure both of them will have a wonderful time," Rian said with more confidence that he actually felt.

"If they don't, you can believe we'll never hear the end of it."

An hour later they stood waiting patiently in the hall for the women in their lives to appear. Rian had just finished making a succinct comment about the amount of time required to pin up a few curls when the change of expression on Liam's face stopped him. Turning, he looked up to see Catherine standing at the top of the staircase, and had to remind himself to breathe. What was this mysterious power she possessed? Rian wondered. Just when he was confident that he knew every facet of her personality, every intimate detail of her being, when he felt sure of his ability to recognize the subtleties of her temperament and nature, she could do something as simple as put on a ball gown...and steal the breath from his body with a single look. It was a gentle reminder that he didn't know quite as much as he thought. And he told himself she couldn't possibly look more beautiful than she did at this moment.

Catherine descended the staircase draped in layers of antique ivory and gold satin that made her skin shimmer as if dusted with some magical fairy powder. The muted blending gave an almost iridescent glow to the blue of her eyes, and in their depths Rian saw a promise he fully intended to redeem later. Her white blonde curls had been caught up in a fashionable design that was entwined with matching gold ribbons and small fragrant flowers, leaving her neck and shoulders deliciously bare.

The only jewelry she wore was the fabulous canary colored diamond, which nestled between her breasts just inside her décolletage. Its partner protectively covered the plain gold band on her left hand. With a smile on his face, Rian gently hooked his finger beneath the gold chain and pulled the jewel free so it lay outside her bodice.

"Your eyes look exactly as they do when you take me inside you," he said, leaning down to murmur in her ear. His remark was rewarded by a deep pink flush that began somewhere below the neckline of her gown, and spread rapidly up her throat to brand her cheeks.

A polite cough from above their heads told them that another Mrs. Connor was waiting to make her own grand entrance. The periwinkle blue of Felicity's gown was complemented by an elaborate silver and pink brocade trim, which brought a delightful warmth to her normally pale skin. The subtle glow was further enhanced by multiple strands of creamy pearls at her throat. Liam had given the necklace to her not long after she had announced her pregnancy. Ropes of companion pearls encircled both wrists while more had been cleverly woven in the upswept elegance of her dark hair. Liam could only stare, his mouth falling open slightly. His little mouse was gone and had been replaced by the fabulous goddess standing before him. His wife. The mother of his unborn child. His soul mate.

"You are so beautiful," he told her as she reached his side, his voice cracking with enough emotion to elicit an anxious look from his wife, before she graciously accepted the compliment he paid her.

"Come," Liam said taking his wife's arm and addressing his sibling. "We have waited long enough for these beautiful creatures to appear. Let us share them with the world, and prepare to be the envy of all we meet!"

Chapter 15

The house was bathed in light. Hundreds of flickering flames protected behind glass, shone in elaborate wrought-iron candelabras on the outside walk and stairs leading up to the main entrance. Inside, additional light reflected brilliantly from crystal chandeliers. The sound of merriment and bright music assaulted them the moment they stepped over the threshold, and curiosity dispelled whatever nervousness Catherine may have been feeling as she looked about her. Isabel's home was grandiose on a scale she'd never imagined.

Enormous detailed paintings, idyllic landscapes for the most part, decorated the walls. Marble busts and statues were displayed in the alcoves and recesses. Looking about her, Catherine tried to discern whether there was a theme or purpose to the groupings of paintings, statues and furniture. She was forced to conclude that if there was one, it escaped her. To her mind the display was nothing more than a vulgar show of wealth.

Her nervousness returned along with a queasy feeling the moment she heard Isabel's voice. Unmistakable, it cut through the general mélée, ensuring that all attention was turned their way. Catherine gripped Rian's arm as he squeezed her other hand reassuringly.

"Ah, finally you have arrived!" Isabel exclaimed, coming toward them with her hands outstretched and a welcoming smile on her face.

It seemed to Catherine that she paused, waiting for the assembled guests to clear a path so all eyes would be on her as she moved toward them. Clad in scarlet from head to toe, Isabel looked like something out of the Old Testament. Jezebel turned to a pillar of flame. Catherine wondered what secret she employed to keep her bosom from spilling out of the bodice of the gown.

Felicity, it seemed, was having similar thoughts. "Barely enough fabric to cover her assets," she murmured as both women watched their hostess cross the floor.

"Even so, you cannot deny she is still very beautiful," Catherine stated in a low voice.

"So was the whore of Babylon," Felicity snorted. "A prerequisite for the appellation, I am sure," she added with a sly grin as both women measured their hostess with a critical eye.

Covering the last few feet of tiled floor, Isabel looked only at Rian as she held out her hands. A choker of large, blood red rubies and diamonds encircled her throat while similar gems dangled from her ear lobes. More cuffed both wrists. She wore a ring on every finger, and her dark tresses were elegantly pinned up with a variety of feathered and jeweled combs. Having taken a sweeping look from head to toe, Felicity saw nothing to change her initial opinion. Isabel's appearance was offensive and more suited to a brothel than an elegant ballroom.

Rian bent over Isabel's outstretched hands and politely kissed the back of each one. The smile she gave him held more than a hint of caution. They were all playing roles it would seem.

Turning to Catherine, Isabel embraced her warmly. She kissed her on both cheeks before addressing Liam and Felicity, greeting them with an equally expressive show of cordiality. It was as if they were all old friends.

"Marriage appears to suit you," Isabel said with a charming smile.

It was uncertain whom her remark was directed at, but Felicity chose to answer. The lack of warmth in her response was ignored by Isabel, along with the guarded smile that accompanied it.

"Thank you both so much for coming," Isabel said, turning her attention back to Catherine and Rian. "You have no idea what this means to me."

"Thank you for receiving us," Catherine responded demurely. "You have a beautiful home."

"Then you must allow me to show it to you, though I fear it may not be possible to do so tonight. Come," she said, linking arms with Catherine, "let me introduce you to some people who are most eager to make your acquaintance."

It seemed as if everyone invited wanted to make their acquaintance, and Catherine found herself pausing every few steps to be introduced to *Lord this* or *Lady that*. She also noticed that, despite being on the receiving end of a great many admiring masculine glances, an equal number of feminine ones were not so approving. She was being coolly assessed from head to toe and though many of the smiles appeared to be genuine, an equal number were definitely hostile. It was an uncomfortable feeling, reminding her of Emily's warning about murky waters.

"Do you really know all these people?" she whispered to Rian before turning to smile at another pair of faces waiting to gain their attention as Isabel made the introductions.

"Sweetheart, I have been away a long time. I hardly know anyone at all," he whispered.

"Then why does everyone want to meet you?"

"Who says I am the one they want to meet?" He winked playfully at her, enjoying the view he was afforded down the front of her bodice every time she sank effortlessly into a deep curtsey.

Somewhere between Lady-my-stays-are-laced-too-tight and Marquess-Fussy-And-Oh-So-Full-Of-Himself, they lost Liam and Felicity. Rian's reassurance that Liam had taken his wife to a quiet place to rest eased Catherine's anxiety. In the past few days they had all noticed that Felicity was beginning to tire more easily, but as long as she was given ample opportunity to sit and rest, she suffered no adverse effects.

On reaching the ballroom Isabel politely begged their forgiveness as she was called away to deal with a matter requiring her personal attention. She kissed Catherine once again on both cheeks, and made certain that everyone present witnessed the familiar interaction between herself and the newlyweds. It could now be reported that stories of any ill-will between Isabel and her former lover had been greatly exaggerated. Nothing more than fabrications spread by malicious tongues. Before the night was over the gossips would be telling each other that Isabel was the one who had introduced the happy couple.

"Thank God that's over with," Rian said, watching Isabel walk away. The train of her red gown followed like a tongue of fire.

"Please tell me she's saved enough of her dignity," Catherine murmured with a sigh. "My face is starting to ache from having to smile so much."

Liberating two glasses of wine from a passing servant, Rian handed one to his wife. "Let's hope so," he said, referring to Isabel's dignity. "I don't think I could stand to be introduced to any more useless people."

"Oh hush now!" Catherine reprimanded lightly as she playfully fluttered her eyelashes at him. "Lady-What's-Her-Name-With-The-Big-Jewels was very keen to meet you, and I'm sure she's not completely useless."

"Are you suggesting I ought to find out the exact measure of whatever skills she does possess?" Rian asked, bending to nuzzle his wife's neck.

"Not if you know what's good for you!"

Entering the ballroom on his arm, Catherine found her good humor temporarily subdued. She swallowed uneasily as she watched the numerous couples engaged in a seamless execution of intricate steps as they danced. Side by side they glided holding hands, now releasing. A curtsey here, a bow there. They wove a colorful tapestry across the highly polished floor. It seemed as if she was looking through a prism that captured the white light and threw it back across the room in the form of a rainbow. The bright fabrics of the ladies' gowns and the equally vivid gentlemen's coats formed a dazzling array of color. Ironically both Liam and Rian had chosen to dress almost completely in black and they stood out with a somber starkness that was positively elegant next to the glittering popinjays who swarmed about them.

Catherine gulped her wine, waiting for the drink to calm her sudden attack of nerves. She barely noticed as Rian replaced her empty glass with his own, dispatching the contents with ease. He looked down at her with an expression that was a mix of protectiveness and pride. She had been the epitome of flawless grace during her interaction with Isabel.

"Oh look, Rian," she said, clutching his arm as she pointed in the general direction of the dance floor. "There's Liam and Felicity. Don't they make a handsome pair?"

"Yes, they do," Rian said, taking the now empty glass from his wife's hand and returning it, with its mate, to another passing waiter as the dance ended. "Shall we join them?" He took her by the hand and led her onto the ballroom floor before she could utter a word of protest. "Follow my lead, and it will all come back to you," he told her as they waited for the music to begin.

He led her first in one dance and then another and then graciously relinquished his place to Liam, content to keep his sister-in-law company as they watched from the edge of the room. When the music stopped and Catherine returned to them, her face was aglow with happiness.

"How did you know?" she asked, as Rian handed her a glass of something lighter and more refreshing than wine.

"Know what?" Rian asked innocently.

"That I could dance?"

"Well, I recall an inordinate amount of foot-tapping and humming at the Oakhaven ball," he reminded her.

"That was country dancing, and I don't know how you could possibly have been aware of what I was doing. As I recall you were too busy with a certain pair of twins to ask me to dance."

“Then allow me to take the opportunity to make amends.” Taking hold of her hand, Rian led her back out onto the ballroom floor.

They made quite a striking pair; Catherine bathed in creamy gold and Rian’s black attire accentuated only by the hint of gold thread that decorated the cuffs of his coat and matching waistcoat. The entire ensemble complimented by a snowy white jabot at his throat. On another man such ruffles would have looked foppish, but Rian’s height and broad shoulders made the accessory nothing but completely masculine. Isabel stood just inside the doorway to the ballroom, her eyes fixed on the dancers.

“A handsome couple, are they not?” someone pointed out as Rian and Catherine glided by. Isabel’s response, while polite, was not as warm as the speaker would have expected.

The hours swept by and it appeared that Isabel had indeed been forgiven by her peers. No longer needing to make a public display of affection, she kept herself busy with her other guests, allowing Catherine and Rian to relax and enjoy themselves. Felicity danced with only Liam and Rian, but Catherine found herself very much in demand. Thankfully Rian did not object. Every man present knew exactly who he was, and the nature of his relationship to the beautiful woman they danced with. He enjoyed their envious stares when she returned to his side after every dance.

The arrival of her parents brought a squeal of delight from Felicity. Her father was not an enthusiastic dancer and was grateful to both Rian and Liam for making certain that Emily was not disappointed. Light on her feet, she proved to be a graceful partner, and both Connor men took turns escorting her around the floor.

Having barely managed to swallow two bites of their midday meal, Catherine was famished. The last turn around the ballroom had also left her feeling a little lightheaded. The salon immediately adjacent to the ballroom had been set aside for refreshments, and supper proved to be a sumptuous affair. Her plate piled high with savory treats, sweetmeats and fruit, Catherine felt like a greedy child, but Rian merely laughed and told her to enjoy herself. She felt supremely happy, and her joy spread like a contagion, infecting those around her.

Chapter 16

It was almost midnight when Catherine, forced to disappoint a potential dance partner, took a seat next to Felicity. Liam had gone to join his father-in-law at the billiards table, and Rian was across the room engaged in conversation with a small group of men, all of whom wore serious expressions. Emily had retired to another, less noisy room, to gossip with friends she had not seen for a while.

"Are you having fun?" Felicity asked.

"Oh yes!" Catherine exclaimed, fanning herself as she scanned the room. "I know I have never danced so much in one evening, and you never told me what an excellent partner Liam is," she chided gently.

Felicity laughed. "It does him good to be away from the concerns of Oakhaven for a few hours. He can be very serious, and I worry he will forget how to take joy in more lighthearted diversions." She rested her hand gently on her slightly rounded stomach.

Catherine took her other hand and squeezed it gently, a smile on her face. "I doubt you will allow that to happen."

Pursing her lips, Felicity blew out a breath. "Is it me, or does it feel terribly warm in here?"

"It is a little stifling." Catherine turned and looked over her shoulder. "Come, let's go out onto the terrace. It will surely be cooler outside." Taking Felicity's arm, she steered her toward the large French doors that opened to the terrace and gardens. "Better?" she asked once they were beyond the glass doors, and the cooler air embraced them.

"Oh yes, much," Felicity replied.

They stood shoulder to shoulder, next to the marble balustrade and peered over the edge at the garden below. It was difficult to see anything of note, as the rear of the house was not as brilliantly lit as the front. What light there was illuminated little beyond the tiled veranda itself, and for the most part, the gardens remained in deep shadow. It was the perfect setting however, for a lover's tryst, Catherine and Felicity agreed with a giggle. From inside the ballroom the sound of the musicians playing the next dance was muted, but still loud enough to muffle the sound of approaching footsteps.

"Ah, there you both are."

Two heads, one blonde the other brunette, turned in unison as Isabel made her way toward them from the opposite end of the wide terrace. A footman bearing a tray followed. Isabel's smile was all warmth and friendliness as she waited for the servant to depart after placing the tray on a small table in the alcove behind them.

"I have been very neglectful," she apologized. "Please forgive me by sharing a toast."

"No apologies are necessary," Felicity told her, "and I don't think either of us could complain about being neglected."

As Isabel busied herself pouring the wine, Catherine and Felicity exchanged looks. Felicity's raised brow received a shrug in response from Catherine. Neither of them noticed Isabel using her body to block their view of the glasses on the tray, and so they did not see her flick open the hinged clasp of the ring on her little finger and sprinkle a white powder into one of the wine glasses. It took only a matter of seconds, and then Isabel poured the wine and the powder dissolved.

"I do want to thank you both so much for coming tonight," she said brightly, handing them each a glass. "I know that this wasn't easy for you, and I am certain your husband did not want to be here." The last remark was addressed to Catherine, who acknowledged it with a tilt of her head. "You have no idea how much it means to me," Isabel told her.

Felicity opened her mouth, but Catherine spoke first. "You are most welcome, Isabel. It has been a wonderful evening." She looked at her sister-in-law, her expression a request to say nothing cutting. "Now, what shall we drink to?" Catherine asked, looking back at Isabel. She was determined that nothing should spoil her happiness.

"To new friendships," Isabel declared.

"To friendship," Catherine answered, while Felicity mumbled something under her breath and smiled sweetly.

The delicate sound of clinking crystal echoed in the night air as they joined their glasses and sipped their wine. The light on the terrace may not have been bright enough to see the gardens below, but it caught Catherine's diamond and made it sparkle with a brilliance all its own.

"I must confess I recognize your necklace," Isabel commented, giving the gem a covetous look. "Did your husband tell you it comes with some silly tradition about having to give it up?"

"Yes, he did." Catherine frowned. How did Isabel know about that?

Isabel smiled and sipped her drink. "He told me too, although I'm not sure I would be so willing to part with it."

"I suppose it all depends on one's priorities," Catherine said as she covered the diamond with her hand. Many of the guests had remarked on the beautiful stone, some were even aware of the legend, but only Isabel's comment made Catherine feel uneasy. Why would Rian have told her anything about the diamond? Had he been planning to present her with the necklace? A sudden wave of doubt washed over her, followed closely by a panicky feeling that began to churn her stomach. Wishing Rian was by her side, Catherine took a sip from her glass.

"Oh, how clever! Rian has managed to find you a wedding ring to match." Isabel gushed, catching sight of the jewel as Catherine raised her glass. "May I see?"

Hesitantly Catherine placed her fingers in Isabel's outstretched hand.

"I can't imagine how my brother-in-law told you about the pendant, but never mentioned there was also a ring. After all, you cannot have one without the other, and can have neither without the man." Felicity's tone, while pleasant, was a slap in the face.

With two brief sentences she had made it clear that Isabel's comment regarding the fabulous gem was based on common gossip. The existence of the necklace was not a secret, nor the reason for its surrender, but the matching ring was not as well known. For reasons of their own, very few Connor women had chosen to wear the ring. Catherine was only the third bride who'd wanted to wear it. Rian had never told Isabel about the necklace. The two women stared at each other before Isabel graciously conceded defeat.

"Perhaps I was mistaken," she murmured as she placed her glass back on the tray. "If you will forgive me, I think I am needed inside."

They watched as she turned and unhurriedly made her way back to the other end of the terrace, a column of fire burning more than just the air around her. The sudden clear sound of music playing was muffled again as she reentered the house.

"Oh my goodness, would you look at that!" Catherine held out her hand to show how much it was shaking.

Taking the glass from Catherine's hand, Felicity placed it on the smooth marble surface of the balcony rail, next to her own. "Come now," she said, taking hold of Catherine's hands, "surely you didn't expect to get through the entire evening without at least one minor skirmish."

"I think I rather did."

"Well, be grateful you have come out unscathed."

"All thanks to you."

Felicity waved off her thanks. "I did nothing."

"How did you know she was lying about my necklace?"

Catherine's proprietary claim made the corner of Felicity's mouth twitch as she asked, "Did you really think Rian told her about this?" Hooking the chain with her finger, she allowed the fabulous gem to twirl and sparkle in the night air. "I don't think he ever mentioned it to her. He had no reason to," she snorted before adding, "It's priceless, you know."

Catherine's gasp caught them both by surprise. "No!"

Felicity laughed quietly as she laid the pendant back against Catherine's bodice. "If it makes you feel better, just think of it as a piece of colored glass."

"I cannot unhear what you said." The diamond suddenly felt very heavy as Catherine gently placed it inside her bodice, letting it nestle comfortably between her breasts. "But I definitely won't be wearing it that often."

"You should make the most of it. It has been placed into your safekeeping, but for only a short time, I think."

Catherine's hands fluttered across her own abdomen as she stared at Felicity. "I have heard tales that women with child are sometimes gifted with second sight. Do you know something I do not?" The fluttering fingers now formed a protective shield over the area below her waist.

"Oh goodness me. Heavens, no!" Felicity protested before the twinkle in Catherine's eye let her know she was being teased. They both giggled as Felicity turned and retrieved their glasses. "I don't know which is which," she said apologetically.

"Does it matter?" Catherine laughed, taking one of the glasses.

"I would like to propose a toast of my own," Felicity said, turning solemn. "To the joy of receiving unexpected gifts."

"Unexpected gifts?"

She nodded. "The sister I never knew I wanted…until I got her."

"I am going to miss you so much," Catherine whispered in a voice that wobbled with tears.

Arms about each other's waists, the two women drank and then hugged. They were still embracing when Catherine felt Felicity stiffen in her arms.

Pulling back, she saw the color drain from Felicity's face, and the glass she still held slip from her fingers to shatter on the tile flagstones.

"Felicity! Are you ill?"

Beads of perspiration now dotted Felicity's forehead and upper lip. "I don't know…I need…sit down…"

With Catherine's help, she managed to stagger to a chaise placed in the small alcove.

"Felicity!" Catherine reached out a hand, placing it on her friend's cheek, and was alarmed at the cold, clammy feel of her skin. She called her name again, but Felicity's eyes rolled up, and her head now lolled back against the cushioned headrest. Her breaths turned shallow, coming in a pattern of uneven gasps through parted lips. Though she hated the idea of leaving Felicity alone, Catherine knew she had to find Liam and Rian. There was no other choice. "Stay with me, Felicity. I'm going to get help," she said frantically, unsure if her words were heard.

Catherine stood, fighting a wave of dizziness that gripped her as she came upright. Her arm wavered as she sought to steady herself while trying to fight off the sudden woolly feeling in her head. Looking around she almost cried out in relief when she saw Isabel standing at the balustrade, watching her. The rubies at her throat and around her wrists reminded Catherine of violent bruises.

"Isabel, thank goodness! I need…Felicity is unwell…need to get help… she has fainted…"

"So I see," Isabel agreed with no sense of urgency at all.

Catherine stared at Isabel in confusion. She must not have understood what Catherine had said, or grasped the urgency of the situation. Although how that could be was beyond Catherine's ken. She took a couple of steps forward and was forced to stop as another wave of dizziness threatened. Whatever was wrong with her would have to wait. Felicity's need was more pressing.

"I don't think you understand," Catherine said, trying not to scream in frustration.

"Oh, I understand perfectly." Isabel moved past her to the recumbent figure on the chaise. After picking up Felicity's hand, she let it fall listlessly back into her lap. Trying to find a plausible excuse to separate the two women had been something of a challenge, but now, much to Isabel's delight, it proved unnecessary. Obviously the glasses had been switched, and Felicity had also ingested the drugged wine. "Too much to drink, I expect," Isabel said in a disdainful voice. "No doubt someone will find her."

"No! It's not the wine it's—oooh!"

Catherine put her hands to her temples as a sudden bolt of pain sliced through her head. It seemed an eternity before it passed, but when it did she noticed Isabel was now standing just a few feet from her. The rubies and diamonds at her throat caught Catherine's attention as they winked in the candlelight. She couldn't understand why she would find them so fascinating, but try as she might, she could not take her eyes from Isabel's neck. The gems merged together. No longer resembling bruises on Isabel's alabaster skin, they now formed a straight blood-red line as if her throat had been cut. Catherine blinked and shook her head. The slashed throat disappeared and the necklace became nothing more sinister than a piece of ugly jewelry. The sneer on Isabel's mouth twisted itself into a line of cruelty. Lady Howard no longer resembled a pillar of fire, but instead reminded Catherine of a large red spider sitting in the center of an intricately woven web, with Catherine caught in the silken, poisonous strands of Isabel's weaving.

"I know what happened to you," Isabel whispered softly, coming closer, "and I know the name of the man who scarred your body."

Catherine jerked her head up, Felicity momentarily forgotten. What was Isabel saying? How could she possibly know who had hurt her? And what was happening right now? This game Isabel was playing had moved from petty spitefulness and turned vicious, and Catherine had no time for games. A low moan from the alcove brought Catherine back to the present. If Isabel wasn't going to fetch help for Felicity, then she must. She stepped forward, but Isabel caught hold of her upper arm in a painful grip.

Baffled by her behavior, Catherine stared uncomprehendingly at the fingers digging into her flesh. She demanded Isabel let go of her, but the woolly feeling was getting worse, and she couldn't be certain if her words had been spoken anywhere but inside her head. Thinking was difficult, speaking more so, and though Catherine knew she was opening and closing her mouth, what came out was incoherent and muffled.

"The…wine?" she finally managed to mumble. Isabel congratulated her as the sneer became malicious. "Why?" Catherine's tongue was now swollen and thick, impeding her efforts to talk.

"Because you took something from me and I want it back."

"Rian."

Isabel reached out and cupped her face in her hand, her long nails stabbing Catherine's cheeks painfully. "With you gone he will return to me, and how long do you think it will take for him forget everything about you? In my bed he won't even recall your name."

No, never. Not true.

Catherine's mind screamed and she tried desperately to concentrate, but her focus was slipping, sliding into confusion. As she fought to remain lucid she could feel something strange happening to her body. Something she couldn't explain and was powerless to stop. Her limbs began going numb. Her arms became heavy, and she was unable to raise them. Similarly, her legs tingled and a deadening feeling crept its way up from her feet. She blinked rapidly as Isabel's face swam, but she managed to hold on to her faculties long enough to see her tormentor beckon to the shadows, from which a figure emerged.

With her brain screaming wildly that she had been poisoned, Catherine tried to scream. She prayed that someone—anyone—would hear her through the closed French doors. Her legs gave out before she could utter a single sound, and a pair of strong arms caught her before she fell and struck her head on the marble paving.

"Rian…"She sighed, certain it was her husband's strong arms that held her. But the face that swam over hers was that of a stranger. "Who—" was all she could manage, the word sounding like a soft breath escaping her lips before the drugged wine completed its task. Her eyes rolled back in her head, and John Fletcher stood on the terrace with her unconscious body in his arms.

"You know what to do?" Isabel asked, needing to return to her guests before her absence was noticed.

"Of course, everything is as planned," John assured her.

Looking at Catherine, Isabel leaned forward and spoke. She didn't know if Catherine was able to hear her, but she did not care. "Take comfort in knowing that while you are suffering the most painfully cruel tortures, your husband will be warming my bed, kissing my mouth, taking his fill of this body," she whispered malevolently. Then seeing the gold chain around Catherine's neck, Isabel pulled the diamond from her bodice and with a vicious jerk she snatched it free, breaking the clasp.

"This was meant for me!" she hissed triumphantly at John. "Now hurry. Hurry before you are seen."

Chapter 17

Rian was still deep in conversation when Liam interrupted him. "Where did our wives disappear to?"

Apologizing to his companions, Rian looked at his brother for a moment before scanning quickly over the room. "I think I saw them go outside," he said, indicating the French doors, and recalling the flushed look on Felicity's face. "They probably were in need of some air."

"Do you know how long they have been there?" Liam did not wish to disturb them unnecessarily if they were sharing secrets.

Rian frowned. Some time had passed since he recalled seeing either woman last, and he felt as if they should have returned by now. "I'm not sure, but let's join them, shall we?"

The night air had gone from pleasantly cool to chilly enough that any lady venturing forth would be in need of a wrap. Seeing no sign of either woman on the terrace, Rian glanced over the balcony to the pockets of blackness that made up Isabel's garden. "You don't think…" he said, gesturing to the shadows below him.

Liam shook his head. "No, it's far too dark to tempt Felicity to wander about looking for ideas," he said. "What could she see?"

"They must have gone back inside. Perhaps they are with Emily?"

"No, both Charles and Emily left almost an hour ago."

"I didn't get to say goodnight." Rian frowned.

"Worry not, Catherine said it for you, and I am certain Charles much preferred being kissed by her than you."

A sudden chill ran down Rian's back and he knew it had nothing to do with the cool night air. He shivered. "Just someone walking on my grave," he said, seeing his brother notice the tremor.

He had his hand on the lever that would open the door and take them back into the ballroom when a sound made him freeze where he stood. Looking quickly at Liam's face, Rian saw that he had heard it too. Both men paused, straining their ears and waiting for the sound to repeat itself. It did. A barely audibly whisper that made Liam's chest tighten as he ran the length of the terrace searching for his wife. He almost didn't see the secluded alcove where Felicity lay. Her face was now a ghostly white and her skin clammy with beads of perspiration dotting her skin. The pulse at the base of her throat fluttered erratically, and her breathing was an uneven rattle.

"Felicity!" Liam cried, gathering her into his arms, his face filled with wretched despair.

* * * *

Dipping a cloth into a small basin of cold water, Liam gently sponged his wife's brow. Though the fire in the room blazed brightly, the color had not returned to her face and she remained listless. He didn't need a working knowledge of medicine to know something was very wrong with her. Under his breath he cursed the footman. How long did it take to fetch a doctor?

One of Isabel's servants, alerted by the sight of Liam holding his wife's inert body in his arms, had had the sense to take them directly to a small receiving room, thereby avoiding any curious stares from the other guests. Rian had sent the man to fetch a doctor, and then gone to look for his wife. Liam felt as if hours had passed even though a glance at the clock ticking quietly on the mantel told him it had not even been ten minutes. He reasoned that finding a physician might prove problematic at this hour of the night, and all he could do was pray the man would be sober. In the meantime he anxiously awaited Rian's return with Catherine. The fact that Felicity had been found alone gave him a terrible sense of foreboding.

His wife suddenly began tossing her head from side to side, muttering unintelligibly. "Hush, hush," he soothed, passing the cool, damp cloth over her forehead. This was definitely more than just too much wine or rich food. Damn it! Where was the doctor? He started at the sound of the door being opened and relief flooded through him as a round faced man with ruddy cheeks entered, with Isabel close on his heels. Relinquishing his position next to his wife, he allowed the doctor to take charge and examine Felicity, which he did with an efficiency that Liam found reassuring.

"What happened?" Isabel asked. "Felicity seemed to be in perfect health just a short while ago."

"I don't know. She was like this when we found her."

"We?"

"Rian was with me."

"Where is he now?" Isabel sounded concerned.

"He has gone to find his wife."

Isabel said nothing more, and they both turned their attention to the physician, who had his ear pressed against the narrow end of a small conical instrument lying upon Felicity's chest. After a few moments he raised his head in concern. Liam watched as the doctor gently pushed back Felicity's closed eyelids, shaking his head at her unresponsive state. After sniffing the breath that escaped her parted lips, he stood up and addressed Liam directly.

"Mr. Connor, your wife needs to be moved, and with all haste."

Liam grabbed the doctor's arm. "Good God, man, what ails her?" he demanded in a voice that shook with fear.

The rotund man shook his head. "I cannot say for certain, and speculation will be of benefit to no one—" The rest of the doctor's sentence was interrupted by a worried husband's frustrated curses. Taking no offense, the man waited until he was certain he had Liam's full attention again. "I do believe, however, we should remove your wife to a quieter setting as soon as possible. Is your home far from here?"

"Not so very far," Liam replied with a shake of his head.

"Good, then let us get her safely in her own bed so I may perform a more detailed examination that will tell me more."

From out of nowhere Isabel produced a blanket for Liam to wrap around Felicity. "It might be best if you used the back stairway," she told him. "It will be quicker, and you will be able to avoid needless speculation." Opening the door, she spoke quietly to the footman outside. "I have ordered that your carriage be brought around, post haste." Seeing Liam holding his wife in his arms, she beckoned him to follow her.

Isabel took them down a long corridor that led to the servant's stairway, past the scullery and through the kitchen, surprising most of the staff with her presence. After being told their assistance was not required, they went back to whatever tasks they were occupied with. Though he was in no position to comment on it, Liam couldn't help but find their reaction strangely unsettling. Had either he or Rian walked through the kitchen at either of their residences, carrying an unconscious woman in their arms, the sight would have generated a great deal of curiosity. Either Isabel's servants took the concept of discretion to unheard of heights, or the picture they presented was so familiar an occurrence, it caused no alarm.

When they reached the small courtyard, the doctor helped him get Felicity into the carriage before entering himself.

At that moment Rian appeared in the kitchen doorway. He stepped past Isabel and looked up at his brother. "I'll send a boy to rouse Dr. MacGregor." It would not hurt to have a second physician in attendance, and their faith in the Scotsman was absolute.

"Where's Catherine?" Liam asked, seeing Rian was alone.

"I don't know, but I'm sure she's all right.I just can't find her at present." The chill he had felt earlier returned, intensifying and clawing at his chest.

"No doubt she, too, is looking for you, and has possibly become lost. My house is large and unfamiliar to her," Isabel said. "I am sure your wife is sensible enough to remain in one place and wait for you to find her. That way neither one of you will keep going in and out of different rooms, missing each other."

"Thank you, Isabel. I am sure you are right," Rian replied. Liam, however, was not fooled by the calmness of his brother's tone. Rian was worried, but could only deal with one crisis at a time. He would resume his search for Catherine once Liam and Felicity were safely away. "Now hurry," Rian urged, "and get Felicity home. Catherine and I will follow directly."

"But we are taking the carriage." They had all ridden together.

"Don't worry, I will send them in mine," Isabel offered as she stepped forward. "Quickly now, attend to your wife."

Liam was able to nod his thanks to her just before Rian closed the carriage door and gave the signal to the driver to be on his way. He then gave directions to the boy who had been holding the horses, sending him to Dr. MacGregor and slipping him a coin for his trouble.

"I am sure all will be well," Isabel said, placing a hand on his arm. "Dr. Wilson is a respected man, and no doubt he will conclude that Felicity is simply suffering the effects of too much rich food, good wine and overall excitement. An opinion I am sure your own physician will agree with."

Rian nodded. "I'm sure you're right, Isabel. It's just that Liam is so protective of her now, given her condition."

"Condition?" Isabel raised an eyebrow.

Rian gave a little shrug. In a month or two a glance would reveal their wonderful secret to the whole world. "It is not common knowledge yet, but Felicity is with child."

"Oh, I see." Isabel moved ahead of him through the outer courtyard toward the door that would lead them back into the kitchen. The clever apothecary had warned her about all the possible side effects of the powder she had procured, but he had not mentioned any concerns should a woman be with child. Of course Isabel had not really cared about such things, and she supposed it was unfortunate that Felicity had shared her sister-in-law's glass.

"Please excuse me, Isabel, but I need to find my wife," Rian said, interrupting her thoughts as they made their way back through the narrow hallway. Rounding the staircase, he paid no attention to the door he heard opening behind him, and did not see the large, burly man who stepped forward with his arm raised above his head. There was a slight *whoosh* before Rian crumpled to the ground.

A moment of panic gripped Isabel until she reassured herself that he was still breathing. She glared at John Fletcher's man, who now stood over the motionless form, blackjack in his hand. "You didn't have to hit him so hard!" she hissed angrily.

"He's a big 'un, missus," the man said in his own defense. "I had to be sure he wasn't going to give me any trouble."

With one hand on her hip, Isabel pressed the other to her forehead. "Well, don't just stand there, you bedlamite. Get him moved before someone sees you."

Grunting, the hefty man took hold of one of Rian's arms and hoisted him over his shoulder before following Isabel up the staircase to a bedroom on the upper floor. She watched as Rian was deposited none too gently on the bed.

"Make sure you are not seen leaving," she instructed as John's man moved past her.

After closing the door she remained where she was, content to simply stare at Rian. Then she walked over to the bed, and sat next to his unconscious body. Lost in thought she looked at him, marveling again at the rugged handsomeness of his features, especially now, when he was curiously defenseless. She leaned forward and kissed him softly on the lips. He did not move.

"It did not have to be like this, my love," she whispered in a trembling voice, "but you left me with no other choice."

Getting to her feet, she smoothed an imaginary wrinkle from the front of her skirt before checking her appearance in the mirror. She adjusted one of the jeweled combs in her hair, and then left to join her guests, closing the door quietly behind her.

* * * *

John Fletcher made his way through the dark shadows of Isabel's lower garden. The burden in his arms was cumbersome only because of the number of petticoats she wore beneath her gown. But he was able to reach the gate in the stone wall without mishap. He had unlocked the gate and eased the latch earlier that evening, and now it swung open readily at the touch of his boot. A carriage stood waiting on the other side of the garden wall. Obscuring the windows with dark shades, John made sure that, even if the conveyance caused some attention at this late hour, no one would be able to give any detail if asked. Even the horses were unremarkable. A pair of nondescript brown beasts, they snorted mildly as they waited, impatient to be about their business.

The man who had been standing holding onto a bridle with each hand, now hurried forward, and pulled opened the carriage door. John was pleased to see the interior floor had been covered with pillows and blankets, per his instructions. He carefully laid Catherine on top of the padding. Knowing she would be insentient, he could not have set her on the seat where she could roll off and hurt herself, so he had made the floor of the carriage as comfortable as possible. It had the added advantage of providing less room for her to be jostled about.

He had just placed a pillow beneath her head, and was carefully tucking a heavy blanket around her when Catherine suddenly reached out and gripped his arm.

"Please...take me home," she begged, her voice sounding raw and husky, her eyes bottomless pools of azure blue. "Don't give me back...to him."

Although startled, John spoke cautiously. "Back to whom?" It was imperative to know how aware Catherine was of what was happening to her. Obviously she had not consumed as much of the drugged wine as Isabel had thought, or else the effects would not be wearing off this quickly. Her eyes, though still glazed, were rapidly clearing as she tried to scan his face. "Who do you mean?" John asked again in an urgent whisper.

"My cousin...Phillip."

After climbing into the carriage, he pulled Catherine into a sitting position and put his arm around her for support. Her head lolled back against his arm, and she blinked rapidly as she looked up at him. Taking a small, green vial from his pocket, John carefully eased the cork stopper from the top with his teeth, and spat it out.

"Here, open up now. There's a good girl."

He put the small bottle to her lips, knowing Catherine would have knocked it out of his hands had her arms been working. Able to pour the contents into her mouth, John massaged her throat, making sure she swallowed. Some of the liquid spilled down her chin, but more than enough went down her throat, easing her back to oblivion. The drug's effect was practically instantaneous. Time was of the essence, and John knew he had to make haste. Carefully he laid Catherine on the floor of the carriage and clambered over her slumped body. The man with the horses earned an extra gold piece to ensure his silence. John climbed on the driver's seat, took the reins in his hands and urged the animals forward at a pace that would draw no attention.

The brief exchange with Catherine had rattled him, though he was hard pressed to understand why. His past was littered with a great many incidents he was not proud of. Acts he had committed that were both illegal and immoral in nature. The law, from John's point of view, was an unreliable guide. Enforced by those who, more often than not, would willingly turn a blind eye if it proved beneficial for them to do so. So what if his actions were not always to the advantage of those who employed him? It was what it was, and this was how he managed to survive in the world. This time, however, something felt different, but what it might be remained a mystery. He had never questioned Isabel's judgment before, yet recently he found himself questioning the rationale of her instructions. How dangerously close was she to taking a step that would prove her undoing?

John Fletcher was under no illusions about what was going to happen to the blonde woman after she was handed back to her cousin. He had known from the very first, given Phillip Davenport's perverse predilections. Rape would merely be a way to whet the bastard's appetite.

"Bella, what have you involved yourself in this time?" John muttered as the carriage rolled along dimly lit streets toward its destination. He thought about Isabel and her ill-fated lust for Rian Connor. Even he knew that this was not the way to bring any man, much less one of Rian's temperament, back to her bed. But he'd been on the receiving end of Isabel's temper in the past, and was in no hurry to repeat the experience.

Isabel had told Phillip that she was not concerned with Catherine's welfare, but that was only because she did not know the man's aberrant nature. There would be no bedroom in a back alley brothel waiting for Catherine when her cousin was done with her. Phillip Davenport could not take the chance that Catherine might escape a second time. Or that Rian Connor might find her.

Outside of a dark alley, John brought the carriage to a stop. Another conveyance waited at the appointed place. He frowned, recognizing that a part of him had hoped Phillip would be delayed by some unfortunate occurrence. Then John could have taken the unconscious woman somewhere else. Perhaps keep her safe while he persuaded Isabel to abandon this course of madness she was hell-bent on pursuing. But Phillip Davenport was here, and his agitation as he exited the carriage told John he was not pleased at having been kept waiting.

"You're late," he snarled.

John shrugged. He was not intimidated by Phillip's show of temper. Jumping down from the seat, he opened the door and reached inside for Catherine, but Phillip‘s voice stopped him. "Don't touch her!" he snapped, as he licked his lips in anticipation of receiving his prize.

Unable to hide his disgust, John stepped back as Phillip awkwardly pulled Catherine into a sitting position before roughly hoisting her over his shoulder. Her long hair had come loose from its elegant arrangement, and now fell free. White curls and ribbons swept the dirt of the street as she was moved from one vehicle to the other. John could only assume the driver of Phillip's carriage was under similar orders to offer no assistance.

"I had to give her an extra jolt," he told Phillip. "She did not drink enough of the wine, and was coming around. I took the liberty of presuming you did not wish to have her kicking and screaming before you were able to secure her."

Phillip cursed. "How much did you give her?"

"All of it." John held the green vial aloft. Even in the dark it was easy to see the bottle was empty. Another string of obscenities filled the air. "You've waited this long," John said, keeping his tone calm and even. "What difference will another twenty-four hours make?"

Phillip gave him a long, hard stare. "Tell your mistress any business between us is now finished."

The last glimpse John had of Catherine was an image of her seated on her abductor's lap, her head cradled against his chest. There was something about the way Phillip's hands fluttered over her, touching her skin and smoothing her hair, that struck John as obscene. For a long time he stood and stared into the dark street, his eyes following the route Phillip's carriage had taken. Coming to a decision, he put his hand into his pocket and pulled out the ring he had slipped from Catherine's finger. He admired the diamond's luster for a few moments before returning it to its hiding place. Back on the driver's seat, he turned the carriage around, and headedback the way he had come. Isabel would be furious with him, but that was something he would deal with. His mouth twisted into a grim line. Perhaps it was time to remind her ladyship that the past was not always so easily buried and forgotten. Especially when it was your own.

Chapter 18

Rian groaned and rolled over. His head hurt like the devil and he cautiously ran his fingers through his thick glossy hair, halting when he reached a sizeable lump. The swelling was enough to make him wince. Opening his eyes, he was relieved to find that the rest of his head was remarkably clear. No headache or tell-tale throbbing from too much wine, or anything else.

He lay back on the pillow for a moment, and stared at the painted ceiling. A group of cherubim, with rosy cheeks and angelic smiles, looked down on him as they rested on white clouds in a dazzling blue sky. They all wore the same slightly naughty expression, as if telling him they knew a secret that he did not. The decorated ceiling reminded him of something else, something he felt he ought to know, something he shouldn't have any difficulty remembering…except he did.

He groaned again as he pushed himself up and swung his legs over the edge of the bed. A frown pulled his brows together as realized he was still dressed in the elegant attire he had been wearing for Isabel's ball. Warily he looked about him. There was nothing immediately recognizable about the room he was in. It was a bedroom, but not one in the family townhouse. None of those boasted an angelic ceiling. Still, there was something about the décor that felt familiar. It pricked his brain like an aggravating itch that was just beyond the reach of his fingers.

The drapes at the window were partially open, and from the shadows on the opposite wall Rian estimated it was close to noon. Unfortunately he carried no pocket watch and a cursory glance revealed no timepiece in the room. Getting to his feet, he unsteadily made his way to the washstand, where he soaked a cloth with cold water and placed it carefully on the back of his head. The effect was instantaneous. He groaned and soaked the cloth again, suddenly remembering what the ceiling reminded him of. It wasn't the chubby cherubs, but rather the blue sky behind them. An almost exact match for Catherine's eyes. In his haste Rian turned and knocked the porcelain basin off the washstand, where it landed on the floor and broke into several pieces. But he was already out the door. He knew at once where he was, whose house he was in, and he decided this time she had gone too far.

"Isabbbelll!"

He crashed through the bedroom door, jolting her awake. Isabel sat up, trying to focus as she covered herself with the sheet. For a moment Rian was slightly flustered, her disheveled appearance halting his progress into her boudoir.

"Oh Rian, good morning, or is it afternoon?" She blinked sleepily at him, and then, noting his attire, came wide awake. "Good God, have you not yet returned home?"

"You know damn well I haven't been home," he snarled through clenched teeth. "What the hell did you do to me?"

"Do to you? Whatever are you talking about?" The affronted look Isabel fixed on him would have made a saint question her involvement. "Rian darling, I don't know how much you had to drink last night—"

"Nowhere near enough to have been made insensible!" he snapped.

"But you did slip and hit your head."

Instinctively his hand went to the back of his head.

"You were rendered unconscious," Isabel told him.

"I *wasn't* drunk!" he repeated firmly.

She shrugged. "If you insist."

"What happened after Liam left with Felicity?"

"You went to find your wife. That's the last I saw of you until a footman told me about your fall. As you were still breathing, it seemed prudent to find a more private place for you to regain your senses. I honestly didn't realize you were still here." Her offended manner turned to petulance. "And I really don't appreciate your attitude."

"I don't give a damn what you appreciate. Where's Catherine?"

Smoothing the bed sheet around her, Isabel stopped. "How would I know? If she is like most wives, I imagine she is pacing the floor in *your* home, wringing her hands and wondering where her errant husband could be." Rian stared at her. Was she being truthful? Her voice held just enough indignation to be believable. "Besides, what makes you think I would know anything regarding your wife's whereabouts?"

Without realizing it, Isabel had overplayed her hand. Now Rian knew she was hiding something. "Because the last time I saw her," he said, "she was in this house, and I know Catherine would not have left without me unless it was by coercion."

"Careful, Rian." Isabel narrowed her eyes. "Do not make accusations without being in full possession of the facts. Perhaps you don't know your wife as well as you suppose."

"And you don't know her at all." His voice was low and his temper rising. "Where is she, Isabel?"

"Why do you keep insisting that I know?"

"Because I know when you're hiding something, and you never were a very good liar. At least not with me."

Her laugh was unconvincing. "I'm hiding nothing. Now, I suggest you return to your own home as I have no wish to continue this ridiculous conversation."

On the surface Isabel appeared to be irritated, angry even, but the slight catch in her voice belied the sincerity of her words. Had she forgotten so quickly how well he knew her? And now Rian realized something else. Isabel was trying to conceal something from him. It had been a guess on his part thinking that she knew more than she was telling him, but it seemed he was right. It wasn't Isabel's voice that gave him the answer but the sudden change in her body language.

"I will give you one last chance to tell me, Isabel. Where is my wife?"

Her alabaster skin flushed angrily, her mouth twisting to an ugly line. "How many ways can I say this? I don't know what you're talking—"

He was on her before she had time to finish her sentence, capturing her wrist in a grip of iron. His voice became a growl. "I know you're lying, Isabel, so perhaps I should save us both some time and just beat the truth out of you."

"You wouldn't dare!" she shrieked, her long black hair tumbling about her shoulders as she struggled to pull her wrist free.

"Poor choice of words. You should know me well enough to know I never back down from a challenge."

Rian had never raised his hand to a woman in his life, no matter how extreme the provocation, and he wasn't about to start now. Not even with Isabel. But he was desperate, and it wouldn't hurt for her to think he was not only capable of committing such an act, but that she might have pushed him far enough he would actually make good on his threat.

Tightening his hold on her, Rian dragged her out of her bed. She yelped, and awkwardly clutched the sheet with her free hand, pulling it with her while attempting to cover herself as she staggered off balance. Isabel always slept naked, and Rian was fully prepared to see her body. He had even steeled himself against the possibility of becoming aroused. But there seemed little chance of that happening as Isabel, in an uncharacteristic display of modesty, tried desperately to cover her nakedness with one hand.

"Come now, Isabel, why so shy? It's not like your charms are unknown to me."

Her foot became tangled in the sheet, and hopping on one leg, she almost fell. Under different circumstances, and not so long ago, Rian would have found her antics comical. Now he simply found her behavior irritating, but concerned that she would fall and hurt herself, he stepped in to help.

Letting go of her wrist, Rian reached for one corner of the sheet and pulled. His action left him with an armful of fine linen, and Isabel standing in the middle of the floor as naked as the day she was born. His expression turned from anger to bewildered shock as his brain registered the change in Isabel's appearance. And the only possible reason for such an alteration.

The draping panel of material on Isabel's ball gown had effectively covered her abdomen, cleverly hiding what her current state of dishabille could not. It seemed that Rian stared at her rounded belly for an eternity before dragging his eyes up to her bosom. Her breasts were fuller, heavier, and the faint markings of blue milk veins contrasted with her pale skin. He stared at her face, waiting for her to deny his unspoken question, and realized she would not. Isabel, who was not opposed to using her body to get what she wanted, had deliberately allowed this to happen. There could be no other answer.

She walked past him, head held high, to the chaise where her robe lay. Slipping it on, she tied the sash about her thickening waist.

"When?" Rian asked, closing his eyes, his voice flat.

"Sometime this winter."

He ran his fingers through his hair. "When did this—"

Fire flashed in her emerald eyes, making them glitter wildly. "The night at Oakhaven," she told him. "Has your memory improved sufficiently? Do you remember making love to me now?"

Rian took a step back, shaking his head. "No. It's not possible," he muttered.

It was only a dream.

Except now he knew it hadn't been.

He wanted to shout his denial at her. Tell her that it couldn't be true. It was not his seed that had brought forth the life she carried in her belly. But deep inside he knew she was not lying. Whatever had happened that night at Oakhaven, whether he remembered it or not, the consequence was now staring him in the face. Isabel was pregnant with his child.

She took a step toward him, her voice softening as she held out a hand. "Rian, I was going to tell you—"

"And just when were you planning to do that, Isabel? After the child was born?" His voice, cold as ice, cut through her. It hurt that he had said *the child*. Even though she saw in his eyes that he acknowledged the truth, he refused to verbally admit his part in her condition.

"It has been difficult for me since we parted."

Rian glared at her. "The ball last night was all for your benefit, wasn't it? I know you too well, Isabel. You had no intention of making amends. The entire night was nothing more than an elaborate show on your part." The look in his eyes changed to contempt. "Tell me, what were you hoping to accomplish?"

"No, Rian, you're wrong!" She came toward him and put her hand on his arm, her expression pleading. "I did want to apologize. I do want to be friends with Catherine. I—"

"Lying bitch!" The words came out as a vicious hiss, and he shook her hand off his arm.

"How can you speak to me like that when I'm going to have your child?"

Tears welled in her eyes as Rian stared at her, finally seeing the woman she truly was. Any hope of Isabel's reclaiming his affection was now dashed by the detached indifference with which he addressed her.

"I give you my word I will not deny paternity, and, should you wish it, I will also make arrangements to take the child."

The utter disdain in Rian's voice cut more than his actual words. He was rejecting her a second time, and she staggered under the weight of crushing disbelief. But only for a moment. The pain quickly changed, rearranging itself into something malevolent and evil, and smoothing her face into an impassive, unreadable mask.

In that moment Isabel knew beyond the shadow of a doubt that Rian was lost to her forever. The possibility of a reunion between them, happy or otherwise, had been nothing but a fool's dream. Though he would publicly claim the child as his own, raising it as such if she asked him, for Isabel it was not enough. Even though what he offered was more than most men in his situation would have agreed to, Rian did not want *her*.

"I would like you to leave," she told him.

"Isabel, where is my wife?" Rian asked one last time.

This time she answered him.

"Where she belongs. In hell."

Chapter 19

Returning to consciousness, Catherine hurt all over. Every muscle throbbed with a pain that was far different from the ache she'd experienced as a result of imbibing too much blackberry brandy. It reminded her of the time she'd slipped and lost her footing in the barn, falling from the rafters. If Edward had seen her, he would no longer have called her Cat, but it was one of the few times he had not been with her. Landing in a pile of loose straw, Catherine had counted herself lucky not to have broken anything. As it was, she spent a full day in almost unbearable, pain before Old Ned had guessed what was wrong, and bound her ribs.

What she was feeling now was almost as bad, but it was difficult to know which of her symptoms was worse. The stinging soreness that infused her muscles, or the horrible aftertaste coating the back of her throat. Thick and slimy, it had a rotten flavor, like a piece of fish that had turned or meat that had spoiled. She struggled to recall the glass of drugged wine at Isabel's party, but that seemed a lifetime ago, and she had no idea how much time had passed since then. It could be hours or only minutes. Either one was plausible.

The few candles that still burned offered enough light for Catherine to see she was lying on a large four-poster bed. Carefully she raised her head and peered at the gloom beyond the end of the carved bedposts. Her eyes slowly adjusted, allowing more of her surroundings to reveal themselves, and as she stared at the dresser, its shape and design struck a nerve. There was no need to describe the toiletry items lying on its surface. The silver backed hairbrush, and the two tortoiseshell combs were as familiar to her as the birthmark just above her left hip. They were all she had left of her mother, and she recalled all too clearly the last time she had held them, and where she had placed them. An icy chill skittered down her spine.

With eyes now opened wide, Catherine scanned the rest of the room. Even though she had only been within these walls for less than a single day, she could describe each piece of furniture, the exact shade of silk on the walls, and every horrifying terror that had taken place. She raised her eyes to the pink colored canopy and matching bed curtains, and felt her stomach lurch. Nothing had been changed. Her surroundings brought forth a feeling of dread that seized her by the throat and intensified with each panicked breath.

Holding her fist to her mouth, Catherine smothered the scream that tried to escape as the memory, unfettered at last, broke free inside her head. Every sadistic moment resurfaced, forcing her to suffer through it once again in her mind. And it felt just as real as it had the first time. The memory of her cousin's touch, the feel of his hot breath against her skin, nearly made her convulse. The nightmare had returned, only the fact that she was not sleeping made it all the more terrifying.

Rian! Rian! Where are you?

Without thinking she sat up, giving a startled cry at the fiery burst of pain exploding from hand to elbow. Her arm felt unnaturally heavy, and she stared in bewilderment at the iron manacle cuffed to her wrist, its partner securely fastened to the heavy chain secured around the wooden bedpost. It took a moment or two before she understood her predicament. She was chained to the bed. Following the iron links with her eyes, she found an additional length pooled on the floor, allowing for some movement.

Rage welled up inside Catherine and, grasping the chain in both hands, she pulled with all her strength, but all she did was fill the air with a loud clanking sound that offended her ears. These links had been forged by a master craftsman. It would take more strength than she possessed to break free. Anger was quickly replaced by a sudden overwhelming sense of hopelessness, and tears fell from her eyes.

Stop crying! For heaven's sake, get a grip on yourself! At least this time you know what you are up against. Find a way to use that to your advantage. Rian will *find you, he* will *come for you. You must never doubt that. All you have to do is make sure you survive until he does.*

Wiping her face on the sleeve of her gown, Catherine sniffled. Her head felt a little better. The awful tightness, like a steel band around her skull, was still there, but it was beginning to fade. The foul taste in the back of her throat still lingered, and it was now joined by another sensation that was quickly becoming far more bothersome. Thirst. Her throat was dry and scratchy, and it hurt to swallow. With careful fingers she explored her jaw line, and down her neck, searching for any tenderness or bruising that might account for the discomfort. She found none, which meant the source of her irritation had to be internal.

At the end of the bed, tucked inside the shadows, stood a small table bearing a tray with a glass pitcher and tumbler. It had escaped Catherine's notice during her preliminary sweep of the room, but she reasoned her terror at being back inside this house could make her miss any number of things. When she was calmer she would make a more thorough search of the room. Her eyes narrowed as she focused on the pitcher. It was full of water. Licking her lips, she could almost taste the cool liquid sliding down her throat and easing the burning ache. Carefully she got off the bed, maneuvering her way to the end of the iron links, only to discover the length of chain did not permit her to reach the refreshing liquid. Twisting her body, she tried reaching out with her other arm, stretching her fingers to their limit as the manacle bit cruelly into her wrist, but still the table stood beyond her reach. She was trying hard not to succumb to another round of tears when a sound came from the darkness enveloping the room beyond the bed. A giggle that was almost falsetto in tone, it made the hairs on the nape of her neck stand up. Slowly Catherine turned her head and watched as her cousin stepped into the circle of light shed by the candles.

"Thirsty, my love?" Phillip smirked, moving closer. Catherine scrambled back onto the bed and then off the other side, trying to get as far away from him as possible. Or at least as far as the chain would allow. Fear uncoiled itself in the pit of her stomach, exploding through her in a wave of paralyzing terror. Intuition told her this was precisely what her cousin wanted, what he needed. Her fear was the elixir necessary to fuel his sordid desires, and she could not let him see just how frightened she was. "I am told that one of the more unpleasant side effects of Lady Howard's wine is a terrible burning thirst," Phillip told her. "Does your throat feel dry, my pet?"

Catherine forced herself to swallow, even though her hands clenched at the raw burn in her throat as she did so. "It is not so severe that I would quench it with anything offered by your hand," she declared bravely in a voice like ground glass.

Phillip came to the end of the bed and stared at her. An ugly smile tugged at the corners of his mouth. "It soon will be, I can promise you that," he said confidently. "Soon you will beg me for a drink of water, and in return you will agree to do *anything* to ease your discomfort."

He went to the small table and picked up the pitcher. The pale flickering candlelight seemed to gather inside the glass jug as he held it up, pinpoints of radiance dancing inside the clear liquid. Catherine brought her free hand up to her mouth to stop herself from crying out in desperation, but a sound escaped her, making her tormentor laugh as he poured the water onto the floor. Catherine was aware of every drop that fell to the carpet, and was immediately absorbed by the weave. One hand trembled against her mouth, while the other circled her throat in an effort to prevent herself from screaming at her cousin.

She watched warily as Phillip set the empty pitcher on the table. He picked up the glass tumbler, balancing it on the palm of his hand as if surprised by its empty weight. With a sudden whirl he turned and threw it, shattering the glass against the wall above her head. The noise was deafening and Catherine shrieked as she covered her head with her hands, making the chain rattle loudly as shards of glass showered her head and shoulders.

"You belong to me, Catherine, make no mistake about that," Phillip snarled. "And I will have you, willingly or not."

"You're mad!" she cried out, feeling a tongue of fire lick down her throat as she did so.

"Am I?" Phillip asked, opening the door and looking back at her. "Then how is it that you are the one in chains?"

Catherine waited until she was certain he had left before sliding down the wall to crumple in a heap on the floor. Why wasn't she stronger? Why had her courage deserted her? How could it be that she had managed to escape from this nightmare once, only to be thrown back into the same cesspool?

Her weeping surprised her, because she felt sure she had no moisture in her body to produce tears. Wiping her wet face with her hand, she licked the salty drops from her fingers. She stopped crying after a while, and as she did so she became aware of a dull ache where the manacle chafed her skin. Tearing a strip from one of her petticoats, she poked it between the iron and her skin in the hope it would act as a cushion. Then she carefully shook her head and ran her free hand through her hair, removing any remnants of broken glass before climbing wearily back onto the bed.

Bringing her knees up to her chest, Catherine curled into a ball. She forced herself to take deep breaths, exhaling each one with a deliberate slowness past dried lips. As each breath passed she could feel the wild, jerky drumming in her chest begin to quiet itself. Once a calmer, more soothing, rhythm had been established, she was able to focus her mind and think.

That Phillip had totally lost his grip on reality was a certainty. It made him dangerous and unpredictable. Whatever his intentions, she would have to be prepared to expect anything. Including the probability that violating her body was only a matter of time. But it was what Phillip would do once his sexual appetite was satisfied that frightened her even more. From the maniacal glint in his eyes she had the feeling what had happened to her before would be nothing compared to the punishment he planned to bestow upon her now.

Her thoughts turned to Lettie. Was she all right? Did she even know Catherine was once more a prisoner in her home? Was Phillip aware that Lettie had helped her escape? Was he forcing her to be a participant in this recurring nightmare? This last was something Catherine refused to believe. Instead she held on to the hope that Phillip remained ignorant of his wife's involvement in Catherine's previous escape. Surely he would have said something if he knew? Would Lettie find the courage to help her again?

Pulling her brows together, Catherine forced herself to take a couple of deeper breaths. Panic was nipping at her, and she could not afford to give in to it. Rian would find her. He would save her from the clutches of this despicable madman. Rian would come. He had to come, before it was too late!

But what if he did not? He had no idea where she had been taken, and who was there to tell him? Certainly not Isabel. To do so would admit her complicity in Catherine's abduction, and she would have surely thought of a plausible reason to explain her disappearance. Perhaps even now she was filling Rian's head with her cleverly worded lies.

No! No! No!

Catherine refused to even consider such a monstrous thing. With every fiber of her being she believed that Rian was even now, someway, somehow, searching for her. It was up to her to find the strength to endure until then. This was her last thought before the sedative John Fletcher had forced her to swallow reclaimed her, pushing her back into the realm of insensibility.

* * * *

When Catherine woke again, she had no idea if it was day or night. What little light crept through the draped windows had come and gone, moving silently over the walls and across the ceiling. Still slipping in and out of consciousness, she had even less idea of how many hours had passed than before. Time had become a perception she could not grasp with any lucidity. She could have been imprisoned within the silk lined walls of this room for either a few hours or a few days.

Someone had taken the trouble to cover her with a light woolen blanket. Unfortunately they had not released her from her restraint, and she was still tethered to the bedpost. Hesitantly, Catherine pushed the blanket aside with her free hand, and sighed with relief to see that none of her clothing had been removed, although the laces on her gown had been loosened. She had no doubt as to who was responsible for this, and wondered if Phillip had taken pleasure in seeing the scar on her back.

Uncertain whether she was alone in the room, Catherine turned her head, straining to hear the telltale sound of someone else breathing. There was nothing out of the ordinary, but through the closed and covered window she was able to hear a songbird trilling. As she concentrated, other sounds came to her. The muffled bark of a dog, followed by the clip-clop of horse's hooves, and the rumble of carriage wheels. Although the exact hour was a mystery, Catherine knew it was still daytime beyond her window.

Sitting up, she tilted her head to one side and closed her eyes, forcing her mind to focus. There might be no other sounds from inside her room, but there were also no other sounds from the rest of the house. The odd, eerie quiet filled her with an inexplicable dread. She may not have been in this house long, but it had been long enough for her to know there were a good number of servants for a residence of this size. Why then could she hear no sounds of chores being performed? She ought to have been able to hear some movement, but all that came back to her was a deep, impenetrable silence.

Her first thought was that everyone was abed, but the sounds beyond her window said this could not be so. Catherine might be a little disoriented, but she wasn't that confused. No, the house was unnaturally quiet because there was no one to make any noise. Which meant that Phillip wanted to be certain whatever happened to her would be a private affair with none to witness his actions.

Her eyes had already adjusted to the dim light, and Catherine was able to see that the pitcher had been replaced and fresh water was once again on the small table. Another glass had been placed next to it. She wasn't sure, but it seemed as if the table had also been moved, and was now possibly within reach.

Water! She craved a drink of water! The sight of the clear liquid made her throat begin to burn, and she would have licked her lips, but her tongue was thick and swollen. Positive now that the table had been repositioned, Catherine pushed back the blanket and scrambled across the bed. As she moved forward an odd, lightheaded feeling came over her, but she pushed the sensation to one side as an overpowering need to quench the dryness in her throat drove her to reach for the lifesaving liquid.

She would have wept with gratitude if she had not used up the last of her moisture in her previous bout of crying, because she was more than capable of reaching the pitcher now. The table had definitely been moved. Eagerly she filled the glass tumbler that had replaced its shattered mate, and repeating the word *slowly* in her mind, she put the glass to her lips and sipped the water. Catherine only managed a single sip before greedily tipping the glass and gulping the contents, feeling it spill down her chin and neck as she did so. With a sigh she stared at the empty glass, and then, as her parched throat begged for more, she abandoned it and picked up the pitcher with both hands and soothed the ragged fire in the back of her throat in a more direct manner. The pitcher was three-quarters empty when she put it back down on the table, turned her head and vomited violently on the carpet.

The awful burning sensation of acrid bile now joined the raw feeling, nullifying whatever comfort the water had provided. She continued to retch long after the meager contents of her stomach had been expelled. With trembling hands, Catherine managed to pour what was left of the water into the glass, and rinse her mouth, spitting the tainted liquid back into the now empty pitcher before slowly drinking what was left in the glass.

Finished, she climbed wearily back onto the bed and closed her eyes. She was completely exhausted. The lightheaded feeling remained, but she paid it little mind because her stomach and throat hurt more. Wearily she turned her face into the pillow, gasping aloud when she saw what lay next to her. Another example of Phillip's mean, petty cruelty.

Chapter 20

The footman who opened the front door was knocked off his feet as Rian came crashing over the threshold. Muttering his apologies, he extended a hand to help the man back up before taking the stairs two at a time, calling out Catherine's name as he did so. He had no idea how he was supposed to explain his absence or the fact that he had spent the night at Isabel's house, but his only concern was to see his wife with his own eyes. He could make everything right once he knew she was safe. Nothing else mattered.

He flung open the door to the master suite, expecting to find her with an arm pulled back, prepared to hurl something at his head. Either that or curled up and weeping at his disgraceful behavior. He hoped for the former. Her anger and fury he could deal with far better than her tears, but Rian would accept either. How his wife sought to punish him was her prerogative. He deserved whatever she gave him.

What he did not expect to find was an empty room. It was now early afternoon and the chamber looked exactly the same as when they had left for Isabel's ball. Although the room ought to have been attended to at this hour of the day, he could tell it had not. The day dress Catherine had worn yesterday was still draped across the chaise when it should have been put away, and the bed itself was still turned down. Catherine's nightgown, waiting to be filled with her shapely form, stared accusingly at him.

"Rian, whatever is the matter?"

Turning around, he came face to face with his brother, and noted with some puzzlement that Liam was also still wearing his clothes from the night before. He appeared physically drained, with exhaustion showing in every line of his young face. It was as if he had aged suddenly overnight, and his condition was such that it made Rian pause before asking, "Where is she?"

It was obvious the younger Connor had not yet been to bed. A state made all the more obvious by the show of weary confusion on his face. "Where is who?" he asked.

"Catherine."

Liam stared at Rian as if he had suddenly grown another head. "I have no idea. I—we—assumed she was with you."

"She didn't come back?" Fear seized him, cruel fingers twisting around his heart, and Rian could not hide the escalating anxiety in his voice.

"No, I haven't seen her. I thought it strange when you did not return, but I imagined something must have kept you at Isabel's."

"Why in God's name would you think that?"

Liam shrugged and rubbed his hand across his face. His fingers rasped the stubble on his jaw. "I don't know, Rian. I wasn't thinking."

Something in his voice, the hesitancy, the unspoken plea for understanding, made the hairs on the back of Rian's neck stand up. A warning that something dreadful had taken place. "Liam, has Felicity recovered?" Rian asked. "Does she know what happened to Catherine?"

The younger Connor stared at him, his mouth moving, but the ability to form coherent speech deserted him. Rian had never seen so much anguish reflected in another human being's face. Liam's dark eyes swam and his breath hitched as he tried to speak. "Sh-sh-she…lost the b-b-baby," he managed to say before a torrent of grief overcame him.

"Oh, dear God in heaven, no!"

Pulling his brother into a fierce embrace, Rian offered what comfort he could as he momentarily put aside his own concern. Waiting for Liam to compose himself as best he could.

"What happened? Did Dr. MacGregor get here?" Rian asked gently, keeping his hand on Liam's shoulder.

"Yes, Dr. MacGregor arrived almost at once. He agreed with Dr. Wilson that losing the baby was not a natural occurrence." He wiped his eyes on his sleeve, the gesture suddenly making him look very young and vulnerable. "He asked me if anyone would want to hurt her. Hurt my darling Felicity? Why would he ask such a thing, Rian?"

The stricken look returned, filling Rian with a sense of overwhelming guilt. Liam had always asked so little from him, and the one time he had truly needed the comfort of an older brother, Rian had not been there for him. He would punish himself for this transgression at a later date. Now was not the time.

"Did the doctors say what might be the cause?" Rian asked quietly.

"They both seem to agree that somehow Felicity took some sort of highly potent sleeping draught. One strong enough to harm our baby."

Reaching out, Rian put his hand on his brother's shoulder. "How is Felicity now?"

"She is sleeping." Liam's mouth twisted at the irony of his words. "She was almost insensible with grief when she realized what had happened, so much so Dr. MacGregor feared we might lose her also. He was forced to give her a very mild potion to settle her. He stayed with me all night, watching over her." Liam allowed Rian to lead him to a chair and he sat down wearily. "He said we must keep Felicity calm and quiet for the next few days, and she is not to be moved until he says she can be." He nodded as if making his mind up. "But then I intend to take her back to Oakhaven." Rian squeezed his brother's shoulder in agreement. It was the most sensible course of action. "Emily and Charles will be here soon. It was selfish of me, but I wanted to wait until Felicity had passed the crisis before sending for them."

"They will forgive you," Rian said, watching Liam chew his lower lip in worry. "And I'm sure they will understand your reasoning."

"But where were you?" Liam asked, his voice suddenly cracking under the strain.

The words sounded more like an accusation than a question, but Rian was not about to color the truth no matter how painful or how much it might compound their collective misery.

"I seem to have spent the night at Isabel's." He turned away, unable to face the look of disappointment on his brother's face. "I have no justifiable reason to account for my absence, and so can give no explanation for it." Running his fingers through his hair, he winced audibly as they made contact with his wound.

"What's wrong?"

"I have quite a sizeable lump on the back of my head."

"Let me see." Getting up, Liam made Rian take his place on the chair. "That's quite a knot you've got there," he remarked with concern.

"I'm sure it played a part in why I was not here, where I ought to have been," Rian told him grimly. "I'm positive someone hit me from behind although, according to Isabel, I slipped and struck my head on a stair. She also said I was drunk."

"Nonsense!" Liam retorted emphatically. "You were as sober as a judge when you helped me get Felicity into the carriage."

"What did I say to you, Liam?"

"You said you were going to find Catherine and then come straight home. But this is the first I have seen of you since then." He shifted a little as embarrassment colored his next question. "When you awoke this morning, whose bed were you in?"

"I was in one of Isabel's guest rooms."

"And were you…alone?" Liam's face turned pink.

"Yes," Rian answered somberly, adding, "and I was dressed as I still am."

He saw Isabel again in his mind's eye, her rounded belly proclaiming the presence of his child. She would not be able to hide her condition for much longer, and then the race would be on to see which tongue could spread the gossip fastest. If he were a betting man, his money would be on Charlotte Maitling.

"But Catherine was not with you?" Liam asked, interrupting Rian's brief reverie. He shook his head as cold panic formed once more, and his brother looked even more worried, if such a thing was possible. "If Isabel had no intention of being intimate with you, why would she be so determined to keep you, incapacitated, in her house all night?"

"So you think she is behind this?"

"Of course," Liam snorted. "Who else could it be? But the question remains, why would she want you to spend the night in her house, but not her bed?"

In a strange twist, Rian was glad to be the unintentional source of his brother's focus. It meant Liam could put aside, at least for the moment, his own grief and sorrow. "Perhaps because I am now married?" he offered, but the look his brother gave him was one of disbelief. They both knew marriage was no deterrent for Isabel.

Liam muttered to himself as he thought. "Why would she?. Why would she not?Well she wouldn't, would she, not unless—" He suddenly stopped and grabbed Rian by the arm, staring at him in horror. "What if Isabel's aim was to prevent you from being with someone else?"

"You mean Catherine? But why would she—you think she *took* my wife?" Rian could barely believe that Isabel was capable of such a monstrous act.

Liam nodded. "It's the only thing that makes sense. Tell me exactly where Catherine was the last time you remember seeing her."

Rian rubbed his hands over his eyes as he tried to get his thoughts into some sort of logical order. He rose and paced. "It was in the ballroom. I was talking with Lord Carfell, and I saw both Felicity and Catherine sitting across the room by the French doors. Catherine had been dancing, and I think she was warm—no, they both were—because Felicity was fanning herself." He looked up at Liam with haunted eyes. "They must have gone outside on the terrace for some air."

"Which was what you suspected, and where we found Felicity," Liam said slowly.

"And Isabel was the one who said Catherine must be waiting for me in another room, staying in one place so I could find her." Rian frowned. "I remember you leaving with Felicity, walking back along the hallway, following Isabel and then nothing until I woke up this morning." He thumped the side of his leg with his fist. "God, I'm such an ass!"

"You were not at fault, Rian. How could you have possibly known?"

"I couldn't, at least not with any certainty, but damn it all to hell, I should have suspected!" He put a hand to his forehead, shading his eyes as he shook his head.

"If Felicity took ill while Catherine was with her, and we have no reason to suppose otherwise, we both know she would never have left her side," Liam continued. "And as she is nowhere to be found, there can only be one explanation."

"Yes?" Rian mumbled morosely, not wanting to hear his brother's conclusion for it would be the same as his own.

"She is being kept from you, brother."

"Dear God, no!"

Liam, though emotionally exhausted himself, put a compassionate hand on his brother's shoulder. "I'll wager Isabel's hands are dirty," he said gravely.

Rian stared at him, doing is best to contain his anger. "That may be, Liam, but she will never admit to it."

"She could be made to."

"No, not this time."

"What makes you so certain?"

"Because Isabel has other reasons for her actions, compelling reasons that have nothing to do with my wife."

Liar! She's carrying your child, and that has everything to do with your wife!

Liam gave him a puzzled look. He could always tell when Rian was keeping something back, even when they were children.

"Then you have spoken with Isabel since last night?" Rian gave a weary nod, grateful that Liam did not ask for an accounting. "Stuart Collins!" Liam suddenly burst out. "We must send for Stuart. If anyone can find Catherine, he can."

"Of course!"

Rian's need to find his wife was like a white-hot fire in the pit of his stomach, but he recognized that he owed his brother a duty as well. He prayed that Catherine would understand and forgive him, and hoped that a few minutes' delay would not mean the difference in finding her. He would never forgive himself if it were so.

"It will be quicker if I go to him," Rian said, "but before I leave, I need you to promise me something, little brother. I want your unbreakable oath." He spoke so gravely, so seriously, that Liam was taken aback.

"Of course, anything at all."

"You must not let Felicity think losing the baby was in any way her fault."

Heartsick that such an idea would have crossed Rian's mind, Liam felt his legs weaken, and he gratefully accepted the support of an arm at his elbow. "Of course, it wasn't her fault! Why would you suppose I would ever—"

"I don't think that, but she might."

Closing his eyes, Liam took a deep breath to calm himself before opening them again and staring at Rian. "Why would she?"

"I don't claim to know how a woman's mind works, but it is a possibility you must deal with before it becomes something more. Something terrible. Something that could stand between the two of you for a very long time." There was a horrible finality to Rian's words. A somberness that showed a side of his brother Liam had never seen. He said nothing, waiting patiently for Rian to continue.

"It is only natural that the death of a child will affect a woman more profoundly than a man. They are more sensitive to the loss, will feel it more keenly and mourn more deeply. It matters not that your child did not draw a single breath outside his mother's body. Believe me when I tell you, Felicity will carry this memory always in her heart until the day she dies."

"What can I do for her?" Liam spread his hands. "How can I be of any help when I feel so useless, so inadequate."

"Stay with her, be constantly at her side until she is strong enough to move on, no matter how long that might take. Nothing else is more important. Felicity needs to know that you do not hold her at fault, and do not now think her weak or frail because she could not keep the babe within her." He held up his hand, silencing Liam's protest. "She will not be in a rational state of mind at first, and may accuse herself for the babe's loss or, worse, believe that you do. Talk to her, Liam. She must hear from your own lips that you do not blame her for this tragedy." Rian suddenly dropped his eyes, unable to look at Liam's face. "Do not, I beg of you, repeat my mistake."

This last was said with such sorrow that Liam could only speculate as to the size and magnitude of the heartbreak that had left such a scar on his brother's life. "Sophie?" he whispered hesitantly and Rian nodded silently.

What little Liam knew about his brother's first wife had been gleaned from letters over the years. She was the only daughter of a neighboring plantation owner, and her father had vehemently disapproved of Rian and considered him an upstart. But he had not reckoned with his headstrong daughter's willingness to defy him. She was in love—they both were—so she had married Rian against her father's wishes.

For a while his brother's letters were deliriously happy, and then inexplicably, nothing. No word from him, no correspondence for almost a year. The silence was finally broken by a short, tersely written page that told Liam Sophie had died, and nothing more. No details given, no circumstances shared. After a while Rian took up writing to his brother again, but he never mentioned his dead wife, and Liam did not press the issue.

"It was no one's fault," Rian said in a gruff whisper. "The baby came too early and I was away on plantation business. Sophie tried hard to be strong, to bring him into the world, but he never drew a breath."

"He?" Liam said softly.

"My son." Rian looked up, his eyes bright. "I know how it is to feel helpless, brother. Believe me, I know. I was unable to find the words to comfort my wife, so I said nothing. I did nothing. And my darling Sophie, who was so brave, mistook my silence for censure, believing I held her responsible for the death of our child. It became more than she could bear. Unable to face me any longer…she took her own life."

Liam let out a gasp as his heart skipped a beat. Now he understood why Rian had kept this a secret from him. The guilt he carried was a choice he had made, and it was something he would never surrender or expect another to share.

"Rian, I am sorrier than you will ever know."

Rian stared at him, wondering how, having suffered the loss of his own child just a few hours before, he could find the compassion to ease another's sorrow. Shaking his head, he took Liam by the arm.

"I carry her with me still. And every day I think of her. I think of them both. They are always with me. It is a cruel fate that decrees that brothers should both lose their firstborns. Now"—he pushed Liam toward the open door—"go sit with your wife. Hold her hand, kiss her cheek, and speak kindly to her. Make certain that when Felicity opens her eyes, yours is the first and only face she sees."

"I will," Liam said, swallowing hard as he tried to reconcile himself to this shared sorrow.

"Promise me, Liam," Rian said seriously. "Do not leave her side." As they had when they were boys, Liam made his vow by covering his heart with his hand and closing his eyes for a moment. Rian gave a small smile at the childhood gesture and nodded, but the moment was interrupted when voices rose from the lower level of the house. "I think your in-laws have returned," Rian noted, glad that he would not be leaving Liam entirely alone while he went to meet with Stuart Collins.

Shaking his head, Liam corrected him. "That is not Charles's voice," he said, but before either of them could speculate further, a footman, slightly out of breath from exertion and with his wig askew, found them.

"Oh, Master Rian, thank goodness you are still here!" the man exclaimed, clearly agitated. "There's a man below, says he knows where Miss Catherine is."

Chapter 21

Both Connor men stared at the fellow who now sat across from them in the downstairs drawing room. It had taken all the restraint Liam possessed to make sure his brother didn't resort to beating the man bloody in order to get whatever information he claimed to possess. It had been a close call, but apparently having an idea of the type of welcome he might receive, the man had come prepared. Calmly he pulled a pistol from the inside of his coat and leveled it at Rian, effectively slowing his descent down the stairs.

"I can assure you that not only am I a very good shot, but you present too large a target for me to miss," the man said as Rian came to a shuddering halt at the foot of the staircase. Behind him Liam continued at a slower pace. He crossed the foyer, giving the appearance of having all the time in the world to wait for the stranger to dictate their next move. He was, after all, the one with the weapon.

"If I can have your word that we can all behave like gentlemen, this will not be necessary," the man said, tilting his head toward the pistol.

Hearing his brother mutter something vulgar under his breath, Liam took it upon himself to speak for both of them. His tone was frigid as he said, "Entering my house and brandishing a weapon hardly constitutes gentlemanly behavior."

The man raised a brow. "A matter of self-preservation, and a prudent precaution it would seem." Having decided the older Connor was far too volatile to deal with, the man gave Rian a hostile look before turning to address Liam. In a strange way, he was grateful for the younger sibling's more rational attitude. "May I have your word, as a *gentleman*, that you will keep your brother calm, at least until you have heard what I have to say?"

The brothers looked at each other, silent communication passing between them. With the barest of nods, Rian indicated that he would keep his temper in check for as long as their visitor proved useful. After that, he would not be held accountable.

"Would you care to introduce yourself?" Liam asked, adding no warmth to his voice.

"My name is John Fletcher." The man did not bow or even incline his head as was customary, not wishing to take his eyes off either of them.

"He's Isabel's man!" Rian exploded, making Liam step quickly in front of him. "Did that bitch send you?" he snarled over his brother's shoulder.

John Fletcher took a half step back as the violent outrage in Rian's voice confirmed what he already suspected. Isabel had put herself in a situation that was far beyond her understanding. She had seriously underestimated both Rian Connor and Phillip Davenport, and the consequences for her would be disastrous once her involvement was discovered. John's instinct had been right. Somehow he had to extract a promise from Rian Connor, the equivalent of a pardon that would show leniency for Isabel's part in the abduction of his wife. He hoped the man would listen to reason because looking at Rian's muscular build, John Fletcher doubted he would be able to best him in a physical fight. He wondered briefly if the younger man could restrain his brother long enough to allow an escape out the front door. As if sensing his plan, two footmen suddenly came and stood before the closed door, each crossing his arms over his chest and blocking his way. The idea of making an escape was abandoned.

John turned and stared at both men, each of whom seethed with anger. He decided to get to his business quickly.

"Lady Howard did not send me, and is completely unaware that I am here." He did his best to act as if Rian's outburst was nothing more than a schoolboy's tantrum. "I expect my dismissal will be immediate when she discovers my actions."

"This does not concern you?"

"If she did not threaten to dismiss me at least once every month, I would think something was amiss. This time, however, I do believe she will have no choice but to make good on her word."

Liam looked over his shoulder at Rian, but a movement in his peripheral vision distracted him. Mrs. Hatch stood at the top of the stairs, worry on her face. The commotion had brought her from Felicity's bedside.

"Come, we should conduct whatever business we have in here." Liam gestured to an adjacent open door that led to a receiving salon. He fixed Rian with a look that told him to keep a tighter hold on his temper before leading the way. With an unhappy sigh of resignation, John Fletcher followed. Once seated both Connor men looked at John fixedly, but he did not flinch under their ferocious scrutiny. He had withstood worse. Carefully he put the pistol down on a small table, where it remained in easy reach.

"Do you know what has happened to my sister-in-law?"Liam asked directly.

"Yes, I do."

"Well, for God's sakespit it out!" Rian gripped the wooden arm of his seat with enough force to blanch his knuckles.

"In time." John paused, and his gaze flickered briefly to the clock on the mantel."She is safe enough…for now."

"What exactly does that mean?" Liam asked.

John Fletcher sighed. Faced with Rian's enraged manner, he wished he could deal with the younger Connor alone. As if he could read John's mind, Liam reached out and put his hand on his brother's arm. The effect was almost instantaneous, and John looked at Liam in surprise at the sudden change that permeated the air between them. Rian physically locked his rage away, and allowed a breath of calm to wash over him.

Liam repeated his question, "What do you mean when you say my sister-in-law is *safe enough*?"

"It means that she still has a few hours left until the potion in her system wears off completely." John narrowed his eyes.

"What potion would that be?" Liam asked.

"The one that was put in her wine," John answered, grateful to turn his attention away from Rian.

"By you?"

The man shook his head, making both Connor men wondered if he realized he'd just condemned his mistress.

"How can you be so sure that she is safe?" Liam asked curiously.

"Because he will want her to be fully conscious, and completely lucid before he proceeds. Besides," John continued hurriedly, seeing the furrow in Rian's brow, "I gave her an additional dose before handing her over."

"Handing her over to whom?"

John's expression became quizzical, and it took him a moment to process the fact that neither of them knew anything about Phillip Davenport's existence. He had been told that Catherine's memory had returned, but now it was clear that some critical gaps still existed.

Rian spoke though gritted teeth. "Exactly whom has my wife been handed over to?"

"You'd best answer him, Mr. Fletcher," Liam advised, allowing the other man to hear the edge in his own voice.

The fragile calm was being rapidly replaced by a naked hostility that told John he was walking a very fine line. If he had any hope of coming out of this unscathed he need to speak, and quickly.

"I need certain assurances from both of you." Picking up the pistol, he casually placed it in his lap. "Before I reveal the location of the lady in question."

"Assurances? What type of assurances?"

Liam flashed his brother a look that, while full of empathy, requested that Rian allow him to ask whatever questions were necessary.

"I want your guarantee that you will not seek any form of retribution for my mistress's misguided part in this…unfortunate incident." Resting his elbows on the arms of the chair, John Fletcher steepled his fingers beneath his chin as both men weighed his words.

"You bastard!" Liam exclaimed vehemently. "How can we be sure that you are speaking truthfully, that you even know where Catherine has been taken? It would seem more reasonable to believe that you are here on the express orders of your mistress."

John seemed genuinely nonplussed. "To what purpose? What would my mistress gain from such a ploy?"

"To confound and prevent us from actually finding my sister-in-law."

Rian wanted desperately to believe John Fletcher was telling the truth but he needed more than his word. He needed—no, he demanded—irrefutable proof. For all Rian knew, the man could have been listening behind a closed door to his altercation with Isabel earlier that morning.

It would seem that John Fletcher was thinking along similar lines. Reaching in his pocket, he brought out an object and handed it to Liam, who gasped before handing it to Rian. Capturing the light, the gemstone sent up an arc of brilliance, creating a kaleidoscope of color that danced on Rian's cheek. It was almost as if Catherine's diamond wedding ring was kissing him.

"How?" Rian couldn't say any more as he closed his fingers over the ring, securing it inside his fist before putting it to his mouth.

"I removed it from her finger before she was taken from me," John said quietly.

"Who has my wife?"

Liam and Rian were not the only ones with fluctuating emotional states. For the first time in a very long time, John Fletcher was going against Isabel's wishes. By deliberately spoiling her plans, he would save the life of another woman, and as this understanding came to him, he was struck by the oddest notion. John felt that if he told either man his reason for defying his mistress, they would, without question, believe him. Although he needed to save Isabel from her own folly, as well as from the very real predicament she had put them both in, he was acting to save the only truly innocent victim he had ever come across. Catherine. It would be John Fletcher's one good act. Something that could not begin to atone for a lifetime of wickedness but perhaps it might help to tip the scales in his favor on Judgment Day.

"Please, gentlemen, let me speak as it will save all of us a great deal of time," he said before revealing in detail the events of the previous night. When he was done, Rian turned to Liam.

"Your assumption was correct. Isabel meant to prevent me from discovering Catherine had been taken in the first place," he said, sounding both angry and horrified.

"So it would seem."

"Gentlemen, your assurance?"

Two pairs of eyes turned toward him, and John Fletcher shifted a little uncomfortably in his seat.

"My guarantee would be better kept if your mistress realized the full extent of her actions and understood how far my retribution can reach," Rian told him grimly.

"Of course." John had known that some bargain would have to be struck and being allowed to get Isabel to a place of safety was more than he could have hoped for. "I think her estate in Ireland would be a good place for reflection. Would such a distance be satisfactory?"

Hades would not be far enough, but Ireland would suffice.

"What makes you certain she will go willingly, or even at all? What if she refuses?"

"I will persuade her that it is in her best interest," John said firmly.

"And why would she heed your advice?" Rian asked in disbelief.

"There are times when circumstance dictates the choices that we make," John snapped, clearly irritated that Rian doubted his influence.

"Circumstance?" Now it was Liam's turn to question. "What circumstance?"

"Gentlemen, I am not as stupid as you might wish me to be. I know that Lady Howard has become involved in something that has consequences far beyond those she anticipated. Leaving these shores is the best course of action. Besides, there is now another concern that must be weighed. One that changes everything."

Though he did not look directly at Rian, John Fletcher's expression was mocking. The man knew exactly who had fathered the child his mistress carried in her womb.

"What other concern might that be?" Liam asked with a frown. "Just what exactly is your relationship to Isabel?"

John smiled at him, an oddly smug lifting of the corners of his mouth. "I am in her ladyship's employ. Nothing more, nothing less. Over the years I have proved useful, and Lady Howard values my insight on a wide variety of matters."

Liam was not convinced. Clearly the man was hiding something, and if his relationship with Isabel was a longstanding one, the secrets would be dark, and numerous. But what could be so important that he would risk coming here, without her knowledge, to bargain for her safety and return Catherine to them in exchange? Whatever the relationship between them, Liam could sense it was far more involved than that of a loyal family retainer.

"Tell me, Mr. Fletcher, just to satisfy my own curiosity, do you actually have any balls, or did you allow Isabel to castrate you a long time ago?" Rian spoke so softly that Liam wasn't sure he had heard him correctly. Had his brother lost his mind? A glance was all he needed to see John Fletcher also had excellent hearing. "It must have been particularly galling," Rian continued in the same tone, "to know she would lift her skirts and spread her legs for the lowliest farm boy if he caught her fancy, but still deny you, eh?"

John's face darkened, his expression turning murderous, and Rian grinned broadly at him.

Liam wondered if he should try to keep Isabel's man back or simply let his brother have at him.

"Would you like me to share the secret of pleasuring her?" Rian's voice now dropped to a dangerous level. "It would be to your advantage, surely, because you're in love with her, aren't you?"

For a moment there was nothing but silence, a heavy, dangerous quiet, and then John Fletcher began laughing. It was not the reaction Rian was expecting, and the look he cast his brother said one of them had miscalculated. But which one? Why else would John Fletcher risk so much to bargain for Isabel's safety?

"Forgive me, Mr. Connor, but I could probably better educate you as to how her ladyship likes to be pleasured, both in bed and out of it," John told him scornfully. "And perhaps if I had, the need for this conversation would never have occurred." He shook his head. "Your assessment is quite wrong; I am not in love with Lady—"

"No, you're not," Liam interrupted. He spoke slowly, weighing each word with care. "I should have seen it before, and I suppose I did, but I thought—"

"—it too preposterous to be true?" John finished for him.

Liam nodded while Rian fixed him with a blank stare. "It's all in the shape of the mouth and the eyes," Liam told him. "Stupid of me, really, not to have noticed right away, especially as their eyes are so similar in color."

It was now Rian's turn to stare at the man sitting across the room from them. Of course! How could he have missed it? "Isabel is your sister?" he asked incredulously.

"You see, Rian, he does *love* her, but he's not *in love* with her," Liam clarified before addressing John again. "But she doesn't know blood ties you to her, does she?"

John shook his head. "How, if I may ask?" Liam was, as always, unfailingly polite.

"Different fathers, but the same whore of a mother." John Fletcher shrugged as if the entire matter was of little consequence, but that careless gesture spoke volumes.

"And her marriage to Lord Howard, I suppose you had a hand in bringing that about also?"

John permitted himself a wry smile. "I can take credit for the introduction only. What happened afterwards, well, Bella managed that all by herself." He stared at both Rian and Liam, sensing a shift in his favor. "Perhaps we should get back to the matter at hand. Do I have your assurances, gentlemen?" He spoke with a firmness that said he would not be swayed from his course.

"And if we choose not to give any?" Rian said, wanting his adversary to know he, too, could be stubborn.

John Fletcher sighed. "Then we will be at a stalemate, which will not be to your advantage. Time is running short." He made a point of looking at the clock before turning back to Rian. "I will not divulge your wife's whereabouts without an agreement in place."

"When you next see your mistress you may tell her I will seek no reprisal," he said, and then his gaze bored into John. "Provided she follows your advice, and departs for Ireland before the day is out."

John Fletcher inclined his head, thankful that neither man could see his relief. He had not been as confident as he appeared.

"Tell my brother where his wife is," Liam said, placing his hand on Rian's shoulder and squeezing lightly. Another gesture from their childhood games, saying it was over, finished. John Fletcher gave them the address he knew Catherine had been taken to. "Who lives there?" Liam asked.

"Has your wife ever mentioned a man called Phillip Davenport?"

Rian looked at Liam, who shook his head slightly. "No, I've never heard the name mentioned."

"He is your wife's cousin, and the reason she was taken from you."

"Come." Rian stood up. "You will take me there."

"But you have the location," John protested. "There is no need for me to accompany you." The last thing he wanted was to be trapped in a claustrophobic carriage with Rian Connor.

"Your presence will assure me that there is no trickery on your part," Rian said, fixing John with an icy stare, "and you are going to tell me everything you know about this so-called cousin."

Chapter 22

Lettie had been awake for most of the night, sick with worry over what was happening behind the locked door down the hall. She had heard Phillip go in twice now, the second visit lasting considerably longer than the first. Grace told her that he had been in the kitchen opening cupboards, and rummaging through drawers looking for something. He finally left carrying a pair of shears, and wearing a smile that Grace did not like. She thought it a good thing he did not know she had been spying on him from the scullery. Hearing the child's words, Lettie knew her worst fear had come to pass. God had truly abandoned her, because Catherine was back inside the house.

This turn of events made Lettie decide to keep Grace with her during the night. It would be safer than letting the child sleep alone in the servants' quarters on the topmost floor of the house. She had been touched by the child's gratitude. Most of the other servants were now gone, and Grace was afraid to sleep by herself. In the short span of her life she had never slept alone, and so she gave not a second thought to climbing into the big bed. Lettie was thankful for the resilience that allowed the girl to sink into a deep, untroubled sleep.

All through the dark hours she stayed awake, listening for sounds of Phillip. She expected him to enter her room, gloating over Catherine's return. Though she heard his heavy tread in the hallway, he did not stop or pause by her door. The house was unnervingly quiet and the silence filled Lettie with a fear she had never experienced before. Not even when Phillip was at his worst. This was the quiet of the grave. A deep, penetrating silence filled every space. A portent that something horrifying and terrible was about to happen.

She didn't remember falling asleep, but she must have dozed because when she opened her eyes, Grace was gone and Lettie was alone. Without thinking she pulled back the covers, swung her legs over the side of the bed, and carefully made her way to the door, where she pressed her ear against the paneling listening for sounds.

"How nice to see you getting around so well." The sound of Phillip's voice made Lettie's insides churn. "I had been laboring under the assumption that you were confined to your bed. Apparently I was mistaken."

Caught like a rabbit in a trap, Lettie turned her head to see her husband sitting on the small stool by her dressing table. How could she have not noticed he was there? It had been so long since he had visited her room for any reason, it never occurred to her to look for him. And now he knew her secret. She tried to be stoic, but the fear was too strong to hide, and her façade broke down. It seemed that Phillip's maniacal outrage had damaged more than her leg. He had broken something inside her, twisting and bending it beyond repair.

Lettie stared at her husband, feeling an uncontrollable trembling course through her. Her palms were damp with perspiration as she clutched the neck of her nightgown, and her anxiety increased tenfold as she noticed the item Phillip now held in his hands. The small, black velvet pouch contained the few items of any value she had managed to hide from him. It was to be her means of starting anew when she was finally able to walk out of this room, and this house.

Phillip smiled slyly, holding the bag for her to see. The silken cord that pulled the neck closed was wound about his fingers as he let the small sack dangle in midair. "Does this appear familiar?" he asked, knowing full well that she would recognize it. "I believe it belongs to you."

He pulled open the silken cord, carefully extracting the items from within, and placing them on her dresser. Her mother's ring, a pair of ruby earrings, and a small diamond and sapphire brooch given to her by her father. Seeing them sparkle and shine, Lettie felt her heart sink. Any hope of escape was now dashed, and she let out a strangled sob.

"Did you really think I would allow you to leave me?" Phillip asked as he cruelly pocketed the means of her freedom before carefully smoothing out the empty bag.

Lettie did not answer him. Her throat had tightened, constricting her vocal cords. Terror marked every plane and hollow of her face as her husband stood, and held out his hand to her.

"Come dear, I have something I want to show you," he said, beckoning to her with curled fingers. A lifetime of obedience made her place her hand in his.

Slowing his pace to match hers, Phillip took her through the door and down the hallway, coming to a stop at the room where Catherine was imprisoned. Removing a key from his waistcoat pocket, Phillip inserted it into the lock. The mechanism clicked loudly and Lettie jumped, her free hand covering her throat as the door was pushed open. Tightening his hand around her fingers, Phillip led his wife into the room.

Despite the morning hour the heavy drapes remained closed, making it difficult for Lettie to see in the gloom. There was nothing wrong with her nose however, and she wrinkled it in disgust as the odor of vomit reached her. A part of her brain suggested the room be subject to a good airing as soon as possible.

Catherine was awake and sitting on the edge of the bed, her upper body partially hidden in the shadows. She raised her head, staring with dull, lifeless eyes, and gave no sign that she recognized the small woman standing next to her jailer. Catherine's expression was one Lettie imagined those sentenced to death must wear. It was a look of deep resignation that said their fate was sealed, with nothing to stay the drop from the hangman's noose.

Unable to bear the bleak despair on Catherine's face, Lettie glanced instead at the movement in her lap, watching her hands as they twisted restlessly. At first glance, Lettie thought it a skein of pale yarn that Catherine's busy fingers nimbly smoothed and plaited together. It seemed oddly out of place given her surroundings, but then Catherine moved out of the shadows, so the candlelight illuminated her head and shoulders.

"Your hair!" Lettie cried out, realizing what Phillip had used the shears for. In a purely self-conscious movement, Catherine raised one hand and held it to the bare skin at the nape of her neck.

Taking advantage of her final dive into oblivion, Phillip had decided to teach his prisoner a lesson. Wrapping her long hair about his fist, he had simply chopped it off at the base of her skull, leaving it as a gift on her pillow. It was the spiteful act of a spoiled child, and now Catherine's mouth twisted into a grim line as Phillip pulled his wife forward so she could better admire his handiwork.

"Not your fault, Lettie." Her voice was a rusty croak, and it was plain to see how much even those few words pained Catherine to say.

"But your hair...your beautiful hair," Lettie stammered, recalling her envy at the cascading locks.

"Of little consequence." Fighting to keep the tears from spilling over, Catherine held out the long braid and fixed Phillip with a stare before opening her fingers and allowing the mass of white blonde curls to fall to the floor. She refused to give him the satisfaction of knowing how much it had hurt to discover he had cut off her beautiful hair. The hair that Rian so loved to run his fingers through. Catherine had never thought of herself as a vain person, but her hair had always been a source of quiet pride. And now it was gone. So much for vanity. "In time, it will grow back."

"Oh Catherine! I am so s-sorry. I am so, so very s-s-sorry."

Big gulping sobs racked the small woman's frail body, and Catherine knew she was apologizing for much more than the pale braid at her feet.

As Phillip put his arm around his wife's shoulders, turning her to go, he saw Catherine notice the unsteadiness of Lettie's gait. "Punishment for helping you escape," he said with a smirk. He looked down at the pale, trembling woman beside him, her cheeks wet with tears. Placing a finger beneath her chin, he raised her head so she had no choice but to look at him. "If she tries it again," he said softly, his voice a gentle whisper that could just as easily be a promise of paradise, "I will kill her."

Catherine did not need to see Lettie's face to know her terror. She sensed that whatever strength this petite woman had found to help her before, it had been all she possessed. Despair washed through Catherine and she closed her eyes, but not before a single tear rolled down her cheek, landing with a splash on the back of her hand.

"Come, Lettie," Phillip whispered."Our dear Catherine has had a long journey finding her way back to us, but she is home now, and we must let her rest."

One hand on her elbow, and the other wrapped about her shoulders, Phillip steered his wife out of the room, pausing only to relock the door. Back in her own bedroom, he solicitously helped her settle in the big bed, fluffing the pillows and arranging them comfortably behind her.

"As you can see, my dear, escape is quite useless," he told her. "I will always find a way to get back what is mine. If Catherine was not able to elude me, what hope could you possibly have?" He paused with his hand on the door knob, and the look he gave her froze the marrow in her bones.

The years of living in constant fear rose and completely paralyzed Lettie as decidedly as if her spine had been snapped in two. She became incapable of any rational thought. Phillip was right. Phillip was always right. If Catherine had not been able to escape his poisonous, grasping reach how could she hope to? Catherine was the strongest woman she had ever met, both physically and mentally. In a single, glorious moment she had dared to defy Phillip. Defy him, fight him, and win. It had been a moment of triumph. At least for a while.

Lettie hoped Catherine had been happy in her freedom, and she was sorry it could not have been forever. But now it was over. Phillip had brought her back. He had won. He would always win. Turning on her side, Lettie ignored the fiery pain that flared in her lower back and hip as she curled herself into a ball. She needed to find her own escape, so she let her mind slip to another place. One far away from the misery that had become her daily existence.

Chapter 23

Isabel sat at her dressing table, head in her hands, weeping bitterly. How could everything have gone so horribly wrong? All her carefully laid plans were ruined, shattered like the small porcelain figurine she had once destroyed in temper. How was it possible that she, always so shrewd and cunning, could be guilty of such a terrible error in judgment?

She had made the mistake of assuming carnal pleasure would be enough to bind Rian to her. God knows other men had been willing to tether themselves to her for less. But Rian was not other men, and he had surprised her. Lust, though enjoyable, was not nearly enough for him. He desired something more meaningful, more substantial. A basis on which to build a future. It was a foundation he believed Isabel was incapable of providing, and that had been a betrayal of the worst kind. What possible future could he want that she was not a part of? She shook her head as fresh tears spilled, and her body trembled with the deep ache of his rejection. It made no difference that Rian had told her many times, in many ways, that he would never marry her. Pride had refused to let her see the truth of his words. Taking the affection he was willing to give, she had twisted it into something it was never meant to be. And now it had spoiled, becoming ugly and unrecognizable.

"And you wonder why he turned away from you?" she said bitterly, staring at the disheveled, red-eyed, weeping woman who looked back at her from the mirror.

A sob caught in the back of her throat and she made a raspy hitching sound.

"Weeping, Isabel? My, my, I thought you were incapable of producing tears. How very touching."

Raising her head, Isabel looked at the figure leaning against the doorframe. She frowned and pulled a handkerchief from her sleeve so she could wipe her eyes before staring in disbelief. Of all the people she might have expected to see this day, he was not on her list.

"Liam?" Her concern was genuine. He looked terrible. Fear and worry had worked their own particular brand of destruction on the handsome, boyish face, leaving him exhausted and shattered. He still had not changed his clothes, and he looked creased and rumpled. "Liam, what are you doing here? Shouldn't you be with your wife?" Isabel's voice rose a few octaves. She didn't know why, but the sight of him leaning so casually in her doorway sent an unexpected shudder through her. Felicity had surely made a full recovery by now.

"Ah yes, my wife. How nice of you to remember her."

Charles and Emily had almost collided with Rian and John Fletcher at the front door of the townhouse. His in-laws had asked no questions regarding his brother's hasty departure, nor the identity of the man who accompanied him. But they were not so forgiving with him, and he had to beg them to stay with Felicity.

"Liam, where are you going?" Emily had asked anxiously.

"There is a matter I have to attend to."

"It cannot wait?"

He had looked over Emily's head, directing his answer at his father-in-law, "No, it cannot."

Charles Pelham did not need to know details. Instinctively he understood the necessity of his son-in-law's departure. He nodded supportively and took his wife by the arm. "Of course we will watch over Felicity," he assured him.

"How is Felicity?" Isabel asked, her voice bringing Liam back to the present. His presence unnerved her. He ought not to be here, in her private apartments. She watched, eyes narrowing, as he came into the room, his walk so like his brother's. "Is she quite recovered?"

As Liam proceeded toward her, Isabel swung back around on the stool and watched him in the mirror. She picked up her hairbrush, and began passing it through her raven locks, her hands trembling slightly as she did so. Liam was now directly behind her, and he placed his hands on her shoulders, gently smoothing his fingers over the alabaster skin. His behavior was uncharacteristic, but even so Isabel was confident she could easily deal with the younger Connor.

"Liam, what about—"

"Shhh," he hushed her. "Don't speak, Isabel. Don't say a word."

This was most definitely not the Liam Connor that she knew. Despite her concerns she felt her body responding to his strong fingers as they expertly worked on relieving her tension. Closing her eyes, she tilted her head to one side as Liam continued to knead the tight muscles with one hand while the other, after moving her hair, now stroked the smooth column of her neck.

"You really are a very beautiful woman, Isabel." Liam sighed, his lips grazing the sensitive spot below her ear as he spoke. "It would be a shame to disfigure such a lovely face."

Her eyes flew open at the same time his hands stopped moving and his fingers dropped to circle her slender neck. With a sudden gasp she reached up, trying to free herself, but he only squeezed tighter.

"Stop it," Liam ordered in a voice that was completely calm. "Stop it or I swear to God I will snap your neck right here and now." Immediately she ceased struggling. "Good, that's better," Liam murmured as his untroubled eyes met her wary ones in the looking glass. For the first time in a very long while, Isabel felt afraid.

"Your man, John Fletcher, graced us with a visit a little while ago," Liam continued softly. "He put forth a most interesting proposition." He disclosed how John was able to secure her freedom from his brother's retribution for her part in Catherine's abduction. He did not reveal the reason behind John's desire to protect her. Though she tried to suppress it, Liam felt Isabel's shudder of relief, and in the looking glass he saw her eyes close, and felt the muscles move beneath his fingers as she swallowed.

"It has been generally agreed upon that a visit to your estates in Ireland would be most beneficial," Liam said. "The sooner the better. I trust you see the sense of this proposal." He loosened his hold just enough so she could nod in affirmation. "Good, but there is one more thing you need to know before you go." Leaning forward, he exerted pressure again. "Felicity lost the baby she was carrying—our baby—because of you."

Isabel instinctively dropped a hand to her lap and pressed it against her stomach. Was Liam going to dispense his own brand of justice, an eye for an eye, a life for a life? Her baby for his?

"Your man made one small mistake when he bargained for your safety, Isabel. He only secured an agreement with Rian." She looked at him in the glass, her face pale and her lips trembling. "Most likely he did not think that your actions had had any effect on me directly. Go to Ireland, stay there and don't ever come back. If I see you again or if I hear that you have returned"—Liam released his hands from around her throat and let them rest lightly on her shoulders—"I will kill you. On that you have my solemn promise."

Not once had he raised his voice above a polite whisper, speaking smoothly and softly, and that made his words all the more deadly.

Chapter 24

Catherine lay quietly on the bed, watching the waning light outside the window through a gap in the heavy brocade drapes. It had been a shock to see Lettie looking so pale and gaunt, dragging her injured leg. She bore little resemblance to the woman who had helped her escape, and none to the one who had welcomed her into this house. What had Phillip done to her, and how had she been injured? Her mind began throwing up one horrific scenario after another, until she threw her arm over her eyes to block out the images. Lettie's life was miserable and wretched enough, and the last thing Catherine had ever wanted to do was to add to her burden. She was deeply sorry to be the reason for her most recent injury.

A light knock on the door made her turn her head. What new torment had Phillip dreamed up? "Come in," she rasped.

A girl entered the room, carrying a tray which she placed on the table next to the empty pitcher of water. Catherine started to tell her to mind the floor—she did not want the child to step in the stale vomit—but the carpet had been cleaned. She frowned. When had that happened? The girl took the cover off the dish and the aroma of hot beef stew elicited a growl from Catherine's stomach. Her last meal had been the plate of sweet and savory treats at Isabel's party, and from the alarming gurgles her stomach was making, it would appear that was some time ago. Saying nothing, Catherine watched as the girl picked up the empty pitcher, left the room, and a few moments later returned with a full one.

"The master says you gots to eat," the girl told her, keeping her eyes fixed on the floor. Her tone seemed unnaturally subdued for one so young, and her brows knitted as if she was trying to remember something. It unexpectedly cleared, and she dropped Catherine a wobbly curtsey.

If the sight of a grown woman manacled to the bedpost with her hair shorn alarmed the child, she gave no sign. Catherine had to wonder what she might have witnessed in so short a span of years that such brutality raised no distress whatsoever. What possible reason had Phillip given to explain Catherine's presence? Why presume he had given a reason at all, Catherine thought dully. This was his house. He had no need to explain himself to anyone. Least of all to a child.

"You can tell the *master* that I would rather starve to death than accept any food from his hand," Catherine said softly, her throat aching as she spoke.

The girl's eyes darted toward the open door, her impassive expression quickly replaced by fear. She plucked nervously at a fold in her dress as she stood waiting. Turning her head slowly, Catherine saw the reason for her dread as Phillip now joined them. Obviously he had been outside the door, listening to their exchange.

"Grace, come to me please." He spoke pleasantly, motioning with his hand in the girl's direction. She obeyed, but Catherine could see the tremble in her shoulders as she stood next to him.

Ignoring his prisoner, Phillip gave his full attention to the child, making certain that Catherine had an unrestricted view. Poverty and hardship had not quite taken everything. A trace of hope lingered still, hope at the possibility of a better life. It told Catherine the child was too young to be in this house.

"Did you tell the lady what I told you to say?" Phillip asked.

Grace nodded.

"And what was her reply?"

Just as softly, Grace repeated Catherine's words, exactly as she had spoken them, word for word. Saying nothing, Phillip turned and l stared directly into his captive's eyes, a cruel sneer curling about his lips as she stared back at him. No longer dull and lifeless, her eyes sparked with defiance. Phillip made a sound in his throat that reminded Catherine of a fussy hen.

"What a ridiculous notion to think that I would allow you to starve yourself," he said. "No, my dear, this just cannot be tolerated." He placed a hand on the girl's shoulder and Catherine saw her flinch as Phillip continued. "I will admit that the last time we were together you managed to inflame my passions to such a degree that I quite lost control of myself, but that will not happen again. This time I am better prepared." Idly he moved his hand and pulled a curl from beneath Grace's bonnet, twirling it around his forefinger as he continued to watch Catherine. "You are refusing my hospitality, Catherine dear, and that is most rude of you. Your lack of manners I will forgive, but not your disrespect. I see no merit in punishing you, so I will punish the child in your stead."

"No!"

Catherine's shriek of protest was not enough to cover the sound of Phillip's backhand slap across Grace's face. So brutal was the blow, it lifted her thin body off her feet, sending her across the floor to land in a heap by the open doorway. Blood trickled from the corner of her mouth. Phillip smiled at the look of horror on Catherine's face, and then walked over to Grace. He raised his hand, as if to deliberately strike her again.

"No, Phillip, don't! I'll do whatever you ask!"

He gloated in triumph. The injustice of his action had created a fire that made Catherine's skin glow and her eyes light up. She was filled with so much rage, Phillip could almost taste it. It was a fury that promised to make his flesh sing when he took her again. Already he felt the slow burn of anticipation and his face flushed with excitement.

"You will obey my every command and fulfill my every wish?" he asked with conceited arrogance. Defeated, Catherine nodded wearily. He had found the weakness in her armor, and they both knew he would, if given the chance, exploit it to the fullest extent. He was barely able to prevent himself from rubbing his hands together in glee. "Well, you had best finish your meal, and get some color back into your cheeks," he said in a cheerful tone. "Here, Grace will help you." He gave a vicious kick to Grace before stepping over her and locking the door on both of them.

Scrambling off the bed, Catherine stretched as far as the chain would allow, but it was not enough to let her reach the child. "Grace?" she called, but her throat hurt too much for her to do more than whisper.

She clasped her hands anxiously, hoping that Phillip's boot had not caused an injury serious enough to warrant a doctor's care. It was doubtful the child would receive it. The next few moments were some of the longest in Catherine's life, relieved only by the sight of Grace's limbs moving. Opening her eyes, the child blinked a couple of times. There was a puzzled look on her face as if she could not recall how it was she came to be lying on the floor. Or why her body ached so. She struggled to a sitting position, groaning and clamping a hand to her lower back. Her breaths came out as quick, short gasps to counteract the pain. She crawled toward Catherine, who lifted her in her arms, being careful not to hold too tightly, and placed her on the bed.

Tears streaked down Grace's small, pinched face, an ugly welt marring her cheek. She sniffed loudly, wiping her eyes on her sleeve. "Sh-shall I take it away?" Grace asked, pointing to the stew.

Catherine shuddered as she picked up the spoon. "No, sweetheart. I will eat it." She eyed Grace's rail thinness. "But I think it may be too much for me, and I do not want the master to become cross. Would you help me?"

During the course of their shared meal, Catherine learned a great many things. Holding Grace close to her, she spoon fed both of them, and discovered that during the past few days most of the remaining household staff had been sent away.

"Who is left?" Catherine asked.

"There's cook, an' Rosie who keeps to the scullery, an' me to look after the missus, oh an' some men I never saw before." Grace gave Catherine a grave look. "They came this morning."

"But why would everyone else be sent away?" Catherine asked.

Grace's thin shoulders moved under Catherine's hand. "Dunno, Missus, but the Master promised me a sovereign if I stayed 'til the end of the week to help with the other missus."

"Why only until the end of the week?"

"The other missus won't need anyone after then."

A cold shiver went through Catherine. Either Lettie was far sicker than she had realized, or else her demented husband was planning something horrible. Tucking a curl beneath the cap Grace wore, Catherine contemplated the freedom with which the child could move about the house.

"Grace, can you get in and out of Miss Lettie's room?"

The girl nodded.

"Good," Catherine said as a spark of hope ignited within her. "I need you to get a message to her." Looking around the bedroom, Catherine pointed to the bureau against the far wall. "See if there is any paper there and pen and ink also. I will write a note for you to take to Miss Lettie for me."

Moving away from Catherine, Grace shuffled her feet and hung her head. "Can't do that, miss," she said, putting her hands behind her back, and refusing to look at her. "Please don't make me."

"But Grace, it's just a note."

"If the master finds out, I'll be skinned alive so help me!"Her belief in the threat was so absolute, terror smothered her like a blanket.

The small spark of hope that had ignited in Catherine sputtered and died before it had a chance to burn. She had neither the words nor the time to convince the frightened child that if she was careful, she would be safe. Not wanting Grace to see her disappointment, Catherine looked away. It wasn't the child's fault. Having already witnessed Phillip's cruelty to her, there could be no doubt that it had not been the first time Grace had tasted his temper. He had managed to hobble her courage just as effectively as he had crippled his wife.

Catherine's mind was racing. There had to be a way out of this nightmare, and she was determined that when she found it, she would leave neither Lettie nor Grace behind. She could not, would not, escape without them.

Giving Grace a reassuring smile, Catherine put her finger to her lips. "We'll say no more about it," she whispered softly as the sound of a key turning in the lock made them turn their heads toward the door.

Phillip entered, smiling when he saw the empty dish on the tray. "Much better," he said. "You may take it away, Grace."

She scurried to do his bidding, her eyes darting nervously to Catherine as she picked up the tray. Giving Phillip as wide a berth as possible, she headed out of the room. Once Grace was safely away, Catherine stood by the side of the bed and looked at her cousin. Her expression was calm and her eyes clear, and she showed no sign of the fear that Phillip craved. He in turn became thoughtful as he looked at her. His goal was to have her cowering before him in abject terror but, he reasoned with himself, perhaps this show of defiance was not such a bad thing. It would make the effort of breaking her that much more rewarding. The result so much sweeter.

The door opened and two men came into the room. Presumably these were the two new arrivals Grace had told her about. She was not surprised by the hip bath. They were in use at both the townhouse and Oakhaven, but she was surprised Phillip had one. Vaguely she recalled Lettie mentioning something about the desire to bathe in private being one of her husband's peculiarities. It was a shame she had not thought to mention his other 'peculiarities.' Forcing herself to show no emotion, she watched as the bath was deposited in the middle of the room.

The men's rough, unkempt appearance suggested whatever talents they possessed were probably better suited for more reprehensible undertakings. They spoke not a word as they busied themselves with buckets of water which were dutifully poured into the bath. Finally, their task complete, they stood on either side of the door, awaiting further instructions. Phillip moved toward Catherine.

"I am quite distressed by your...*disarray.*" He gestured to her appearance with a wave of his hand. "It would give me great pleasure to have you bathed and perfumed. These *gentlemen*"—the word rolled off Phillip's tongue with heavy sarcasm, and the glance Catherine gave both men told her the mockery was meant for her—"are to ensure that once released from your restraint, you do not attempt anything foolish. Such as attacking me."

Leaning over her, he took a small key from his vest pocket and unlocked the heavy iron manacle, opening the two hinged halves and enabling her to slip her hand free. She rubbed her wrist gingerly, grimacing at the ugly red welt that had formed. The protective strip of petticoat had been taken along with her hair.

Settling himself comfortably in a chair, Phillip gestured toward the hip bath. "If you don't mind, my dear."

Holding her wrist, Catherine moved around the side of the bed and walked over to the waiting water. In a show of willful insolence she stepped directly into the bath, sitting down in a gold cloud as the skirt of her gown billowed up around her. Phillip's face turned almost purple with fury as he struggled to bring himself back under some measure of control. Then he gestured to the two men.

"Strip her," he ordered, spitting out his command between clenched teeth.

Catherine was grabbed roughly by her upper arms and hoisted her to her feet. Tearing at the lacings of her bodice, the men quickly ripped the beautiful gown from her body, leaving her clad in her petticoats and chemise. They paused, wisely looking to Phillip for direction. "All of it," he instructed in a cold voice.

Though eager to follow Phillip's command, both men relished the opportunity to fondle her body with their rough, calloused hands. They took their time, but when they saw her back, Catherine felt them hesitate. She couldn't tell if the sharp hiss of breath she heard was in admiration or disapproval at the scars she bore. Once she was completely naked, and her clothing piled in a sodden mess on the floor, Phillip got up from his seat and came toward her. Their chore complete, the rough men resumed their place by the door. The look on each man's face was enough to suggest that Phillip had promised them a great reward for their part in his obscene, perverted scheme.

Slowly Phillip circled her, stopping to admire his previous handiwork. He clucked his tongue loudly. "I must be losing my touch. I really would have expected more show for my previous efforts, although"—he reached out and traced a finger down the long ridge of mutilated skin before declaring arrogantly—"this signature of mine is quite magnificent."

Fear and revulsion at Phillip's touch made gooseflesh rise on Catherine's body. She sat in the water and began lathering herself with the scented soap. If she could have scrubbed the skin from her bones, she would have gladly done so, but Phillip, observing the furious movement of her hands over her skin, ordered her to stop. She scowled, her mouth set in a tight line.

"Think of Grace," he warned.

With one fluid motion Catherine stepped out of the hip bath, and stood dripping water. She took the towel Phillip handed her, and wrapped it around herself. The hip bath was now considerably heavier, and the two men grunted as they carried it from the room, sloshing a good amount of water over the sides as they did so.

"Perfume and prepare yourself," Phillip told her, "and make sure you wear this for me." He picked up a handful of sheer material that had been draped across the back of the chair where he had been sitting. "I shall return shortly."

Tremors racked her body as Catherine sat before the dressing table. She held out her arms, gripping the edge of the polished wood, waiting for the spasms to pass. She was surprised Phillip had not cuffed her with the manacle, but then he had Grace to use against her if she did not cooperate, and she was certain the two thuggish henchmen would not be far away. A shiver of loathing ran through her as she recalled the feel of their hands pawing at her flesh. Phillip would not make the same mistake twice. Escaping would not be such an easy matter a second time.

In the mirror she looked at the tattered remnants of her ball gown. It had been a lovely dress, and she had felt beautiful wearing it. Tears filled her eyes as she saw Rian's face swimming in front of her. Where was he? Desperately she wondered how long she would be able to keep Phillip at arm's length, because in her heart she knew Rian was searching for her. And God help Phillip when he found her.

Chapter 25

The carriage came to a halt at the entrance to a secluded square where half a dozen elegant houses sat back from the street. The destination took Rian by surprise. Hearing John Fletcher calmly discuss the manner of man his wife had been turned over to, Rian had expected the surroundings would be as filthy as the man's intentions. But this was no squalid hovel.

It had been almost impossible for him to sit and listen to Isabel's brother speak without wanting to reach out and crush the breath from him with his bare hands. Each word that fell from John Fletcher's lips was another drop of poison turning his world a little darker. Rage burned through him, making him curl his hand into a fist. If such knowledge was having this effect on him, how much worse had it been for Catherine, experiencing it firsthand?

Only Liam's words, falling like a cool spray of water, had kept his temper in check.

"Remember, he knows where Catherine is," Liam had cautioned though his tone was urgent and fierce. "Getting her back safely is the *only* important thing."

The carriage came to a stop. John Fletcher leaned forward and pointed out the house where Phillip Davenport lived. "He brought her to his home?" Rian asked skeptically.

"Of course, why would he not?" John answered. "He believes he is safe. The only people who know he has your wife are as guilty as he. Betraying him would mean revealing their own involvement." The matter-of-fact manner in which the explanation was given grated on Rian's already taut nerves. Leaning forward, John opened the carriage door. "I trust we will never see each other again," he said, pushing the door with his foot until it swung open.

"There's just one final thing I ought to mention." Rian paused, the muscle in his jaw working furiously. Liam would have recognized the warning sign that said his brother's temper, while not at the exploding point of uncontrollable fury, had nevertheless reached the point where release of some kind was needed. John Fletcher, for the first time in his life concerned with another's safety, had no idea the jeopardy his words had put him in.

"Yes, what is it?" he asked irritably, oblivious to the danger sitting across from him.

With lightning fast reflexes Rian reached out, and slammed him against the back of the seat. His fingers closed around John Fletcher's throat, threatening to crush his windpipe. "Be assured that if I ever see you again, I will snap your neck and throw you in the gutter to rot like the filth you are," Rian snarled, flexing his fingers. He squeezed, and then shook the helpless man, much like a terrier with a rat. "Do I make myself clear?"

The frantic, panicked look in John Fletcher's eyes was all the answer Rian needed. Releasing his hold, he climbed out of the carriage and walked quickly away. He didn't look back, but waited instead for the sound of fading hooves to tell him Isabel's man was gone. Turning his attention to the other houses in the square, he noted the similarity of architecture. All were comparably proportioned, and in more than one he saw a few illuminated windows. It was not so very late, but the day was beginning to wane, and soon the last hour of the afternoon would give way to twilight.

The Davenport house was cold and uninviting, with no windows offering a warm glow. It seemed to Rian an air of abandonment lingered over the house, and in a strange way it reminded him of his first impression of The Hall. But with Catherine's home he had felt a residue of happiness. This house, despite the elegant brick and decorative ironwork, spoke of nothing but darkness and sorrow. He proceeded with caution, not knowing what might lie in wait for him. Catherine was so close yet still so far away, assuming Isabel's brother had not lied to him.

Isabel's brother!

Rian found it difficult to believe, but Liam was convinced of the truth and that was the only confirmation he needed. As he stared at the solid front door a frown wrinkled his brow. Had John Fletcher lied to him? With a decisive grunt, Rian knew he had not. Isabel meant too much to him. Any deceit on his part would put her safety at risk, something Rian knew her brother was not prepared to do. Else why would he have come to them in the first place?

But now he put all thoughts of Isabel Howard and John Fletcher out of his mind, so he could focus on the house and its surroundings. He kept to the lengthening shadows, using them to hide his movements should one of the square's occupants happen to glance out of a window. It did not occur to him that he might not be the only watcher in the square. Skirting the perimeter of the Davenport house, Rian made his way around the back, and then nimbly climbed over the brick wall and dropped soundlessly into the garden on the other side. Undetected, he made his way toward the rear of the house, hoping to gain access through the scullery or washroom.

He listened for signs of movement, and hearing nothing out of the ordinary, advanced to the sturdy looking door that admitted entrance to the lower level of the house. Convinced it would be an exercise in futility and the door would be locked against him, Rian turned the handle anyway. He was surprised when it moved easily in his hand, swung open and revealed the room beyond. He never heard the sound of footsteps behind him, but he felt the whisper of air next to his ear just before an arm came crashing down. For the second time in less than twenty-four hours he took the full brunt of a leather blackjack. This time it struck him above the temple.

With a grunt, the man caught Rian, turned and hoisted him over one shoulder. After kicking the door fully open, he carried Rian through the kitchen, past the startled cook and scullery maid to the main floor of the house, where he deposited his burden at the feet of his employer. Phillip's faith in Isabel's ability to take care of Catherine's newly acquired husband was nonexistent. It now appeared his intuition had been right. Kneeling next to the prostrate body, he grabbed a fistful of Rian's long hair, lifted his head and looked at the chiseled features.

"How wonderfully predictable," Phillip said, barely able to contain himself before dropping Rian's head back to the floor. He turned to the man waiting in the doorway. "Secure him, and then bring him to the room," he instructed.

Phillip had often wondered how it would feel to have another watch as he satisfied himself, but his potential audience was limited and, for the most part, as depraved as he. Having Catherine's husband watch as he took her again and again was going to be a thrill beyond his wildest imaginings. Just the idea was making him hard.

* * * *

Catherine sat like a statue in front of the dressing table mirror. Wrapped in the filmy silk robe Phillip had told her to put on, she tied the sash firmly around her small waist. She could do nothing but rub her shorn head dry. With an odd prick of feminine vanity she wondered if Phillip might allow her some scissors so she could tidy up the appalling job he had done of cutting her hair.

"Do you really suppose he's going to allow anything sharp to fall into your hands? You might get ideas about cutting something else," her reflection admonished.

The perfume bottles and pots of powder and rouge remained untouched. She was not going to decorate herself for his pleasure. Whatever Phillip had planned would test her sanity as much as her physical stamina, but what happened to her mattered not. The child was the tool he would use as coercion, and Catherine would do whatever he asked of her if it would spare Grace, even though, deep in her heart, she knew it might not be enough.

Catherine would have to strike while she still possessed the strength and mental acuity to do so, and before Phillip was able to restrain her. She couldn't allow him to break her physically, which meant she had to be ready to seize her moment. And as certain as she was that the chance would come, she was equally positive it would only happen once. Her cousin would not make the same mistake twice.

Taking advantage of the quiet, Catherine thought back to happier times in her life. Moments from her childhood when her mother was still alive, and her father was full of joy. She recalled family picnics on days filled with the warmth of the summer sun, the thrill of her first pony ride, the sweetness that flooded her mouth from strawberries picked with Ned long before he was ever called old.

And then her thoughts turned to Rian, and an unexpected gratitude flowed through her. She was grateful to know what it was to love, and be loved in return, by a man who filled her life with happiness in ways she could never have imagined. He gave her life meaning, a sense of purpose that resulted in a deep and abiding contentment. Accepting her completely for who she was, Rian was more than a husband. He was an adoring lover who delighted in showing her how to give and receive pleasure. A mentor encouraging her to fulfill her potential. A confidant she could share her deepest secrets with. He was all these things and so much more. He was her friend, and her soul mate.

Catherine closed her eyes so she could imagine him standing before her. She pictured the sun highlighting the strands of copper in his dark hair, the crinkles that appeared at the corner of each eye whenever something amused him, the flash of his even white teeth as he laughed out loud. Her days with him were a never-ending adventure of discovery, overflowing with plans for their future. She had no idea what quality she possessed to make him love her with such passion, but she was thankful for whatever it was that bound him to her, and her to him. Visions of him making love to her began to fill her mind, but she quickly shut them away. She would not allow such intimacies in this room, this house. No matter how much she craved the comfort of such moments. She forced herself to lock Rian away in a secret place in her heart.

Madness, Catherine concluded, was the only explanation for Phillip's need to hurt her so terribly. Inflicting pain on another living being for no reason other than that he could was beyond her comprehension. Carefully she thought back to everything that had happened from the moment she'd first set foot inside this house. Examining every gesture she had made at that time, every word she had spoken, Catherine tried to determine when or how her actions had offended her cousin. There had to be a reason for his behavior, but if it existed, it was too complicated for her to grasp.

A small gasp of pain made Catherine whirl around to see Phillip standing behind her with Grace at his side. His fingers were digging into her thin shoulder, and it had been her voice that had startled Catherine.

"Just a precaution if you will, my dear," Phillip told her as he relaxed his hold. "While a certain measure of resistance on your part will be delightful, I need to make sure that you remember the consequences should you go too far."

Catherine watched as Phillip directed Grace to a seat across the room. Already revolted, she found her disgust for him descending to a new level of abhorrence that made her skin crawl. Wanting another to bear witness to whatever sexual depravity his foul mind conjured up was one thing, but having that witness be a child was the worst type of corruption. Phillip wanted Grace to see Catherine's fall into total degradation, to witness her complete and utter humiliation at his hand. And it would be complete, for Catherine would not risk any physical harm being inflicted on Grace as a result of her own insubordination.

"Let the child go, Phillip, I beg of you. She does not need to see this," Catherine pleaded.

Phillip looked at her in surprise. He had expected her to beg, but not on behalf of a street urchin she barely knew. "Oh, you are quite mistaken, my dear. It will serve as a valuable lesson for her."

"She's a child. What lesson is to be learned?"

"Your absolute submission at my hands will reinforce the worth of her own life." The smiled he gave was repulsive. "Which is, of course, absolutely nothing."

Catherine hung her head as Phillip walked past her, his fingers idly stroking the smooth skin of her shoulder through the light fabric of the robe she wore. She shuddered, unable to curtail her physical reaction to his touch, and so missed seeing the cruel gleam in his eyes. He walked over to the bed where her shackle lay on the pillow and picked it up, playing with the length of chain that pooled on the covers. Hearing the now familiar clink of iron, Catherine got to her feet. With one hand holding her robe closed, she held out the other to be secured by the metal restraint.

Phillip snickered. "This will not be necessary," he said, stepping close enough to assault her with his decaying breath. "I have something far better to guarantee your obedience." Her eyes flicked to Grace sitting quietly across the room with her head bent.

Motioning toward the open door, Catherine watched as the men who had struggled earlier with the hip bath, now brought something else into the room. A chair. Ornately carved, it reminded her of a throne, and like a throne, it appeared solidly built. It would have been heavy by itself, but the addition of a figure in the seat was cause for red faces and much panting from both men. It was obvious the figure was male, but his head was covered, and his features hidden. Catherine could only assume the seated man was another of Phillip's equally perverse acquaintances. Someone desiring to witness a display of deviant behavior, but wishing to keep his own identity a secret. Why, she couldn't imagine. It wasn't as if she was going to be permitted to reveal his identity to anyone. Perhaps the hood was part of the game. The voyeur's groan as the chair was placed none-too-gently indicated he had not enjoyed his journey.

"My dear, we have a special guest tonight," Phillip said, adopting a playful tone. "Someone who has agreed, albeit reluctantly, to share our pleasure with us."

Suddenly fearful, Catherine turned her head, refusing to look at the hooded figure in the chair. Cruel fingers grabbed her by the chin as Phillip forced her head around. She closed her eyes, not wishing to see another disgusting, leering face, lips already wet with anticipation.

"Think of Grace," Phillip murmured as his fingers tightened.

Catherine snapped her eyes open, and glared at him before following the finger he pointed. Her brows pulled together when she saw the ropes which bound the hooded man to the chair. Phillip had mentioned reluctance, and there was something terribly familiar about the man. Something she recognized …but didn't want to believe.

One of the henchmen pulled the hood away and Catherine gasped. She had no need to see the handsome chiseled features to know who was tied to the chair. She would know him anywhere. "Rian!" Her hand flew to her mouth as if she wanted to deny the truth, but it was too late. She could not recapture his name and push it back down her throat, and even if she could it wouldn't change his identity. Her head swam, and a wave of nausea rolled through her.

Rian was unconscious. Muscles slack, his body sagged against the heavy bindings securing him to the heavy wood framework. Tears filled Catherine's eyes, and Phillip sniggered as he watched the full range of her despair flood her face. She could stomach anything, anything at all, but not this. She was in some unknown level of hell, caught between two fires and two horrors—a child, and the man she loved, both being forced to witness her debasement.

Catherine sank to her knees and prayed fervently, silently, for God to intervene. She begged him to spare both Grace and the man who was the center of her existence, and the love of her life. She cared nothing for herself, unless there was a way she could be used to destroy the evil that had manifested itself in the form of her only blood relative. Seeing her lips move, Phillip sneered.

"Prayers, Catherine? What makes you think God can hear you, or that he will answer?"

One of the men suddenly poured a pitcher of water over Rian's head. It brought with it an immediate response as Rian jerked up and began spluttering. He was disoriented, and took a few moments to stare uncomprehendingly at his surroundings while also testing his bindings. A trickle of blood ran from a point in his hairline and dripped into his left eye. Blinking rapidly, Rian shook his head, staining his shirt with droplets of blood.

Catherine rose and took a half step forward before Phillip caught her arm and pulled her back. His grip was such that her skin bruised at once, but she did not care. Instead she balled the hand of her free arm into a fist and swung at her cousin, punching him squarely in the face. Shock and surprise allowed her to land three good blows in quick succession before Phillip, snarling like a rabid dog, punched her back, dropping her to the ground.

Fury rolled through Rian at seeing his wife struck. His muscular arms strained against the ropes holding him. Thinking Catherine was unconscious, he was relieved to see the flutter of her eyelids. Unsteadily she pushed herself to her knees, her hands shaking violently as she tried to wipe away the moisture on her face.

"Clean yourself!" Phillip barked, throwing a cloth at her.

Catherine couldn't help the smile that stretched her mouth. Her hand was on fire, but judging from the anger, and the odd thickening of her cousin's voice, at least one of her punches had been successful. She wiped her mouth, cleaning as much of the blood and mucus mixture as she could, but the sound of Rian calling her name was too much. Dropping the cloth, she threw herself at him. With her arms around his neck, she covered his face with kisses that were a mix of blood and tears.

"I'm sorry. I'm so sorry!" she managed to say as she pressed her lips desperately to his, needing the taste of him in her mouth.

A slight nod of Phillip's head brought one of his hired henchmen forward to quickly jerk Catherine's arms free of Rian's neck, pull her away, and dump her on the floor at Phillip's feet as Rian roared like a man possessed.

Ignoring him, Phillip pulled Catherine to her feet and pushed her to the center of the room, turning her so she could look at her husband. The sheer silk robe clung to every curve of her body. Catherine, in a feminine gesture of self-consciousness, put her hand to the nape of her neck, acknowledging the loss of her hair. To Rian it did not matter. She looked beautiful. As beautiful as she had that night in his room when she had first given herself to him. The memory of that moment came flooding back and it electrified his senses.

The love that Catherine felt for him, that they shared, poured out of her like a beacon welcoming him home. If his life were to ever reach a point where agonizing despair became his only companion, where his future was nothing but an endless sea of hopelessness rolling before him, Rian knew all he need do was reach for her, and he would find his haven.

He watched as she raised a finger to her lips, begging him to remain silent. He struggled to keep his face impassive. To not give her bastard cousin anything he could use against either of them. Exhaling softly with relief that Catherine was alive, Rian allowed his attention, which had been riveted on his wife, to focus on the other people in the room. His head pressed against the carved back of the chair, he looked about him guardedly while ignoring the steady throb of his earlier encounter with the blackjack.

The two burly figures in the doorway had come from the docks, judging by their clothes and overall appearance. Though taking on two at a time might require some effort on his part, Rian was certain he could overpower them once he was free. Being tied up was definitely a disadvantage. Turning his head slowly in the other direction, Rian was startled when he found himself caught in the stare of a child who sat, immobile, hands in her lap, staring back at him. Her expression was that of a terrified rabbit caught in a snare. As Rian continued to stare, her eyes, too big for her small face, became even more terrified, and he wondered how she would ever give her trust to any adult again.

There was one other person in the room. A figure that Rian had studiously chosen to ignore because acknowledging his presence would put a strain on his control. It would help no one if rage caused him to make a mistake, and Catherine would pay the price. He prayed he had not already crossed that line. It was Phillip, however, who decided to make the first move.

Chapter 26

"I don't believe we've had the pleasure. I am—"

"Phillip Davenport, and believe me the pleasure will be all mine when I choke the breath from your body," Rian finished for him.

Phillip took a moment to observe him, a look of disquiet on his face while Catherine allowed the tiniest glimmer of a smile to lift her lips. Like any hot-blooded male, Rian was at his most dangerous when his family was being threatened. A fact Phillip could not have failed to notice. Rian did not need to issue threats or warnings. A line had already been crossed and there was no going back. Both men now stared at each other. Rian took in the debauched figure with the sagging flesh and dissolute face. He could not believe Catherine shared the same bloodline as Phillip, yet he knew it to be true. His wife's face told him it was true. This was the architect of her nightmares, and Rian made a silent promise that Phillip Davenport would not leave this room alive.

As if he were the honored guest at an elegant function attended by the very best of the aristocracy, Phillip waved off Rian's interruption and continued to speak.

"Well, I see that formal introductions are not necessary, but allow me to indulge myself and explain why we are all gathered here before we embark on tonight's entertainment." He paused and moved to the dresser, giving Rian a wide berth as he did so. Whether he did not trust the rope, his men or the captive himself, it was hard to say, but Phillip had noticed the way Rian looked at Catherine, and the way she looked back. The man was her husband and her lover, and as such was unpredictable and volatile. It was wise to be cautious. Pouring a liberal amount of brandy into a glass, he gulped the fiery liquid down. The burn in his belly bolstered his courage.

"As you may or may not know," Phillip said, "depending on how loose Lady Howard's tongue has been, Catherine and I are related by blood. We are distant cousins, and have the privilege of being each other's only surviving blood relatives." Rian shared his feelings with a curse, which Phillip admonished by waving his finger back and forth as he took a larger gulp from his glass.

"As I said," he continued, "we are blood relatives, but it seems that my dear cousin's feeble excuse for a father managed to squander away his fortune before making sure his daughter was married." His eyes shone with hypocritical sympathy. "Upon his death my dear cousin was left a pauper. A condition unfamiliar to her, but one that I have more than a passing acquaintance with, given the circumstances of my own wretched childhood." He turned to Catherine. "I really should commend you on the tenacity of your father's lawyer. The man simply refused to give up until he had secured my promise to shelter you under my roof. Personally I would never have agreed except that he guaranteed doing so would not be to my disadvantage." Phillip licked his lips. "And I realized I could profit from the situation."

"Profit?" Catherine asked, bewildered. "How?"

"I was assured that, though penniless, you were handsome enough to attract a husband." Phillip now beamed at her. "Fortunately, I have always been able to see the full potential of any business proposition. If you were such a beauty, I knew a far more profitable arrangement could be brokered, but of course that was before I saw you for myself." He drained his glass.

"I don't understand," Catherine whispered, looking bewildered and lost.

"Sweetheart, he meant to sell you to a whorehouse," Rian stated without emotion.

"Ah, I see your husband is a man of the world," Phillip said, refilling his glass. "I am sure he is quite familiar with the workings of brothels. How much would he have been willing to pay to lie with you, I wonder?"

With his heart aching, Rian watched Catherine's eyes change color as understanding gave way to rage.

"You miserable bastard!" Leaping forward, Catherine knocked the glass from Phillip's hand and slapped him soundly across the face, leaving a stinging imprint on his cheek.

"Bitch!" Phillip returned the blow with more force than Catherine's slight frame had been able to generate. His mouth compressed into a thin line as she fell to the floor, hand covering her face as she fought back tears. Rian let out a howl of rage as Phillip grasped the front of the flimsy garment

Catherine wore, pulling her up so their faces were only inches apart. "Let me be perfectly clear," he snarled. "You will pay for all I have suffered."

More confused than ever, Catherine asked, "Suffered? How? In what way?" Nothing Phillip said was making any sense. His words only convinced her he was more deranged than she had previously thought.

"I *suffered* because everything you ever had was *given* to you. It should have been mine as well. You stole it from me. It was my birthright too!"

"But I didn't even know you existed! Whatever the rift in our families, it happened before either of us were born. You cannot hold me to blame for something I had no knowledge of!" Catherine spoke reason, but the maniacal gleam in her cousin's eyes told her it was useless as an enraged Phillip pushed her back to the floor.

"Of course I blame you," he told her fiercely. "Someone has to pay for my misfortune."

"You're a-a-a monster," Catherine stuttered, but Phillip glowed as if she had just paid him the most charming of compliments.

His glass had landed on the floor and was, surprisingly, still intact. Phillip picked it up and refilled it. "I was quite convinced you had died after leaving me as you had," he told her. "The streets are a cruel, violent place, especially to young girls who know nothing of them. On reflection, it would have been better if you had perished. God knows you should have."

"But she didn't," Rian said.

Phillip sighed and gave Rian a sour look. "No, she didn't. I suppose that was due to your interference."

A terrible form of horror came over Catherine as she listened to the casual way Phillip spoke of her dying.She meant nothing to him, and he held absolutely no regard for her as a living, breathing human being.

Rian spoke in a low voice, "You had best make sure your men kill me, Davenport, because if you do not, then I promise you will not take a breath outside this room."

Hearing Rian's words, Phillip turned and blinked slowly, once then twice. "Why, Mr. Connor," he said, feigning surprise, "forgive me. I should have made my intentions perfectly clear. Of course you will be killed, but only after you have suffered all the agonies of hell as you watch me take this divine creature you care so much for. And I will take her, by force, again, and again, and again. I promise you she will not enjoy one moment of it, and when I am done, there are others who will take their pleasure with her." He nodded at the two men standing by the door, and, unable to help himself, Rian glared at them.

"If either of you so much as lays one finger on her..." He left the rest of his threat unspoken.

"Such theatrics!" Phillip rolled his eyes. "As I said, after they are done with your wife, then you can watch as *I* choke the life from her in the full and complete knowledge that you cannot stop me."

Rian resumed looking at the two burly guards who, finding themselves the object of such intense scrutiny, shifted uncomfortably. Ignoring Phillip, he addressed them.

"You know I will kill you both," Rian said calmly, "before I kill him." He jerked his head in Phillip's direction.

Apparently the full extent of their expected participation had not been explained; Phillip had failed to share with his two henchmen the role he wanted them to play. Neither man was a stranger to thievery, battery or rape, but their curious code of ethics balked at murder for no good reason. If Phillip wanted to kill both the woman and her husband, then so be it, but he would have to do it without any help from either of them. Swinging from the hangman's noose for someone like Phillip Davenport was not a prospect either had bargained for.

A silent communication between the two said they wanted no part of Phillip's peculiar brand of insanity, so they simply turned and walked away. The sound of their boots could be heard as they made their way down the staircase. It was soon followed by the front door slamming.

"They may have gone for help!" Catherine said desperately, her voice close to breaking, but Phillip only laughed at her.

"Nonsense. They have been paid well for their services, and if they want to live to see another sunrise, they know to hold their tongues."

To hear Phillip state that he would murder her had been shocking, momentarily freezing her. Catherine knew that she alone could not prevent him from ending her life. But she was definitely not going to make it easy for him. She was not about to hand herself over to him without taking something in return. The idea of gouging out an eye was very appealing.

As if deciding that too much time had been wasted in conversation, Phillip moved closer to her side. "Come, Catherine, it is time."

"Phillip, for the love of God, I beg of you don't do this!" she beseeched, but her plea only seemed to irritate him. He jerked her roughly to her feet and slapped her.

"At least let the child go!" Rian's roar made Phillip stop to consider the request.

Sensing a moment of hesitation, Catherine added, “Please, Phillip, I promise I will do whatever you ask of me, but let Grace go. She has no place here.”

“Will you do everything I ask of you?” He ran his hands over her body, feeling the warmth of her skin through the light fabric. Catherine nodded, not trusting her voice.

He paused, his gaze falling on the small figure seated across the room. She was so still, she appeared frozen. Phillip did not have to tell her to mind her tongue.

With a jerk of his head, Phillip motioned toward the door, but Rian was the only one who saw the child scramble from her seat and hurry out of the room. He sighed. She had undoubtedly seen too many acts of human cruelty in her short life, but there was no need for her to witness murder.

“Now, let me see how splendid you are, my dear, and how well you have recovered from our last encounter.” Phillip pulled the sash tied around Catherine’s waist and slipped the robe off her shoulders.

* * * *

Lettie lay curled up in her bed, her mind safely locked in a faraway place where bad things did not happen to good people. She vaguely remembered Phillip coming to her room, handing her a glass and telling her to drink. For a moment she’d wondered if he had finally decided to be done with her. Did the glass contain poison? But as if reading her thoughts, Phillip had laughed.

“No my dear, it’s just something to help with the pain, and to give you pleasant dreams. I promise.”

Not daring to refuse him, Lettie had finished the contents of the glass and then gasped as a strange, numbing sensation began to steal over her. “Wh-what did you give me?” she stammered, her eyes already having difficulty focusing.

“Only something to make you feel better,” he said stroking a hand down her cheek. “Now sleep, and let your worries fade away.” She was almost unconscious by the time he reached the door.

Awash in a laudanum haze, Lettie forgot the horrors of her daily life. She willingly embraced the landscape of this new dreamworld that claimed her, drifting mindlessly from one pleasure to the next. Here she had no worries, no husband, no cruelty in her life. The grass was sweet and green, the sky a perfect shade of blue, the flowers an extraordinary mix of perfume, texture and color. Everything was perfect. Only now, something was trying to pull her out of her paradise and drag her back to the ugly reality she abhorred. Someone grabbed her by the shoulders and shook her, and no matter how hard Lettie tried to pull away, she could not free herself from the relentless grip.

"No…no…" she mumbled into her pillow as she tossed her head back and forth. "Won't go…can't make me—owww!" This last was in response to the cold water that soaked her head and shoulders.

Blinking furiously, Lettie sat up, and saw Grace standing by the side of the bed, worrying her lower lip and holding the empty ewer from the washstand.

"What do you mean—"

"Sorry, Missus," Grace said urgently, "but you gots to come quick, and help the lady. I thinks the master means to do something bad to her." She paused to catch a breath. "And I think he means to murder the man as well."

Grabbing hold of Grace's thin arm, Lettie asked, "Man? What man?"

"The one who's come for the lady."

Lettie knew who the lady was, but the man was unknown to her. Had Phillip taken leave of his senses and brought a stranger into their home? Why would he do such a thing? But wait—Grace had said the man had come for the lady. Did she mean he was someone who had come to rescue Catherine?

"Where is this man?" Lettie asked.

"In the lady's room."

"Yes, but where exactly?"

"They gots him tied to the chair."

Tugging on Lettie's hand, Grace got her out of bed, but the moment Lettie tried to stand she became dizzy and had to hold on to the bedpost until it passed. Once she was able to stand without falling, Lettie took Grace's small hand in her own. "Tell me exactly what has happened," she asked, and without hesitation Grace bravely told her all she had seen.

Lettie had no idea how long she had been trapped inside her drug induced hallucination, but she was keenly aware that though she had stepped back to this side of reality, there was no guarantee how long she might remain. Time was of the essence, and she could waste no more of it. Too much had happened already while she had been unaware. She took a step forward, gritting her teeth against the terrible burning sensation radiating outward from her hip.

Step and drag...step and drag...

Refusing to give in to the throbbing ache, Lettie made her way to the bedroom door and pulled it open cautiously. Grace had told her about the two men she had seen leave, but she had no way of knowing if they might have since returned. She peered down the hallway, hearing nothing but an odd muffled sound coming from the direction of the room where Catherine was being held captive.

"And the other man, the one who came for Cath—the lady—is in the room with her as well?" Lettie asked.

"He's tied to the chair," Grace confirmed solemnly. "And I think he knows the lady."

"Why do you say that?"

"Cos when he looks at her it's like he wants to kiss her."

From the pocket of her apron Grace suddenly produced a wicked looking kitchen knife that she had had the foresight to fetch before waking Lettie. No one had seen her take it. Cook was gone, presumably deciding to make her escape while she could and taking the slow-witted Rosie with her.

"Not to worry," Lettie said with a quavering smile. "We two will be enough." They would have to be.

A moment of indecision suddenly rendered Lettie immobile. Fear snaked its way through her, and she almost succumbed to its poisonous charm, but then she thought of Catherine, who had managed to find someone to care enough for her that he had come to her rescue. Lettie could do no less.

"I'm going to fetch a pistol," she told Grace, pushing down her fear. "I know the master keeps one in his room, but I want you to stay here where it will be safe."

"But missus, you gots to go past the other room to get to the master's room." With a dirty finger, Grace pointed to the open doorway.

"I will make sure I am not seen," Lettie told her.

"But you gots a bad leg."

Closing her eyes, Lettie took a deep breath. Bad leg or not, she was the only one who knew where Phillip kept his pistol. It would be impossible to save Catherine without it. Smiling with a confidence she did not feel, Lettie assured Grace she could make it down the hall without being seen. She did not add she was certain Phillip's attention would be otherwise occupied.

It was a torturous journey that took all of the courage Lettie possessed. At any moment she expected Phillip, alerted by the thunderous sound of her beating heart, to appear and demand she explain why she was out of her room. The dimly lit hallway helped to conceal her, and passing by the open door to Catherine's room, Lettie froze as movement caught her eye. But the shadows being thrown upon the wall were too distorted for her to make out, and she closed her eyes for a moment before finding the strength to continue. Her leg was on fire, the throbbing pain encompassing every part of her from the waist down. Lettie willed herself not to fall. If she did she knew she would never rise again, for Phillip would surely kill her. It seemed that luck was on her side, for though her back was soaked with perspiration, and her hands shook uncontrollably, she reached her destination without mishap.

Grace waited until Lettie disappeared. She had taken the knife from the kitchen for a specific reason. Now she, too, inched her way down the hall to the open doorway, ignoring Lettie's command to remain in her room. Grace had seen a great many things in her short span of years. It made no difference to her that the master wore nice clothes, or the missus slept in a grand bed. People were people, and Grace had learned early to tell the good from the bad. More than once seeing the next sunrise had depended on it.

She knew what was taking place in the bedroom was the same thing that her mother used to do night after night. Grace wondered if the lady in the room had also been promised a gold coin when the master was done with her. She thought not. Somehow this was different from what she had seen her mother do. Grace didn't like the master. She hadn't from the first time she had seen him, and she wished with all her heart her mother had sold her to anyone else but him. Rosie wasn't as dimwitted as she made out, and she had told Grace about how the master had done things, horrible things, to the other girls that used to work in the house. Only all the girls had been sent away, leaving behind just Rosie and Grace.

"He won't touch me," Rosie had told her with a knowing smile.

"Why not?"

Rosie had tapped her temple with two fingers and mimicked a lunatic's grin. "You best watch out for yerself," she warned.

But Grace hadn't needed the warning. There was a mean streak in the master that made her afraid. It was easy enough to stay out of his way when there had been others to act as a shield. At first she had stayed in the kitchen, but then the master had said she was to look after the missus. He promised her a gold coin if she did, but the look on his face had made Grace's stomach swoosh with a sick feeling. Her stomach was swooshing again now, but she knew she had to help the man and the lady. The missus was not strong enough to do it all by herself.

Chapter 27

The light from the flickering candles cast a golden honey glow on Catherine's skin as she stood, waiting for Phillip's command. Unable to bear Rian's wretched expression as he watched another man look at her, she closed her eyes. Phillip walked in a slow circle around her, savoring the sight of her nude body. He spent a long time staring at the scar on her back, and Catherine wondered how many others he planned to add to it.

Even though she had told herself to expect it, she still jumped when he took hold of her hand. His palm was damp, his fingers sweaty, and it took every ounce of her resolve not to snatch her hand away. But she wasn't able to completely hide her disgust.

"You do not welcome my touch?" Phillip murmured.

It was the laugh that provoked her. The high pitched, schoolboy giggle that sounded obscene coming from the mouth of a grown man. With no regard for the consequences, Catherine opened her eyes and spat at her cousin, then calmly steadied herself for the blow she was certain would follow. But Phillip did not strike her. Instead he took a handkerchief from his pocket and wiped away the gob of spittle from his cheek.

"You will pay for that," he told her as he moved behind Rian's chair.

Keeping her face as blank as she could possibly make it, Catherine watched her husband rein in his rage. She was not deceived by his calm exterior. He carefully flexed his arms against the rope binding, testing it for weakness. He was close to erupting like some fantastic volcano she had read about, spewing forth the molten lava of his fury, and giving no mercy to those who stood in his path.

"Isn't she captivating?" Phillip asked silkily as both men stared at the woman bathed in candlelight.

Head held high, Catherine stared at an imaginary point in the middle of Phillip's forehead. She did not try to cover herself. Instead she let her arms hang loosely at her sides, keeping her body as relaxed as possible.

"To be able to partake of such forbidden fruit, inhale the sweet fragrance of her woman's perfume, and feast on such succulent flesh…what would a man give for the chance to do all that, I wonder?"

Rian made a low guttural sound in the back of his throat.

"Tell me, my dear," Phillip said, addressing Catherine, "what would *you* give to save *his* life?"

Alarm flashed in her eyes. She didn't trust her cousin, and she had no explanation for his strange obsession with her. But could it be used to her advantage? Would he, in his madness, be willing to strike a bargain with her? Keep her and let Rian go? If there was a chance, no matter how small, she had to take it. In a voice that was strong and unwavering, Catherine gave him the only possible answer.

"Anything. I will do anything."

Rian felt his heart break. He knew what she was doing and why. It would do no good to tell her Phillip was lying. He would never allow Rian to leave this room alive. But his wife, his beautiful wife, was willing to give everything she had if there was any possibility, no matter how small, that she could save him. Rian had never been more in love with her than he was at that moment, or more proud to have her as his own. Or more filled with pain and anguish. He willed her to look at him, and, hearing his silent plea, she turned her head. His warm brown gaze held fast to her deep blue one.

"Shall we put that to the test, cousin dear?" Phillip sounded sly and cunning. "Your willingness to do anything I ask of you."

"How do I know you will keep your word?" Catherine asked. "How do I know you will let my husband go once I have done whatever it is you ask of me?"

"Grace is no longer here, is she?" It was true. He had allowed her to leave, and Catherine was grateful. She gave Rian one last, lingering look, hoping he would not hate her for what she was about to do. "Come here, Catherine," Phillip ordered with a lascivious twist to his mouth as he stared at Rian's face. "And get on your knees."

* * * *

Grace crept closer to the open doorway, listening to the voices coming from the room. The master was speaking, saying things she didn't understand. His voice sounded funny. A little like the cutpurse boys, excited and fearful all at once. The man in the chair was also talking, and though he did not yell or shout, Grace could tell he wanted to hurt the master. Good. She wanted to hurt him too. The master was leaning back against the bed, while the lady was kneeling in front of him. It looked as if she was praying, but Grace did not think so. Her ma had told her you prayed if you wanted to talk to God, but you could only talk to him in a church. And you wore a lot more clothes in church.

Seeing Catherine's fingers move to the fastenings of the master's breeches, Grace put a hand to her mouth to stifle a gasp. She had seen her ma do this many times. One time a man said she bit him, and he hit her in the face hard enough to knock out a tooth and then wouldn't pay her. The side of her ma's face had swelled up something fierce. Grace didn't want the lady's face to swell up, but the smile on the master's face reminded her of the man who hit her ma. It was the same smile that always made Grace's stomach hurt. She didn't like it, and she didn't think the lady liked it either, but then the master closed his eyes and leaned back his head, giving Grace the chance she needed to slip into the room unnoticed.

Thankfully the chair the man was tied to was big enough to hide her. Using the shadows and Rian's body as an additional shield, she took out the kitchen knife and began sawing through the ropes.

Rian jerked at the tug he felt on the ropes binding him. Phillip's two thugs had not troubled themselves with securing his legs, and no one had reckoned with the determination of a ten-year-old girl.

Catherine was in no doubt about what Phillip wanted her to do. A foul, rank odor assaulted her as she loosened his breeches, making her gag. She knew the moment Phillip forced himself into her mouth, she was going to vomit. The sound of his lustful moan made her freeze, and Phillip grabbed her by the back of the neck in a grip of iron.

"Remember," he warned her, "his life will be in your hands, or rather your mouth." Pleased by the cleverness of his own wit, Phillip released his hold on Catherine's neck so she could finish with her task. However, her fingers were shaking so much she was having a difficult time getting the fastenings undone. "Oh, for God's sake!" Phillip declared as he slapped her hands away.

When the flap of his breeches fell partially open, Catherine braced herself with her hands as her body fell forward. His body odor was more than she could bear. Accompanied by the most awful retching sound, she vomited all over Phillip's lower legs and feet. Spitting and coughing, she trembled weakly as tremors ran through her. Kicking her in the side with a dripping foot, Phillip sent her sprawling.

Rian could hear Grace panting from the effort of sawing through the ropes, and he prayed Phillip did not. He thought about making some sort of a disturbance to muffle the sound of Grace's efforts, but that might draw attention to her instead. He stared at Catherine as she lay sprawled on the floor, noting the strange expression on her face. It took him a moment to realize that from her vantage point she could look beneath the chair, and could clearly see Grace kneeling behind it. Cautiously Rian flexed his biceps, and felt the rope give.

The next few minutes brought complete and utter chaos, minutes that would remain with Catherine until the day she died. With a primitive, deep-throated growl of animalistic rage, Rian launched himself from the chair and grabbed Phillip by the throat. He shook him like a dog with a rat, intent on choking the life from him, but Phillip fought back with a maniacal strength only those in mortal peril possess. He struck Rian about the head and temples with his fists, sending blood gushing down Rian's face and momentarily blinding him. Seizing the moment, Phillip kneed him in the groin. Rian stumbled back as pain flared, and points of light danced before his eyes. Gasping for breath, he dropped to one knee.

With a cry of rage, Phillip threw himself on his attacker, using the surprise of this counter attack to his advantage. Well aware that he was no match physically against Rian's size and strength, Phillip fought like a demon. It was almost as if Lucifer himself had blessed him with a savagery to compensate for what he lacked in physical prowess. He clawed at Rian's face, but Rian's answering punch bloodied Phillip's nose and split his lower lip. With an agonized shriek Phillip sprayed blood everywhere, but he still managed to hold on.

Thinking he was never going to free himself from the disgusting piss-pot masquerading as a man, Rian redoubled his efforts. Now he gripped Phillip's throat more tightly, sinking his fingers into the doughy flesh while ignoring the flailing arms and wildly aimed punches. Grabbing Phillip's shoulder, Rian intended to flip him over onto his back, but he was suddenly deafened by a loud retort that made both men drop to the ground. Phillip jerked his head toward the open doorway, a look of almost comical surprise on his face before he slumped forward in an untidy heap. The acrid smell of gunpowder in the air told Rian all he needed to know. He stared curiously at the small woman holding a Queen Anne flintlock pistol with both hands; smoke still curled from the end of the barrel. Her long brown hair, threaded liberally with grey, fell to her waist in a loose braid. The shabby robe she wore was stained and torn, but it was her face that held Rian captive. He had never seen an expression that was more serene or more blissful, and she gazed at him with a smile that was positively beatific.

"Lettie!" Catherine's cry cut across the room.

Rian moved forward, catching the small woman in his arms as she stumbled, dropping the pistol from slack fingers. She did not faint, but her entire body trembled violently and it was a few moments before Rian could determine that shock was the culprit, and she was not suffering a seizure. Carefully he seated her in the chair he had recently occupied before turning and selfishly pulling his wife into his arms.

Sobbing tears of relief, Catherine held up her face, and he smothered it with kisses. Wrapping his arms about her naked body, Ryan buried his face in her neck, his own silent tears of gratitude wetting her skin. All he could do was hold her to him, press her close and feel her heartbeat against his own.

"I thought he would kill you!" Catherine said as she clutched his shirt in her hands. "I'm sorry…I'm so, so s-s-sorry."

"Whatever for? You did nothing wrong."

"I l-l-lost my d-d-diamond necklace, Rian, the one you g-g-gave me!" Catherine hiccupped, her eyes huge and swimming with tears. "And my h-h-hair, he cut my hair!"

Afraid that if he let her go, she might be taken from him again, Rian continued to hold her. He murmured soothingly in her ear while his hands moved gently up and down her bare back, and Catherine shuddered silent sobs against him.

He had come,as she had known he would. He had come.

"Here, missus."

Grace's quiet voice prompted Rian to release his wife long enough for her to take the robe the child held out to her. It was a much more modest garment than the last one Catherine had been forced to wear, and she slipped into it gratefully. Rian's face flushed slightly at the realization that even under such horrible circumstances, the sight of his wife's naked body was arousing a familiar stirring in him. With his forefinger he lifted her chin so he could look at her. She had stopped crying but her cheeks were still wet and her eyes redrimmed and glistening. Rian put one arm around her shoulders, and the fingers of his other hand moved back and forth gently across her lips.

"Your diamond will find its way back to you again, I promise," he told her solemnly. "You are not the first to have lost it and yet, somehow, it always comes home. In the meantime you still have this."His fingers left her lips, he reached into his pocket, and took out the ring that John Fletcher had given him earlier. He slipped it on the third finger of her left hand. “As for your hair”—he paused, and gently ran his hand over her shorn skull—“it will grow back.”

Lettie’s sudden coughing fit made them all jump, and Rian felt a spasm of guilt. In truth he had forgotten she was there, but he looked at her, almost lost in the huge chair.

“Is he dead?” Lettie asked, unable to bring herself to look at the still figure on the floor.

Rian glanced at Phillip’s body. “I would imagine so, but we need to be certain.” Placing his hands on Catherine’s shoulders, he guided her toward the other woman. They sat together, the seat wide enough to accommodate both of them easily. Catherine wrapped an arm around Lettie’s shoulders while holding onto Grace with the other.

Rian rolled Phillip over, seeing the large black hole in the middle of his back. It really was quite amazing that Lettie’s aim had been so true. “He’s quite dead,” he told the two women somberly, as he pulled a cover from the bed and draped it over Phillip’s body.

“God forgive me, but I’m not sorry,” Lettie told him in a voice that ached with weariness. “He was a monster.” She took Catherine’s hands and gently stroked her cheek as fresh tears spilled. “I am sorry for you though, for what you had to endure. I am so sorry that I was not brave enough to come to you sooner, to help sooner.”

Catherine hugged her and pulled her in close, gently stroking her hair. “It wasn’t your fault,” she whispered reassuringly. “He was quite mad.” She stared into Lettie’s face. “You do know that, don’t you?” A shuddering nod was her answer.

“Come,” Rian said, offering his hand to his wife. “We need to leave.”

Like a shepherd with his flock, Rian ushered the three females out of the room, but at the doorway Catherine stopped and turned back to gaze at the room, as if wanting to commit it to memory.

“What is it, darling?”

“I want to be certain…”

“Of what?”

“That this will never hurt me again, not in my dreams, not anywhere,” she told him as she finished taking in every detail, especially the dead body on the floor. It was just a room, she told herself. Four walls covered with silk that had no power over her. Not anymore.

At the bottom of the stairs, Lettie gave Rian directions to the stables, where he would find a carriage and horses. As reluctant as he was to have Catherine out of his sight for even a minute, this was the only way to get them all to safety. He would have taken them all with him, but coming downstairs had drained the last reserves of Lettie's energy. He returned in less than fifteen minutes, driving the coach and pair himself. His relief at seeing Catherine open the front door was palpable.

Lettie pressed Grace's hand into Catherine's. "Get her settled. I'll just be a moment."

Alarmed, Catherine reached for the smaller woman's other hand. "Where are you going?"

"The drawing room," Lettie said, her hand reaching up to cradle Catherine's cheek. "I want my music box. It's all I have left from my father. I'll be but a moment, I promise you."

"A moment, no longer." Catherine nodded as she took Grace down the wide steps to where Rian was now waiting with the carriage. He took Grace from her, settling the child upon the padded seat, but the frown creasing his brow as he looked over Catherine's head made her turn around in time to see the front door closing.

"No!" she screamed, picking up the hem of her robe and running back up the steps. Pounding her fists against the heavy door, she heard the unmistakable sound of bolts being slid home on the other side. "Lettie! Lettie! What are you doing? Come out of there!"

Lettie's voice was eerily calm, and reached her clearly. "Catherine, it is the only way I can expect to be forgiven. Promise to take care of Grace for me. You're a good person. Give her the life she deserves."

Catherine redoubled her efforts, as if striking the door with her fists would change Lettie's mind and stop whatever course of action she was intent on. Coming up behind her, Rian seized hold of her hands. Her knuckles, already bruised, were now skinned and bleeding. Wrapping his arms about her, he pulled her away.

"Rian, stop her!" she implored, clutching his arm frantically and blinking back tears.

A quick assessment of the door told him there was no way it could be forced open from the outside. "Stay with the child," he ordered, pushing Catherine toward the carriage. "I will see if the back entrance is still open."

Grace's high scream wheeled Catherine about, and she followed the thin arm that stretched out the open carriage door toward the house. Both of them watched in horror as Lettie deliberately put a candle to the curtains, setting them ablaze. She must have known they were watching her because she raised her hand to her mouth, and blew a kiss to them before moving to the adjacent window and continuing with her task.

The rooms on either side of the front door glowed with unnatural light as flames licked hungrily up the draperies, consuming all in their path. From the swift passage of the fire, Catherine had to wonder if Lettie had used something to accelerate it. Phillip's brandy possibly? The fire took on a life of its own, spreading quickly through the lower level of the house, and Rian came stumbling back from the dark alley, his face dirty and his chest heaving.

"It's no use!" he gasped as he reached Catherine's side. "The door is bolted, and all the windows shuttered. I cannot get inside."Alarmed by the smell of the smoke, the horses whinnied and stamped their hooves. Rian took charge of the situation. "Get in!" he ordered as he pulled Catherine toward the carriage.

"No. I cannot leave her!"

Framing her face with his hands, he forced her to look at him and ignore the house. "She has decided her own fate, Catherine, and we must leave. Do not let her sacrifice be a meaningless one."

She hesitated a fraction longer, and then nodded, allowing Rian to bundle her inside. He would accept no further protest. She was too precious to him. Jumping onto the driver's seat, he picked up the reins and urged the anxious horses forward.

Chapter 28

Oakhaven welcomed them back once more, and they allowed the soothing balm of the house and land to work its magic, restoring them as only it could. Of course, not everything would be the same. Not everything could be forgiven or let go. Lives had been changed. Lives had been lost.

In the small cemetery behind the family chapel, a place was made for Lettie to lie in peace. Her charred body had been found in the smoking ruins of the house and Rian had claimed her as next of kin. Catherine, overwhelmed by the gesture, had thanked him with tears in her eyes. He had not done the same with Phillip nor, for some strange reason, had either of them been asked to do so.

A smaller headstone had been placed alongside Lettie's, and into the marble had been carved only the year and the words *Our First Love* in memory of the babe lost to Liam and Felicity.

"She would like that," Felicity told them.

"She?" Liam looked at his wife and gazed in awe at the serene expression in her eyes. "You knew it was a girl?"

Felicity smiled. "Only in my heart, dearest, only in my heart."

Reaching for his wife's hand, Liam tried to speak, but the sudden lump in his throat prevented any words from forming. He pinched the bridge of his nose with the thumb and forefinger of his free hand, willing the tears not to fall. Saying nothing, Felicity simply slid her arms around his waist and rested her head on his chest, holding onto her husband and comforting him in his moment of grief.

The road back to recovery is never a smooth journey, especially not if traveled alone. Liam, heeding both the advice of his brother and Dr. MacGregor, spent as much time with his wife as she would allow. They took morning rides together and long afternoon walks and, at other times, when the weather permitted, they could be found sitting quietly in the garden where Liam read aloud and Felicity, fingertips blackened from charcoal, sketched her grand designs for the restoration of the gardens in a large notebook.

Both of them welcomed the opportunity to immerse themselves in each other's interests. Liam made a point of taking Felicity with him when he had to attend to estate business. He found her keen mind and sharp observations to be invaluable. Every tenant they met expressed sorrow for their loss. This, more than anything, touched both of them in a way neither would have expected. The loss of a child was grieved by all.

The path for Rian was a little darker. On the surface, both he and Catherine seemed to be mending well. They also took walks together, went riding and even squabbled good-naturedly as they played cards, each accusing the other of cheating. But since returning to Oakhaven, Catherine had resumed sleeping in his mother's room. Alone.

She had quietly asked to be given the time to recover in her own way from the horrors of that night. Hiding his hurt, Rian had acquiesced and made no demands. He found himself overwhelmed by a sense of helplessness he had never experienced before. Unable to sleep alone in the bed Catherine had once shared with him, he took to sleeping in the library or the den.

"Patience, Master Rian, patience," Mrs. Hatch advised, after finding him sitting on the floor in the middle of the night, staring at Catherine's closed bedroom door. He had said nothing, but looked at the housekeeper with a face that could not hide the loneliness consuming him.

Before leaving the city, Dr. MacGregor had examined Catherine. He assured Rian that she had not suffered any irreparable physical harm, but he could not speak as confidently about her mental state. He shared with Rian his belief that Catherine was holding something back. Before, she had no memory of what had taken place, only the brutal evidence left on her body. But now she knew every sickening detail. Shaking his head and keeping his voice low and his manner mournful, Dr. MacGregor had been blunt. The strain of carrying such a burden would eventually take its toll, and Catherine was walking a razor's edge. It was anyone's guess which way she would fall, but fall she would.

Rian knew his wife well enough to sense that something about her, something deep down, was wrong, but he was handicapped by the strength of his own feelings, and he did not want to do anything that would cause her to lose faith in him. Of course he did not expect her to come through this most recent nightmare with Phillip unscathed. He understood the guilt she felt about Lettie's suicide, and he knew it would be a long time before she felt comfortable enough to share her feelings on either matter. He could accept that, but what he could not accept was the way she had completely cut herself off from him emotionally.

He was at a loss to know how to reach her. How could he make her see that the burden Phillip had placed on her was not hers alone to bear, but his to share also. Stealing from Mrs. Hatch's remedy book, Dr. MacGregor had advised patience, and Rian had given him a wry smile. They had been down this road before. He promised to give Catherine as much time as she needed. And so they embarked on a perilous journey that threatened, with one misplaced sigh, one misread glance, one misdirected inflection, to pull them apart.

* * * *

They had been back a little over a month before Catherine broached the subject that Rian and Liam both seemed determined to avoid. It had become customary for them all to retire to the library after dinner to play cards. Liam cheated terribly, which made them laugh as he was so bad at disguising his efforts. They had just finished a hand of whist when Catherine asked, "What has become of Isabel?"

The silence that followed was like a whip crack echoing around the room. Since their return, they had spoken openly of John Fletcher, examining his role in both Catherine's abduction as well as her rescue, but no one had mentioned Isabel's complicity. Her involvement had simply been ignored. Both men hoped their wives would be content to let the matter lie, but now it seemed that was not going to happen. Liam gave Rian a worried glance that did not go unnoticed by Catherine. He reached for his wife's hand, but Felicity gently removed it from his grasp. Propping her elbow on the table instead, she cupped her chin in her palm, and stared at her brother-in-law.

"Yes, Rian, what has become of Isabel?" she asked in a tone that was neither accusing nor condemning, only curious.

"What have you heard?" he asked nonchalantly, shuffling the cards and refusing to look up.

He had told his brother that this moment would come; if given a choice, each would have preferred the moment to have been put off a little longer. But the subject was out in the open now, and having been raised by Catherine and then seconded by Felicity, both men knew they were not going to be able to do anything but be direct and, above all, truthful.

"She seems to have disappeared from what Mama has told me," Felicity said, picking up her cards and sorting her hand. "No one can confirm it, but there is a rumor that she has gone to her estate in Ireland. Her house has been closed up for the rest of the season, and she has dismissed all but a handful of servants, giving a full year's severance to those she has let go." Felicity paused, watching as both men diligently sorted their cards. "The odd thing is that she did not mention her plans to a single one of her friends. Mama tells me Charlotte Maitling is quite peeved."

"A year's pay seems very generous. A little too generous for Isabel, don't you think?" Catherine asked Rian.

"Perhaps," he replied with a noncommittal shrug.

"Did you know she had an estate in Ireland?" Catherine fixed him with a stare.

He sighed and laid his cards on the table. There was no point in trying to play the hand until this discussion was over. "Yes, I knew."

"Do you know anything about her reasons for leaving so suddenly?" His wife was not going to be dissuaded.

"I would have thought that was obvious," he said quietly.

"Perhaps, perhaps not." Catherine sounded doubtful.

Rian stared at her. "What is it that you are really trying to ask me, Catherine?"

It was Felicity who answered. "Whether there is any truth to the rumors."

"What rumors?"

Felicity turned and fixed Liam with a stare of her own, "That Isabel's hasty departure came as a direct result of a visit she received from my husband."

Rian gave a start. Liam had visited Isabel? Why had he not known about this? Had he also discovered her secret? Surely not, because Liam would have told him, wouldn't he?

Not if he thought you didn't know.

"Cooks and grooms," Rian muttered under his breath quietly, but still loud enough for Catherine to hear him. She gave him a quizzical look, but he only shook his head.

With a sigh, Liam decided it was time to come clean and confess his part in Isabel's departure. He gave his brother an apologetic look.

"After Rian left with John Fletcher, I decided to pay Isabel a visit to make sure that she fully understood why she needed to leave. I wanted to be absolutely certain that she understood the consequences if she failed to do as we demanded. It was not going to be possible for her to return to town, hoping a change of scenery, or missing a season was all that would be necessary to safeguard her health."

"What was wrong with her health?" Catherine asked.

"At that time, nothing as far as I know."

Rian felt a small sigh of relief escape him. Liam's answer said he was ignorant regarding Isabel's pregnancy.

"*At that time?*" Felicity drummed her fingers lightly on the surface of the card table. "What was going to happen to her health if she did not agree to your decision? What exactly did you say to her, Liam?"

"That her man, John Fletcher, had made a mistake by only eliciting a guarantee of her safety from one brother," he raised a brow and gave Rian an unfathomable look before continuing, "and that I would never forgive her for being instrumental in the loss of our child." He stopped speaking as Felicity's hand covered his.

"And?" she asked softly.

Her husband swallowed. On reflection, Liam wished he had been more guarded in his manner with Isabel, but he could not change what had taken place. He had been emotional and grief stricken, and had spoken with his heart, not his head. "I told her that if she was so foolish as to cross my path again, then her life would be forfeit."

Catherine gasped, and Rian could not help the sudden surge of pride and admiration that filled him. He and Liam were more alike than people realized. But it was Felicity who shocked them all. Shy and reserved, she normally avoided any display of public affection, but she squeezed her husband's hand tightly before leaning forward and kissing him full on the mouth. It was the first time since the night of the party that she had shown such physical intimacy, and it took her husband completely by surprise.

"Thank you, my darling," she whispered after releasing his lips. The look in her eyes told him that Isabel's name would never be mentioned by her again.

* * * *

Summer was fading. The days were still long and full of bright light, but in the evening hours, as the sun was setting, a coolness that had not been felt previously now made itself known. Both Catherine and Felicity had taken to wearing shawls when they went walking. Catherine's hair was growing back, more quickly than she had expected, but it would require a little more time before it reached a comfortable length. In the meantime Mrs. Hatch had made a selection of beautiful frilled caps for her to wear, and Catherine had grown quite fond of them. Rian thought they made her look like a beautiful dairy maid, and he couldn't help being struck by the irony of that particular thought. Isabel had referred to Catherine as a milk maid, but she had meant it in an offensive, derogatory way.

"If only she knew," he said quietly to himself, watching his wife make her way across the lawn. He sighed as thoughts of Isabel clouded his mind. He had not told anyone that Isabel was carrying his child, and he especially hated keeping it a secret from Catherine, but in her present state of mind, he feared what the knowledge might do to her. The strong length of steel that bound him to his wife, linking his heart to hers, had been pulled so taut by recent events that it was in danger of snapping. To ask Catherine to accept one more devastating piece of information about her nemesis might be too much right now. It could easily make her turn away from him, and that was something he would not be able to bear.

He sighed wearily and came to a decision. As long as Isabel kept to her estates in Ireland, Catherine need never know the truth. Protecting her was Rian's only thought. There wasn't anything he wouldn't do to keep his wife safe, even if it meant walking a razor's edge himself. It was a risk he was more than willing to take, even though he knew, deep down, secrets had a way of making themselves known. As Catherine disappeared from view, Rian decided he could not wash his hands of Isabel entirely. He needed someone to tell him when the child was born, someone to alert him if she decided to test the boundaries of the agreement with John Fletcher. Someone who, above all, would be discreet. It sounded like a task for Stuart Collins.

The onset of the cooler evening temperatures encouraged the pursuit of activities more suited to the indoors, and so it was that one evening they all decided to explore more thoroughly the paintings in the portrait gallery. The Connor ancestors all seemed to be gazing back at Catherine with austere and slightly disapproving expressions. "Why do they all look so miserable?" she asked Rian. "Is having your portrait painted really such an awful chore?"

He had chuckled softly at her miffed expression. "Perhaps it is the knowledge that they will be on silent display for each successive generation to criticize that makes them look grumpy," he told her. "Although I suspect with one or two the tight lacing of a corset would be a more reasonable explanation."

She turned and looked at him, a smile warming her face. "Why are there no portraits of you or Liam?"

"It's tradition to paint only the owners of Oakhaven," he said, waving toward his ancestors, "and I am sure Felicity will talk Liam into a sitting soon enough."

Catherine stopped and sighed wistfully as she recognized the canary diamond that adorned the ring finger of one woman in a large painting. Absentmindedly, she twisted the same ring decorating her own hand as she looked up at the beautiful but haughty face. She did not fail to notice that she had yet to see a portrait in which the sitter had been painted wearing the matching pendant.

"I am truly sorry I lost the necklace," she said in a subdued voice.

Coming behind her, Rian placed his hand lightly in the small of her back. "It was *your* necklace," he corrected, "and I have every faith that it will find its way back to the family. As I told you before, it always does somehow."

"I remember your saying it has been lost before." Catherine looked up at him, her expression hopeful. It would ease her conscience immensely if she knew she was not the first to have misplaced the fabulous gem.

With his hand on her elbow, Rian steered her down the hall, coming to a stop before a good-sized painting of a woman with flaming red hair and skin as white as snow. On the ground, tumbling around her feet and the billowing petticoats of her elaborate gown, were a mix of some half a dozen toddlers and small dogs. All of whom seemed to be having tremendous fun pulling tails and chewing feet. The subject of the painting was one of the rare few who seemed happy to have her image preserved for her descendants.

"She lost the pendant?" Catherine asked skeptically.

Rian nodded.

"How?"

"Absolutely no idea," he admitted. "Family history says that a detailed account would not only be impolite, it might also prove embarrassing to a certain member of the Royal Family."

"Hmmm, how very convenient." Catherine stared at him for a few moments before turning her attention back to the figure in the painting. "So, if I were ever to have my portrait painted—"

"*When* your portrait is painted," Rian corrected gently, "we will have a postscript entered into the Connor Family history so generations to come will know that you temporarily misplaced the diamond."

"Misplaced," Catherine murmured. "You really are very generous to describe its loss that way." A frown suddenly puckered her brow. "But how would future generations know? You said that only the owners of Oakhaven can have their portraits in this gallery."

"Yes, that's correct."

"Then how would my painting be here?"

"I am sure Liam would make an exception. Besides"—he smiled at the confused look on her face—"do you not have a portrait gallery at The Hall?"

She shook her head. "Well, there's a gallery but no paintings. Not anymore." She thought of the beautiful canvases that had been catalogued and sold to pay her father's debts. They had fetched more for the frames than the subject matter, or so she had been told.

"You have no picture of your father or mother?" Catherine shook her head. It had never bothered her before that neither of her parents' likenesses had been captured, but now she felt the loss keenly. "Then I think it's time the tradition was reinstated," Rian said, sensing her sudden depression. "And your portrait would be the perfect start to such a collection."

She opened her mouth to protest, but snapped it closed as Liam and Felicity joined them.

"Catherine, you really must come and see this!" Felicity took her hand with a mischievous twinkle in her eyes, leading her toward a smaller display.

"Your wife found Uncle Seamus?" Rian asked, giving his brother a knowing look.

"That she did," Liam confirmed, wearing a grin that lit up his face and stretched from ear to ear.

Their heads turned as one when Catherine, in a mix of disbelief and astonishment, declared,"My God, you're right; it is a goat!"

Two feminine heads swiveled to look at them, and Rian decided it was as good a moment as any to tell them the colorful tale of Uncle Seamus and his unabashed love for his beloved goat, Penelope. Before long both Felicity and Catherine were holding their sides as they giggled helplessly. Even Liam continued grinning, never tiring of the story. Rian, meanwhile, managed to keep a pained look on his face as if mortally offended by their mirth.

"Stop it!" Felicity admonished waving a hand weakly at him, her eyes damp with tears of laughter. "I refuse to believe that I have married into a family whose members openly admit to having a relative who slept with livestock!"

"But it's true!" Rian defended in a wounded tone as he dramatically clutched his chest. "Uncle Seamus always claimed he couldn't tell, between his wife and Penelope, which of them had the more beautiful beard. But rumor has it the goat had the better disposition!"

Howls of laughter echoed through the gallery and Rian allowed himself the comfort of a smile when he saw his brother hold onto his wife, and embrace her warmly. Later, when they said their goodnights, he had the feeling that it would not be long before they began trying for another child.

Chapter 29

Catherine was still recalling the story of Uncle Seamus a few days later as she returned some books to the library. A smile lifted her lips and every now and then she would chuckle to herself as she recalled yet another humorous remark made by Rian that evening. She was thankful for his patience with her, and seeing how Felicity and Liam were managing to deal with the pain they had endured gave her hope.

She could not compare her defilement at Phillip's hands with the loss of a baby, but it had caused a pain of a different kind. She knew the bond she and Rian shared was just as strong as the one that tied Liam and Felicity to each other. If her best friends in the whole world could put enough trust in each other to move forward with their lives, surely she could find the same faith in her husband, and he in her. Of course, the difficulty that threatened their love for each other was very different in nature.

Catherine had returned to her previous bedroom because she had been afraid. Afraid of being rejected by Rian. Would he ever be able to look at her again and not see Phillip's hands on her body? How could he take her to his bed and not be reminded of all that had happened that night? Was the image of her, on her knees, burned forever in his mind? Would he—could he—ever want to make love to her again? Had Phillip succeeded in destroying the passion and desire they'd once felt for each other?

Catherine had no answers, but these questions had haunted her every day since returning to Oakhaven. She knew Rian would never deny her his bed, but what if he turned away from her? Or chose to sleep elsewhere himself? It was cowardly of her to seek refuge in what had once been his mother's bedroom, but better that than to lie next to him knowing he could not bring himself to touch her.

It had been different when they'd first escaped from Phillip's house. Once Catherine had convinced him she suffered no lasting physical effects, all attention had been devoted to Liam and Felicity. This did not mean Rian failed to be attentive to her, but Catherine was able to direct his concern to his brother, telling him rightfully that Liam's hardship was greater than hers. When Rian finally returned to their bedroom, the hour was inevitably late and she was sleeping. Not wishing to disturb her, he had spent his nights fitfully dozing in the chair.

But that had been in the city; at Oakhaven it was a very different matter.

As his wife, Catherine was expected to share his bed, but why put him through the torture of making excuses not to sleep with her? So she had decided to take the decision out of his hands and asked to be given her old room. He had agreed, as she knew he would; only now she didn't know how to breach the impasse between them.

Rian was still kind and attentive, giving every indication that he was happy to be her husband and she pleased him as a wife, but she could sense him starting to withdraw from her. At least physically. He had never needed an excuse to touch her. Stroking her cheek or reaching for her hand came as naturally to him as breathing. But he no longer did those things. When they walked, he kept his hands firmly jammed in his pockets and no longer pulled her behind a tree or some overgrown shrubbery to nuzzle her neck or kiss her. And he no longer whispered how much he wanted to take her body. Like a plant that was deprived of water, the intimacy they once shared was slowly dying.

With a sigh, Catherine realized there was only one way to stop torturing herself with unanswered questions. She had to know, to be absolutely certain whether her life with the only man she loved, the only man she ever wanted to love, was over or not. Pushing her fear aside, she searched for the courage to speak about what had happened with the only person who truly mattered. Before it was too late.

* * * *

Rian and Liam were in the study dealing with estate business when the letter was delivered. Recognizing Edward's neat script, Rian quickly broke the wax seal bearing his insignia and unfolded the heavy parchment. The letter was short and, unlike his customary reports, made no mention of The Hall. At least not directly. Rian quickly scanned the two paragraphs, and felt his heart sink. He glanced at his brother, and then reread the letter. The expression on his face remained bleak.

"Rian, man, for God's sake what is it? What has happened?" There was more than just concern in Liam's voice, so Rian handed him the single sheet of paper. He poured them both brandy as Liam read for himself Edward's words and then took the glass from Rian's hand.

"How on earth are you ever going to tell her?" Liam asked.

"I have absolutely no idea."

* * * *

Catherine was in her room, brushing out her hair when a knock on the door interrupted her. "Come in, Rian."

Looking slightly flustered, he entered. "How did you know it was me?"

She turned on her seat and smiled at him. "If you have not forgotten, I spent a great deal of time confined to bed in the townhouse. I learned to recognize who passed by the door by the sound of their footsteps."

His expression made her suddenly embarrassed by her revelation, and turning back around, she busied herself with her hairbrush, hoping he had not noticed the flush on her cheeks.

"Your hair is getting longer," Rian observed.

Self-consciously Catherine put her hand to the nape of her neck and looked at him in the mirror. He seemed out of sorts, distressed and a little agitated. There was a shadow in his eyes, one that made her heart skip a beat.

Oh my God, is he going to tell me that he doesn't love me anymore? Or worse, that he does, but can't be with me?

"Rian, what is it? Is something wrong?" She swiveled around and watched as he came and knelt before her. Oh God! A man only knelt before a woman to either ask for her hand, or to give her the gravest of news. As she and Rian were already wed, he was not kneeling out of joy. Gently he took the hairbrush from her hand and placed it on the dresser. His face was filled with sorrow, and Catherine stared at him, trying to guess what could have caused such misery. "Rian, something has happened, hasn't it? Please tell me what it is. You're beginning to scare me!"

He cleared his throat and spoke in a husky whisper. "I received a letter today…from Edward."

She nodded. A letter from Edward. Well, that wasn't unusual. Edward had written to Rian before. "What did he say?" she asked softly.

Her eyes were a bright summer sky blue, clear and gentle as they stared back at him. The barest hint of her earlier embarrassment still flushed her cheeks, and her mouth, lips full and slightly parted, reminded him how much he wanted to taste the sweetness again.

"Rian, what did Edward tell you?"

There was no way to soften the blow. "Old Ned has died."

For a moment she felt nothing but relief to know he hadn't come to tell her he no longer loved her, but then his words registered and she was immediately ashamed of her selfishness. Guilt and sorrow stole her voice for a moment.

"How?"she asked, barely above a whisper, and had Rian not seen her lips move, he would have missed the question.

"It was very peaceful. His daughter told Edward he died in his sleep." He swallowed. "I know how much he meant to you, Catherine."

She looked up at him and nodded, then dropped her head. Seeing the tell-tale movement of her shoulders, Rian got to his feet and pulled her into his arms so he might console her. Catherine turned her face into his shoulder, and mourned for someone who had shown her kindness her entire life, and who had been so much more than a faithful retainer.

She did not know how long she wept, but when she was finally done, the sense of loss was so strong, the void became a dull, throbbing ache. She did not protest when Rian picked her up in his arms and laid her gently on her bed. She did not protest when she felt him reach for her hand and press his lips to the back of it, but she turned away from him when she felt the threat of more tears. She did not weep for Old Ned. She wept for herself and Rian, and what they were in danger of losing.

* * * *

At Rian's suggestion, Liam left with his wife to spend a few days with her parents. Although she had made great progress, Felicity was still fragile, and he wasn't sure how Catherine's grief might affect her. Liam would tell everyone at Pelham Manor the news of Old Ned's passing in the morning.

Rian frowned as he closed the door to his bedroom. For some reason Mrs. Hatch had only left a single candle burning. It cast a weak light, but it really didn't matter as he could navigate his way around the room in total darkness if need be. Removing his jacket, he sat in the chair and pulled off his boots before rising so he could begin the task of unbuttoning his shirt. Catherine's voice stopped him just as he was done with the last closure.

"Do you hold me to blame for what happened to Lettie?" Her voice trembled.

Fearful that if he turned around the voice would prove to be nothing more than an illusion, Rian remained standing with his back to the bed. He searched his memory, recalling how they had sat holding hands quietly in the chapel, listening to Reverend Hastings deliver Lettie's eulogy. They had remained there long after everyone else had left. "Lettie was troubled," he'd told her, "and, I think, had been for a very long time. Finally, she is at peace."

He had thought that would be the end of it, but apparently this had been weighing on Catherine's mind. Had the news about Old Ned acted as a catalyst, reopening a hidden wound in her? He did not know, but all that mattered was that she was here, in his room, and had come of her own volition. He was not about to send her away.

"Do you blame me?" she asked him again, her voice firmer and a little less fragile sounding.

Rian placed his hands on the dresser, palms down, and bowed his head. "No, I do not hold you to blame for Lettie's suicide." There, it was said. He held his breath, and waited for her to say something…anything.

"Then do you blame me for allowing Phillip to do what he did to me before, and what he tried to do again?"

A wave of nausea washed through him at her words. How could she possibly think he would hold her accountable for the sick perversions of that man's twisted nature? Was this what had been festering in the back of her mind since they had returned to Oakhaven? Was this why she had wanted to sleep alone and not share the warmth and comfort of his bed? And it wasn't just her body that he missed, but her companionship.

Rian took a deep breath and let it out slowly before answering. "I blame only two people for your abduction, and all the subsequent consequences. Isabel Howard and Phillip Davenport." His voice trembled too, but it was with barely suppressed anger. How dare they make Catherine think she was responsible in any way for the events that had almost destroyed her? It took some effort, but he managed to leash his anger, and when he spoke again, his voice was soft and gentle. "Catherine, I hold you blameless for everything that has happened, except making me fall in love with you." The lump in his throat was making it difficult to speak, and he forced himself to swallow it down. "For that I hold you completely, entirely, and utterly accountable."

Rian kept his head bowed, his hands curled into fists on top of the dresser. He sensed her behind him, coming closer but still he did not turn around. Out of the corner of his eye he picked up the movement of her hand as she covered his fist.

"Do you still love me?"

She withdrew her hand from atop his, letting it fall to her side. He uncurled his fists, relaxed his hands and placed them, palms down, on the smooth wood surface.

"I will love you until the day I draw my last breath," Rian told her.

"And do you still want me?" Doubt made her step away from him.

"Do I still—" he whirled and every thought in his head turned to dust, shattered by the image that stood before him.

She wore the same nightgown she had worn on their wedding night; the filmy material clung to every sensuous swell and curve of her body. Her hair was curled softly about her face, reaching just below her chin, and it framed her like a halo of white light as she waited for him to declare himself. He could sense her pride, her defiance and also her sense of shame.

"If you cannot bear to touch me, hold me in your arms, or to be a husband to me, Rian, you must tell me!" Tears fell, glistening on her cheeks, revealing what she had been keeping to herself all these long, lonely nights.

"What happened—" She closed her eyes and took a shuddering breath. "The things Phillip did to me…if you find that you cannot lie with me again because of it, I will understand…but you must tell me, Rian, I have to know." She turned her head, unable to look at him. "I cannot live like this. It hurts too much."

He came at her all in a rush, sweeping her up into his arms and throwing them both back on the bed. The breath whooshed out of her, and she gasped. Like a man possessed, Rian kissed her face, her cheeks, her eyes, forehead and nose. He rained quick lightning bolts of barely controlled passion down the column of her throat, her neck, and the naked skin of her shoulders where her nightgown had slipped loose. And then he stopped, his own body shuddering as he caught his breath and looked into her eyes, watching as they turned a deep shade of indigo, a color he loved so well.

"I love you," he told her simply and eloquently, "and I want you in every possible way a man can want a woman." And before she could answer, he covered her mouth with his, tasting the sweetness of her breath and losing himself in the wonder of her.

Quickly he pulled on the ribbons that closed the sheer gown and then shed his own clothes with as much haste. Covering her body with his, he let her feel the hard length of him as it pushed against her and almost wept with gratitude as she opened herself to receive him. Raising his head, his face only inches from hers, Rian felt a chill run down his spine as he looked into her eyes. Eyes a man could drown in, eyes he wanted to drown in, and without a second thought he gave himself to her.

"I thought I had lost you," Catherine whispered, her voice husky with need and wanting.

He felt the warmth of her mouth as her lips sought his, felt the roll of her hips beneath him, and then he felt her desire eclipse his own as she brought him with her to the point of no return, sending both of them over the edge. And in that moment of breathtaking ecstasy, Rian knew his life was complete.

THE END

Meet the Author

Carla Susan Smith owes her love of literature to her mother, who, after catching her preteen daughter reading by flashlight beneath the bedcovers, calmly replaced the romance book she had "borrowed" with one that was much more age appropriate! Born and raised in England, she now calls South Carolina home where she lives with her wonderfully supportive husband, awesome son, and a canine critique group (if tails aren't wagging then the story isn't working!). When not writing, she can usually be found in the kitchen trying out any recipe that calls for rhubarb, working on her latest tapestry project or playing catch up with her reading list. Visit her at www.carlasmithauthor.com

Meet the Author

[illegible]

Printed in the United States
by Baker & Taylor Publisher Services

Printed in the United States
by Baker & Taylor Publisher Services